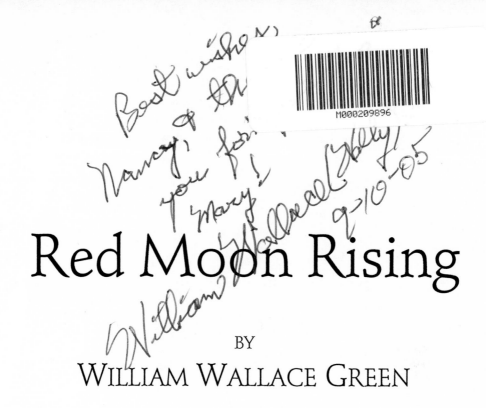

Red Moon Rising

BY

WILLIAM WALLACE GREEN

PublishAmerica
Baltimore

© 2005 by William Wallace Green.

First printing

ISBN: 1-4137-4761-2
PUBLISHED BY PUBLISHAMERICA, LLLP
www.publishamerica.com
Baltimore

Printed in the United States of America

To Robert L. Fenton

Also by William Wallace Green:

Never Say Never

On the Wings of Morning

Diamonds on the Water

Acknowledgments

Many people contributed to the creation of this book and all have my gratitude. I give special thanks to some of them:

Brian Ferguson, Detective Sergeant, Lapeer Post, Michigan State Police,

Bryon Skib, European Studies Librarian, University of Michigan Graduate School Library,

Paul Fischer, Executive Director, Michigan Judicial Tenure Commission,

Mike Benedict, Court Administrator, Michigan Supreme Court,

Glenn Lefeber, Executive Director, Flint River Watershed Coalition,

Bill Zehnder, Owner, Zehnder's of Frankenmuth,

Kenneth Elwert, Director, Lapeer County Parks,

Donald Wyche, lifetime friend, who taught me to use a computer,

Bob Green, my brother, and Marge Green, his wife, who have steadfastly supported all my writing projects,

And finally, my wife, Mary Amelia Green, who has been my constant inspiration.

Table of Contents

Prologue

Paris, France

White cotton candy billows of fog traced the curves of the River Seine. Buildings that were all the same height, thanks to an urban planner in Napoleon's time, radiated out in orderly rows from the center of the city where their hotel, the George V, stood near the Eiffel Tower.

Except for their stunning good looks, they could have passed for any happily married tourists in Paris from America in late September of 2002. She wore a khaki-colored man's shirt while he had on a thick blue terry-cloth robe that matched his eyes.

Holding hands and leaning against the wrought-iron railing of their private terrace, they laughed together in the afterglow of their lovemaking as they watched the city below them turn from gray to gold in the sunrise.

"Those salt and pepper sideburns of yours really make you look distinguished," she giggled, stretching up to playfully nip his earlobe with her teeth, her makeshift top riding up on her hips to reveal black lace panties underneath.

"Not again, you must think I'm made of iron," the man said with a broad grin, then holding her gently by her shoulders with his hands, he stepped back to improve his view, "You look a lot better in that shirt than I ever did."

As the sun cleared the horizon in its mighty leap out of the murky darkness beyond, they went back into their posh suite for another exciting day of making love and visiting the sights of Paris.

Chapter One
Fall from Grace

Black limousines are common in Lansing, Michigan's capital city, so the one coming north down Cedar Street didn't attract much attention, especially in the empty streets at five o'clock of a winter morning.

Completing a left turn onto Kalamazoo, it pulled up to the curb. The prostitute moved wearily towards the limo, hoping that this might be her last trick of the night and that it would be a good one for her.

But the uniformed chauffeur shook his head slightly in the direction of his black sister as he got out to buy a *Wall Street Journal* from the row of newspaper boxes on the sidewalk. Getting back in the driver's seat, he closed the door and accelerated the powerful vehicle away toward the Supreme Court Building.

"Thanks, Jimmy," Supreme Court Justice Robert Preston Foster said, taking the paper through the sliding panel his driver had opened between them. He glanced at the date, Thursday, February 15, 2001, and then laid it on the seat beside him with a heavy sigh. Another one he would never be able to bring himself to read.

Buying it each morning on the way to his office was habit, and a way of holding on to his old life, a very good life, that had begun to slip away from him in the last few months.

* * *

"Oh my God, he's handsome," the curvaceous twenty-year-old reporter from the *Detroit News* said to the photographer she had brought with her as they studied a handful of photographic proofs developed overnight from pictures taken of Justice Foster addressing the Detroit Economic Club luncheon the previous day. "He looks just as hot in these photos you took as he did in that shot *Newsweek* ran with its political piece on rising stars in the national Republican Party."

"Down, girl, you don't get interviews looking awestruck," her middle-aged co-worker, with a digital camera resting on her lap, replied seriously.

They were seated in an oak-paneled waiting room which they had to themselves outside the Justices' offices.

"But it makes me hot just thinking about what he must look like with his clothes off," the reporter said. "He's in great shape for a forty-year-old man," she continued. "Yes, sir, Justice Foster can put his shoes under my bed anytime he wants to," the dark-haired beauty murmured more to herself than anyone else. "He reminds me of Clark Gable."

"Honey, how you talk in these hallowed halls," the older woman scolded in mock indignation. "Besides, this guy has only been a widower for a few months now since his wife died in childbirth. The baby died, too, and my attorney friends tell me he's been behaving strangely on the bench ever since."

"Sex will find a way, it's stronger than any of that other stuff," the reporter observed with a half grin.

"What I want to know is how one as young as you could have gotten so cynical, so fast?" the older woman asked. "Stop staring at those pictures, girl, and go over your interview questions."

"The only one I'm worried about asking him is how he could have written an opinion in favor of a cap on personal injury recoveries," the reporter said as she shifted her attention to a spiral notebook she took out of her purse and was leafing through, "like all those families burned so terribly with gas tank explosions in Ford Pinto crashes, for example. What if something like that happens again, what about them?"

"Sweetheart, you have to think like a Republican, they're against anything that burdens business, and unlimited product liability judgments certainly do just that," the photographer replied, then added in a quieter voice, "Where do you think most of his campaign funding comes from?"

"Now who's being cynical?" the younger woman asked.

"Ladies, I'm very sorry," the male receptionist announced in the direction of the two women as he returned to his desk in a corner of the room. "His Honor has just informed me that he is not granting any more interviews to the press during the balance of this term due to his increased workload."

"The Court's docket isn't any more crowded now than it ever was," the older woman whispered as she rose to leave. "I told you something's up."

"That's what I can't stop thinking about," the reporter quipped with a huge smile on her face.

"You know, you are really terrible, girl," her companion teased as she slung her camera on its carrying strap over her shoulder and they walked out the door together.

* * *

Preston often thought back to better times in the past, especially those of his youth, in order to gather strength to face the present. Although he was riddled with guilt about it later, he sometimes indulged himself in those pleasant memories while hearing appeals with the other Justices on Michigan's Supreme Court.

His favorite remembrance was about the cornfield in the middle of the night. And he chose to think about it this day as attorneys and accountants droned on about the tax ramifications of the case presently before the Court. While the appellant's presenters spoke of complicated accounting terms involving depreciation deductions, Preston remembered years ago as he had stood in a hundred acres of corn listening wonderingly to it grow.

He would have to be careful not to tell anybody about that part of it, they would never believe it. But he could hear the waist-high corn plants moving in the still air, rustling around him as they unfurled themselves in the sticky heat of early August in Michigan.

In his imagination, he'd leaped forward to fly down between the rows once again, feeling the coarse leaves slapping against his flesh. Bounding like a deer, exuberant in strength to spare, he drove his bare feet down hard into the warm, moist earth that smelled of life's beginning.

"Do you have any questions for counsel regarding her presentation, Justice Foster?" The question brought Preston's attention back to the present.

The voice breaking into his reverie was that of his lifetime friend and colleague, Chief Justice Augustus Woodward, whom his fellow Justices called "Woody." Scion of a wealthy founding family of Detroit, for whom a main thoroughfare in the city is named, Woody's great-grandfather had been a Justice on the Territorial Court before Michigan was made a state.

Preston decided not to answer Woody immediately, but instead turned his attention to the rays of sunshine streaming into the courtroom to help transport himself quickly from night in the past to day in the present. From his elevated seat on the podium, he stared at the nearest of the 14-foot-high windows letting in the golden light. All present turned their heads to see what he was looking at and, of course, saw nothing.

The panes of glass had been installed 80 years before. While marvels at the time, of heated sand first made liquid then quartz-hard, age had rearranged their molecules, now making the view through them distorted and untrustworthy.

Preston saw that the tough, old beech trees outside on the lawn that usually gave him inspiration weren't strong at all today, appearing to change shape constantly in the shifting winds of an approaching storm-front. Their limbs seemed to swim in the turbulent air like spaghetti boiling in a pot.

He felt a hand come to rest gently on the sleeve of his robe as Woody whispered, "Are you OK, or should I call a recess?"

The kindness brought tears to Preston Foster's eyes, but he remained silent. In a moment, he heard Woody bang his gavel hard and say, "This Court is adjourned until tomorrow morning at nine o'clock."

* * *

Preston was at his worst when working in his private office. Out in the courtroom, the fear of public humiliation helped enable him to ignore the horrific, intolerable mental image that besieged him whenever he tried to read, at least enough to keep going forward with the proceedings under way.

But alone he was defenseless, without the counter-force of embarrassment to help him push the unwanted visitor out of his mind. Its distraction, but most of all, the strange ritual he performed to temporarily get rid of it, brutally devoured his precious work time.

Purely by chance, when struggling to reinforce his concentration with repetition, he had discovered that the image disappeared when he read things exactly four times. Overjoyed at first with the relief it brought from the paralyzing anxiety the image caused in him, he soon learned his method was a time-consuming curse. Deliverance from being stopped cold by the image came at a high price. The odd, repetitious behavior allowed him to move forward through his work, yes, but at a snail's pace. Opinions that he used to be able to write in a few days, when his late wife, Anna Rose, was living, now required weeks of his time to complete.

He had started coming into the office four hours earlier than usual and worked far into the night to try to get on top of the growing backlog of unwritten opinions. That schedule would have quickly gotten him caught up on his workload in previous years.

He had prided himself on his timeliness back then. But that was all out the window since she had died. The profession he loved was fast becoming a nightmare as he fell further behind with each passing day.

It was a mystery that he struggled to fully understand. Quiet time to work was all he used to need, and his office was always a refuge that provided that. He turned out opinions like Detroit's famous assembly lines turned out cars.

His wife's death had changed everything. She was buried with their son but soon began to haunt him mentally, starting immediately after the funeral. And there was no one he dared talk to about it.

* * *

"How are you tonight, Judge Foster," a custodian, the only other person around, asked as he knocked lightly on the frame of the open door. "I'm taking on an extra shift tonight since Clara is off sick. So if it's okay with you, I need to empty your wastebasket."

"Fine, and you, Harold?" Preston replied, fighting back the sudden, irrational urge to tell this man the truth, that he was afraid he was going crazy.

The intimacy of the situation, being alone together in the empty building late at night with a winter wind blowing sleet against the windows, lowered his guard, but only for a moment. The fact that he had a severe emotional problem of some sort was kept secret from the public and the press by agreement of all the Justices. And he was determined to abide by that compact as a matter of professionalism and self-preservation.

"Clara says you are here every night," Harold said as he returned the basket after dumping its contents into a big, gray barrel he was pushing around on a cart.

"Not quite, but we are jammed up with extra cases," Preston lied, relieved he hadn't foolishly violated a confidence in a weak moment. Of course, they would talk about him anyway.

"Clara says you are the only judge that works late almost every night. They must have given all the extra cases to you, huh?"

"I'd better get back to work, Harold," Preston said, looking quickly down at the papers on his desk so the other man couldn't read his face and see the fear of discovery that gnawed at his gut.

He sat without moving to compose himself until he heard the elevator door close down the hall and then picked up one of the papers that he had been pretending to study for Harold's benefit. It was from the disastrous hearing that morning and was marked "Exhibit D" at the top. A bill, stamped "Paid," for sewer installation at the appellant's factory.

Preston knew what would happen when he began to read it. He would have given anything not to. But this was different than the *Wall Street Journal*s that he had simply ignored over the past few months. He wouldn't be able to comprehend what was going down when the case continued the next day if he didn't understand the financial terms that were now part of the record.

And Woody, so kindly in the courtroom, but unable to restrain himself any longer, had finally blown his stack when they had returned to the privacy of the Justices' chambers area. His message was softened very little by use

15

of Preston's nickname, "Bobby."

His old friend gathered the Justices together in the conference room and on behalf of himself, as Chief Justice, and all the others gave it to Preston straight on, "Bobby, you must either leave on your own or we are going to have to relieve you of your duties, even though we don't want to, there's no choice for us."

They gave Preston a copy of an undated letter addressed to the Judicial Tenure Commission asking for his temporary retirement from the bench on the grounds of a mental disability. It had obviously been prepared in advance and held for use if needed. Every one of the other Justices had signed it. It would be released to the commission, he was told, if he hadn't taken a medical leave of absence on his own volition by the end of the week.

In his own defense, he had reminded them that he had already compromised his principles and allowed them to do some of his caseload after they had complained that he was making them all look bad to the public with his lateness in issuing opinions. In response to that, one of the less tolerant Justices had snapped, "You act like that was doing us some fucking favor."

Preston's grudging admission that maybe he was being "too conscientious" seemed to infuriate them even more as they had gotten up from their large, leather-upholstered armchairs and hurried from the room without further comment. The last one out stopped for a moment to glare at Preston and then slammed the door closed behind him, putting an emphatic, audible period on the ultimatum just delivered.

He and Woody were left alone, sitting across the polished mahogany table from each other. Woody, his face still flushed from the confrontation that had just ended, immediately broke the silence with a rush of words, "You just about screwed yourself with that conscientious crap a moment ago. What about you, Bobby, making litigants wait months too long for your opinions? How does that score on your precious conscience meter?

"I can't hold them back any longer," he continued, "they've done pretty well, actually, at keeping your failures to ourselves, I'm speaking about the failure to pull your share of the workload. They just don't understand your behavior, and quite frankly, neither do I."

* * *

Preston struggled to focus his attention again on the legal exhibits before him on his desk but he knew that he was falling further behind each day, anxiety from his colleagues' ultimatum making it harder than ever to focus on his work. Then, over the howling of the wind outside, he heard the clock in the City Hall Tower across town lugubriously toll the midnight hour. The appeal hearing was now just hours away. He couldn't put preparation for it off any longer.

Filled with dread, he began to read Exhibit D, "Seventy-eight feet of standard twenty-inch-diameter concrete connector line." Halfway through the sentence, mournful music from a pipe organ invaded his consciousness triggering such anxiety that his concentration was totally wiped out. It was a Bach prelude, his dead wife's favorite, that was played at her funeral. Preston knew by now that it was a trick of the mind, the sound would not be heard by anyone else, a personal harbinger of worse to come. Experience had taught him that his beloved Anna Rose was about to appear.

* * *

A full moon, filtered crimson by heat haze, a color that promised rain to the farmers, beckoned Preston to the old, abandoned barn that he had fled to once again in his imagination to head off the arrival of the dreaded mental image. Its leaning sides and sagging roof were silhouetted briefly against what looked like a giant candy wafer sliding up out of the forest to the east.

Never painted, and weathered to silver gray by a thousand storms, the barn's board siding had half-inch gaps between each one. They admitted slivers of moonlight illuminating dust particles that were too new to be part of long-forgotten past harvests.

It was indeed his destination. To mount again in his mind, as he often used to do as a teenager, the tall and powerful, coal-black mare, Sugar Cookie, hidden there with a supply of food and water.

He had been as expert in his bareback ride as an Apache Indian of the western plains. Young man and horse had moved together in perfect unison in their nocturnal gallop over the moonlit landscape, wild and free and beautiful as whitetail deer running through a snowstorm or honking Canada geese crossing a winter sky.

But Preston's exhilarating remembrance back into a better time lasted not more than a few minutes. For once again he heard the clock chime, filling the windswept streets with a haunting refrain, a chilling summons for him to return to the legal task at hand.

* * *

17

Maybe, Preston thought, if he could only read like old times, his gaze passing calmly over the sentences, moving steadily down the page, everything would be alright. After all, like most youngsters, he had learned to read at a young age and had no problems with it over the years, until that day after the funeral when the image first appeared in his mind and changed everything.

With his confidence bolstered a little, Preston tried again to read Exhibit D. Instantly, this time, booming organ music filled his head, a portend of bad things to follow. Sick with despair, and lacking the time to escape again into the past with the hearing so near, he tried the only trick he had left to keep the dreaded specter away.

Hundreds of times over the few months since Anna Rose's passing, it had emerged whenever he tried to read. And by constant trial he had discovered a way of escape. He had stumbled upon the method one morning when reading a letter from a friend.

It was one of the rare occasions that he had a full night's sleep and he had arisen rested and refreshed. He had decided to keep on reading when the image presented itself and see what happened instead of stopping as he had always done before.

He read the letter again and again in an attempt to build some memory of its contents in spite of his mind being made blank by the overwhelming anxiety aroused in him by the image. On completion of the fourth time through, to his astonishment, the image disappeared. Since that fateful day, he read everything four times when the unwanted visitor came to call. But the price of banishing the image was a crushing one. The burdensome multiple reading was the main reason he was falling further and further behind. He knew it must eventually cost him his job, but the alternative was far worse, to live with the unbearable anxiety the awful mental image caused, with its accompanying sweating, nausea and total inability to think.

Strengthened by the memory of his past successes in pushing out the awful apparition, Preston picked up Exhibit D and read it from beginning to end. Quickly, he turned the pages back to the beginning and embarked on the second read, not pausing to allow any time for the dreaded intervention.

* * *

By the time dawn arrived, Preston knew the game was over. Exhausted by five hours of repetitive reading, he leaned back in his chair and rested his eyes by looking out the window for the first time since sitting down at his desk. As he watched the overcast, cold-looking sky lighten to the east, he thought about the dismally small amount of work-product he had created.

He had reviewed eleven of a total of forty-two exhibits entered on the record in the case, which was to be reconvened in a couple of hours, making about seven neatly written notes on a yellow legal pad. It was a mere dribble, really, compared to what he used to be capable of doing in the same amount of time.

It wasn't nearly enough for him to perform adequately during the hearing set to begin perilously soon. And Woody's comment, made with a grim expression on his face, "It isn't fair to me and the other Justices," had deftly played the guilt card against him during that awful meeting yesterday in the conference room.

Yes, Preston acknowledged to himself, his struggle was finally over. He would take the medical leave they demanded. It was a relief, actually, and he was tempted to simply phone Woody now and tell him his decision.

But somehow, he had to muster the strength to hang on to professionalism, and that meant facing them. This time he would be the one to call a meeting of the Justices in the conference room to tell them in person, even though it would delay the opening of the hearing.

He could trust Woody to cover his absence from the bench with the promised innocuous announcement. That would take care of everyone involved in the hearing and those press people that Preston had recognized in the waiting room yesterday that had been tagging after him everywhere.

He would shave and shower beforehand at the room he kept at the Marriot Hotel down the block from his chambers. Justice R. Preston Foster had secretly leased it after he started missing deadlines. He had made it his part-time home so he could slip into the office and catch up without anybody knowing about the hundreds of extra hours he was working since the onset of his mental affliction.

He knew the drill, he had done it many times before. Cleaned up and in a suit just out of the dry cleaners' plastic cover, he would return to the office, exhausted but looking as fresh as possible. He would time it so as to arrive just as the other Justices were coming in, walking in with them and telling them about a meeting he was calling in the conference room to discuss one of his recent cases. That way they would never know he had only been away from the office for an hour.

In fact, the Justice had been staying at the hotel, rather than at his apartment in the suburb of Okemos, about half the days he worked. When he did stay outside the city and rode in with Jimmy, he told his driver he had been out ill the other days and that they had to commute hours ahead of the other Justices to make up for sick time. He probably could have trusted Jimmy not to blow his cover, but you could never be too careful when your behavior had begun to fall well outside the norm.

His "unpaid overtime," as Preston thought of it, in a feeble attempt at humor, had gone far beyond the rationale of the "team player going the extra mile" thing that might have made points with the other Justices in the past. At $165,000 a year in salary, the highest in the nation, no overtime was ever paid of course, and none of the Justices would ever dream of asking for it. Certainly Preston never would, knowing that the extreme number of his extra hours would reveal himself to the world to be the weak link in the court system he knew he had become.

Some small amounts of his work outside of regular office hours that the others had found out about by chance, as when they returned to the office in the evening to get something they forgot, had already generated a confidential warning to him from Woody that "everybody was getting pissed and that Woody couldn't keep the lid on them much longer."

Well, it was finally over. Now the other Justices could do all his cases. Tears came to his eyes as he got up from his desk. At least this time his weeping didn't betray his despair in public.

He knew that he wouldn't feel like hanging around after he informed the other Justices of his decision. Moving about the office, he gathered everything he wanted to take with him. He stuffed it all into a large rucksack for carrying back to the hotel.

As he passed the window, a pair of brilliantly colored wood ducks flashed by, knifing through the morning air just a few feet outside. Foster hurried closer to the glass to better see them hurtle themselves up from the confining rows of buildings. He knew the beautiful birds were seeking the woods and lakes where they belonged.

That was exactly what he, too, was about to do. He had a plan. He would return to his country roots in order to heal. The solace of his ancestral farm near Lapeer, in the Thumb Area of Michigan, seemed mighty good to him about now.

Chapter Two
Diamonds on the Water

His naked body was a sleek torpedo. With head tucked between arms stretched out ahead, he skimmed effortlessly through the deep blue water, above submerged glacial boulders put down 10,000 years before.

A twenty-foot headlong plunge from an oak branch into the lake below a few moments before had provided the energy for his morning dip in the sunlit spring water.

His momentum slowed inevitably by the water's constant resistance, he ended his smooth underwater glide and swam toward the precious air above.

Breaking the surface in a large wave, he breathed deeply, then began a slow crawl stroke towards the shore, skillfully skirting floating beds of white and yellow water lilies, flushing a pair of startled largemouth bass out of one.

Halfway in he stopped, treading water and taking in the comforting surroundings. He had always savored the green of hardwood forests that blanketed the rolling hills and the white of clouds scattered evenly across the blue sky.

He glanced for a moment at the sun's broad path of sparkling diamonds, as his mother used to call them, and then turned quickly away. They were points of light on the water so brilliant that they hurt the eyes if looked at for any length of time. A display born of the sunshine's refraction through the waves kicked up by the fresh morning breeze.

He had been back on the home farm inherited from his parents for almost three months. Riding horseback, watching the deer and wild turkeys and other wildlife, and swimming in this lake at the back of the property had eased his thoughts considerably as well as kept his body in perfect shape.

It had cleared his mind enough to know that a life here in the wilderness of rural Michigan would never be enough for him. His dual career of law and politics had rewarded him so richly, both financially and emotionally, that he was forever spoiled.

He remembered the call from Tom Brokaw he received shortly after retreating to Red Moon. It was made to confirm the Justice's "retirement," as the NBC national television news anchor delicately put it.

Preston knew there was no reason he should have been surprised by the call. The fact that he was the youngest person ever elected to a state's highest court had attracted a lot of national attention a few years back. That, and his brilliant legal track record, had made him a rising star in the Republican Party.

Choosing his words carefully, Preston had responded to Brokaw's tough questions by saying that he was taking an indefinite leave of absence for medical reasons that he preferred not to discuss until he was a little farther down the treatment road. As soon as the brief conversation ended, he called the phone company and terminated his answering service.

His guarded statement was picked up by the Associated Press following Brokaw's comments that night on the *NBC Nightly News* but got only a line or two in newspapers around the country. It had been buried in national news briefs compiled by editors who considered Preston to be politically dead.

He knew better. People loved a comeback. It was one of the few universal truths he was absolutely sure of. Look at Abraham Lincoln and all his defeats. And now that great President was recently discovered to have suffered from the mental illness of severe depression.

As he swam to shore, Preston reveled in his restored physical strength. Freedom, however acquired, from his past long days of sitting did have its reward in renewed vigor. His trim physique slid smoothly along the cool water caressing his sides, his skin glowing with health.

If only he could be as fit mentally. That part was not going well at all. And he had expected that the removal of all that pressure from being far behind in his work would help him become emotionally revitalized.

He remembered his first attempt at recreational reading after arriving at Red Moon. He had picked up the *Farmers Almanac* for the fun of it when he was at the feed store in town, barely resisting the temptation to buy bib overalls and a huge red hanky to complete the picture.

All the joy had gone out of it when he sat down on the farmhouse porch and began to read. Barely a paragraph into the first article on making maple syrup, the organ music had begun to play in his head. He threw the book on the plank floor, bounded across the front lawn, and launched into a six-mile run down the gravel road.

So his mysterious affliction didn't differentiate between serious and light reading. His hopes of a quick cure by simply altering his environment were dashed to smithereens that day. But his curiosity about his frighteningly debilitating condition was piqued even more.

Today he would begin his quest to find a name for it. Having reached shallow water, he stood up on the sandy bottom and waded out. First he had to get the phone turned back on so he could use the Internet. He dried off quickly with the towel he had left draped over a sassafras sapling, leaning close to catch its root beer scent.

Dressing quickly, his excitement building about his plans for the forthcoming days, he loped up the trail leading to the farmhouse and barns. His analytical mind had already begun exploring various avenues of research to pursue. Besides the medical Websites, there were vast libraries at the teaching hospitals downstate full of the latest medical information.

Maybe he would fly out to the National Institutes of Health in Bethesda, Maryland. Even his family doctor might give him a lead. He felt his pulse quicken, as a life force deep in his psyche shifted into drive.

Chapter Three
A Medical Breakthrough

Preston drove slowly to calm himself down as he approached the University of Michigan Medical Center from the east on Fuller Road. A massive complex of connected, multi-storied structures, it crowned the top of the Ft. Wayne Morraine, an elongated mound of gravel outwash from a melting Ice Age glacier. People with his farm background called such geological formations "hogsbacks."

Uncertain in his new and unfamiliar role of patient, he had second thoughts. Was it really his finest hour, admitting he had a problem and seeking help, as his internist described it when referring him here? Or was it the dumbest thing he ever did? What if someone he knew was in the shrink's waiting room?

Turning left and crossing the Huron River bridge brought him onto the Center's campus, the first of the massive buildings looming above him halfway up a steep incline. Feeling dwarfed in the shadow it cast from the morning sun, it crossed his mind that he was like some troubled supplicant approaching a mountain-side Tibetan monastery seeking guidance.

* * *

"Describe this mental image that you suppress by reading everything four times, Justice Foster," the attractive, well-groomed woman said, leaning forward toward him across her desk.

"Aren't there some preliminaries to coast through before we take on the big stuff?" Preston asked, admiring the way her full breasts handled the heavy woolen fabric of her royal blue business suit. Relieved that his assigned psychiatrist happened to be a woman, Rachael Childs, M.D., his confidence had returned.

He was always good with women, especially attractive ones like this shapely doctor, with her thick, dark hair, olive skin, and large, almond-shaped brown eyes, that stirred his loins to a high-alert status.

25

"Why bother?" she replied. "You have a problem, I know how to fix it. Let's get going."

"Hold on, in the law we don't pay much attention to experts until we lay a foundation for their testimony by asking them about their credentials, may I?"

"Justice Foster, are you serious about wanting to get well? Otherwise, don't waste my valuable time. You know from the handout they gave you at registration that I'm a behaviorist, educated here at the university's medical school, with residency training at Johns Hopkins and in London.

"Now let's get to work," she continued briskly. "Surely you understand that your repetition rituals are self-defeating. Tell me about this scene in your imagination that makes a smart man like you do such a stupid thing to forestall it."

But Preston still wasn't quite ready for therapy sessions, saying, "I want us to start out with appropriate attitudes. I am your equal, but in a different field. If you were my legal client, I would not use the word 'stupid' out of respect for you."

"Life is not a popularity contest," the doctor tersely replied. "If you're going to be that sensitive, find another therapist."

"But what about my medical history, my upbringing, the traumatic experiences I've endured? Don't you need to know about those pieces of my personal puzzle?"

"As a behaviorist, I couldn't care less. It's the here and now that matters to you and me. Stop avoiding and answer my question about what's bugging you."

* * *

It was the first time that Preston had dared tell another human being about Anna Rose in her casket with their dead son and the music that was the obsession's precursor.

He spoke of his wife's exquisite face framed in shining black curls even though he had learned long ago not to praise one woman to another, even to an equally beautiful one like Doctor Childs.

Suddenly shy, he left out the part about the loveliness of the curls repeated in miniature upon his wife's pubic mound, instead describing the ornate, golden casket lined in padded red satin like a treasure box designed to showcase the jewel of a woman within it.

Finishing up with a description of his naked, newborn son, umbilical cord still intact, nursing at his mother's breast, he watched the doctor's face for

26

clues to her reaction to his explanation of "what was bugging him" indeed; he saw none.

Her lack of a verbal response, as well, created a silence which, as it lengthened, built a growing tension between them that he finally gave in to. "Am I losing my mind?" he blurted out suddenly and without any warning of his intense feelings.

"Heavens, no, Justice Foster. You're suffering from obsessive-compulsive disorder, along with an estimated five million other people in the United States according to a Gallop poll. Everybody calls it OCD. And since we're talking abbreviations, may I call you something shorter from now on?"

He felt a great weight lift from his shoulders upon learning he was not alone with an illness that now had a name. Almost giddy with relief, he quipped, "A gorgeous lady like you can call me anything you want."

His lame attempt at humor hung heavy in the silence that followed it. Unable, again, to bear the stressful quiet, Preston smiled apologetically and said, "First names for both of us from now on, ok?"

Rising from her chair, the doctor turned playful for a moment, saying, "Hi Preston, I'm Rachael." Then she added in a more professional tone, "Your hour's up now and since it's five o'clock I've got to run off to another appointment, so there'll be no homework assignment until next week."

"Homework?" he said as he stood up and turned to leave, in quick cooperation with her signal that the session was at an end.

"You're going to be doing exposure and response prevention exercises every day," she said sternly. Then to his departing back, in a lighter vein, "I think you need to get yourself a girlfriend."

Turning around to face her when he reached the door, he gave her a long, hard look, letting her have some of the same silent treatment she had used to squeeze information out of him. Then he replied emphatically, "I don't think so." They shared a laugh at the tone of absolute certainty in his negative response, and he went on his way.

* * *

Homework turned out to be a thousand dollars, for an entire-day visitation by Rachael, from nine in the morning to five in the afternoon at his home. These homework sessions in the initial stages of the therapy were frequently three times a week. As the sessions favorably progressed, they would taper off proportionately.

After that first appointment at her office, upon deciding that he could get along with her, Preston had independently researched her background.

Starting with the Center's Website, and following up with phone calls to hospitals where she had been trained and practiced, he confirmed her professional expertise.

She was, indeed, fast building an international reputation with a new approach to treating OCD. Called Cognitive Behavior Therapy (CBT), it was radically different than the traditional treatment with the "talk therapy" of Freudian psychoanalysis.

On the personal side, Preston learned she was 40 years old and the daughter of a prominent psychiatrist at the Mayo Clinic in Rochester, Minnesota.

Her father's first wife had died in the Holocaust but her father had survived the camps and came to the United States, where he was trained by Theodore Reik, another German immigrant, who had been a protégé of Sigmund Freud, the inventor of the psychoanalysis rejected by Rachael.

She was born in the early sixties of her father's second marriage to a Mayo Clinic nurse. Preston imagined there were lively debates between a father and daughter who held such diverse views on how to treat mental illness.

His problem was the enormous cost of treatment. He received disability benefits from Aetna Insurance paid under a policy that was a fringe benefit of working for the State of Michigan. Those covered his living expenses. But his savings account and stock portfolio were almost depleted by his wife's and son's astronomical medical expenses not covered by insurance as well as by the cost of their funeral and burial. And he received no compensation for his leave of absence once his accumulated sick days were used up.

He had promptly forgotten about Rachael's lighthearted suggestion about getting a girlfriend. But he thought of it again when he watched an advertisement on television featuring former Senator Bob Dole pitching Viagra. If the unsuccessful Republican candidate for President could make a ton of money off sex, why couldn't a retired State Supreme Court Justice do the same? A plan had begun to take shape in his mind and he knew just the right person to run it by for final approval.

* * *

Laura Hopkins, at 32 years old, was in her prime. Heads turned to watch her, walking with a strut, and passing through the main dining room of Birmingham's trendy Forte restaurant. A tall, willowy, black-haired beauty of Italian descent, she had "hot dish," an older but quite appropriate description, written all over her.

Preston waited until she reached his table, then stood up, stretching as tall as his six foot two inches would allow, and threw out his muscular chest, to proudly claim her for all to see. He savored the winner's feeling it gave him, something he hadn't experienced for a long time, as he helped her out of the full-length black diamond mink that matched her shining hair.

Gorgeous, with an "if-you've-got-it-flaunt-it" attitude, she had been happy in her role of a multimillionaire's trophy wife. All that ended, when her husband Jake was killed the previous year at the age of 45, in the crash of their private jet on a business trip to South Africa.

She had met Jake shortly after her graduation from high school while working as a flight attendant for his airline, Universal Commuter. Now that she owned the company, returning to her old job would be ridiculous.

Left with no other workplace skills to fill up her days, she had become bored with her life in Bloomfield Hills and West Palm Beach. She dearly loved her three children, but they had a full-time nanny and required little of her time.

Her only real diversion was a daily set of tennis, dressed in skimpily fetching white shorts, with her Brazilian personal trainer, a flirtatious and charming muscle man. She suspected he had his eye on her rather large bank account, some eight hundred million dollars' worth.

Most men were so intimidated by her wealth and beauty that they were too scared to ask her out on a date. She was sweetly eased out of her previous social circle that had revolved around her and her handsome husband by wives skittish about getting her too near their spouses. She had become so desperate for a man in recent weeks that she was teetering on the brink of telling Manuel to meet her in her bedroom rather than at the tennis court.

She had helped Bobby Foster in his most recent election campaign for State Supreme Court, as a volunteer party-planner for socialite fundraisers. There had been five such events, so Anna Rose and he had gotten to know her quite well. They both had found her to be a delightful woman in her flowered silk pantsuits by day and ultra-low-cut black or red evening dresses at her evening cocktail parties in support of his candidacy, all of which were huge financial successes.

He was enraptured by her now, as she talked excitedly to him, waving her red-velvet-gloved hands to punctuate her rapid sentences, in her deep, throaty voice which stirred far more in him than a mild interest in what she was chattering happily about.

Why would a woman this attractive ever need the services he was about to offer her? Hazel, her personal secretary, no doubt spent most of her work-time screening calls from Laura's hordes of ardent suitors. On the spot,

Preston's nerve crumbled, and his plans changed.

He would pitch his idea over this private lunch together, yes, but as something for Laura "to run by a female friend of her choice" to test the waters and report back to him with her "friend's" reaction.

* * *

Steel baron Andrew Carnegie had paid for the Williamsburg-style red brick library, with its white-painted wooden trim, in Lapeer, one of thousands he had endowed across the United States. The pride of the country town, Bobby Foster had bragged about it to his freshman year undergraduate school roommate Augustus Woodward, "Woody," at the University of Michigan, when they met each other at the Sigma Chi fraternity on State Street for the first time.

"Guilt money," his new acquaintance had pronounced in quick dismissal of the town benefactor's generous gift. A child of social workers who did their undergraduate study at Oberlin College, Woody saw things far to the left of his ancestors' politics, conveniently forgetting that it was their capitalistic fur trading and lumbering that accumulated the "old money" that paid his tuition.

If only his old friend could see him now, struggling with the library's computerized index system to find information on anal sex, in his crash course on technique, trying to come up with something "different" that Laura may not have tried. However, all the while he strained to look like he knew what he was doing, so the gray-haired librarian hovering nearby, a high school chum of his late mother, wouldn't glide over and peer at the monitor in her well-intended effort to help him out.

As he scrolled down the list of sex-related publications, writing down titles and call numbers on a piece of scratch paper, he thought about his unforgettable lunch with Laura the day before that had hastily propelled him to the library.

He had eased into his presentation to her with a candid description of being treated for OCD at a staggeringly high cost. His frank disclosure of such a private matter encouraged her to open up, and they quickly became wrapped up in the warm blanket of shared confidences.

She confided in him that she was dreaming of Manuel's great body day and night. Encouraged, he moved on to his innovative way of making enough money to pay for his controversial but promising treatment. He decided it was best not to describe Rachael or even to reveal that his doctor was a woman.

30

"Why didn't you just tell me you are planning on being a gigolo?" she giggled, with an ear-to-ear grin, when he had finished describing the male companion and sexual partner service he had dreamed up and asked her to troll it by a "friend" for a possible strike.

Encouraged by her non-judgmental response, he had rushed excitedly into more details.

He told her how he had already started renovations turning the summer cottage on the shore of the spring-fed lake at the back of Red Moon into an expensive, beautifully-appointed bed and breakfast hideaway as the setting for his new endeavor.

He described to her the 21-foot McGregor cabin sailboat he had bought to spice up his clients' choices of sleeping and eating locations. And how the smell of frying bacon would draw the woman up on deck in the morning sunshine, Bobby having anchored in a secluded lagoon, to prepare breakfast for her when she finally woke up after a glorious night of sexual exploration. A feast consisting of freshly squeezed orange juice, his "famous" blueberry pancakes topped with whipped cream and real maple syrup, and a side dish of thickly sliced bacon, all washed down with Costa Rican Brit coffee brewed from beans ground just minutes beforehand.

Intoxicated by his own sales talk, Preston rattled on, extolling the virtues of the antique shops, golf courses, tennis courts, and restaurants, including Frankenmuth's famed Zehnder's, that were in the vicinity of Red Moon Bed and Breakfast. These treats would be available, he pointed out, in case his lady companion tired of the country life.

Then, saving what he considered the best for last, he had unveiled to an attentive Laura his marketing brainstorm: a $2500 weekend package to be peddled to travel agents in Chicago and Toronto, big-money population centers connected to each other by the Amtrak International that "just happened" to stop at quaint Lapeer located halfway between the two cities.

He closed with what he was sure would be the clincher, "You know how women love the romance of trains."

Smiling at his boyish enthusiasm, Laura had paused for a long moment and then said, "I hate trains, I'll have my pilot, Jason, fly me into Bishop Airport in Flint. That's someplace up around Lapeer, isn't it?"

"It sure is and, I think it's great that you're coming up to take a look at the place."

"Not just the place, honey, I want to check out the entire action and, incidentally, thank you for asking me to be your first guest."

Chapter Four
Setting Up Shop

As the Port Huron Glacier, a mile thick in places, began to melt and recede northward, it revealed the handiwork of its earlier, southbound journey. Nowhere were the lakes and hills it had created more picturesquely arranged than around Lapeer.

A nameless tribe of prehistoric people of the Archiac Era were the first human beings to live on the lake at the back of Red Moon, 8,000 years before Columbus discovered America.

Their primitive stone tools and weapons were found so frequently, both in the water and on the shore, that Bobby Foster chose an archaeology theme for his bed and breakfast.

He was hanging a display board covered with white burlap cloth, upon which he had fastened a circular array of arrowheads and spear points, on the parlor wall when Uncle Earl's booming voice impatiently summoned him to the bedroom.

"I'm in your daddy's playroom," the tall, wiry, white-bearded man called, "and I need you to dirty those hands on some 'real man's' work."

He was holding a ten-by-four-foot piece of drywall against the ceiling with a T-shaped device that he had improvised by nailing together pieces of two-by-four. "If only these walls could talk," he said as Bobby joined him.

"You'd be disappointed if they could, Earl. Mom and Dad worked so hard on the farm that they rarely got back here to use this cottage at all."

"You've become such an overeducated city slicker you probably don't know this little handy-dandy I made is called a 'dead man,'" Earl said, adding with a nod of his head, "You hold this sucker while I do the hard part."

Bobby had hired his father's brother, a retired carpenter, to help him convert his parents' small summer retreat into a top-of-the-line bed and breakfast.

The master bedroom was the last room needing upgrading, the two of them having finished off in the last few weeks the rest of the five-room guest suite, with its private deck overlooking the lake below.

To attractively show off several generations of the family's antique furnishings, they had put up Victorian-style flowered wallpaper, above painted wooden wainscoting that was topped with a chair rail. Built-up crown molding that they installed where the walls met the ceiling gave the small rooms a more stately look.

The wallpaper treatment was repeated within a circle of painted wooden molding, six feet in diameter, above the ceiling fans with their crystal light fixtures that they had installed in each room.

"There," Earl announced as he hammered the final nail through the drywall and into the beam beneath, "slick as snot on a shingle."

The Justice made a mental note that Uncle Earl was definitely not cut out for even the traditional sort of bed and breakfast business, with its genteel clientele of bird-watching and book-reading types, let alone catering to the sophisticated women of the world that would hopefully be coming to this one.

"What's the deal?" his uncle carried on. "First you tell me to take my time and do everything perfect and now we're wrapping up this job faster than Epsom salts through a sick rabbit."

"Not so fast we can't have a coffee break, Earl," Preston said, "I'll bring it out to the new deck. You did a great job building it. You should enjoy it some before the first of my guests arrive this weekend and you won't have access to it anymore."

"Not unless they invite me in to enjoy my charm," his uncle replied with a smile and a wink.

He had his back turned, urinating over the rail onto the ground ten feet below, when Preston arrived on the deck a few minutes later with a pot of coffee and two mugs.

Yes, Uncle Earl had to be kept away from customers, Bobby Foster concluded, which wasn't going to be easy, since his uncle liked to fish.

* * *

However, a much bigger threat to the success of his new business than Uncle Earl occupied Preston's mind.

His therapy sessions had begun in the house he had rented for that purpose in Ann Arbor and, on their most recent appointment, Rachael had given him a prescription for Celexa, which he had reluctantly filled and begun to take.

Rachael had described the new medication's promising track record for

34

banishing the involuntary obsessions that besieged OCD sufferers, and then, without showing any visible signs of embarrassment, she had begun a low-voiced, matter-of-fact description of the sexual side effects of the drug.

"No matter how many times you go in and out, you may still not be able to come," she said as casually as if they were talking about the price of potatoes.

"There must be a more professional way of saying that, Doctor."

"Remember me, I'm Rachael. As you recall, we agreed that we were beyond formalities.

"Look at it this way," she continued blandly, "nobody has to lay in a cold spot."

"Wait a minute," Bobby had said, struggling to conceal his alarm, "what about libido?"

"Same prognosis, it's a 'maybe.' It seems to me," Rachael added, "that if you have to be sexless, this is a good time in your life to do without, having become a widower not that long ago, and spending your weekends alone in the sticks."

"But Rachael, there's something I haven't told you yet."

"Unfortunately, it will have to wait. We have to close now so I can hurry back to my office and pack up some papers. I'm making a presentation at a behaviorists' workshop in Barbados."

"Oh, that's just great, while you're snorkeling on some reef, I'll fill this prescription and neuter myself in the bargain," he quipped.

"No pain, no gain," Rachael said, striding toward his front door.

"Don't tell me, let me make a guess; you won't be back for at least a week. That's after Red Moon Bed and Breakfast's first guest has come and gone."

"How did you know that?"

"I've started stalking you, no, only kidding. Just a hunch from the way my luck has been running lately."

"Not everyone has the same reaction to the meds," Rachael said, more seriously, picking up on his suppressed anger. "You might be pleasantly surprised," she added, trying to leave him on an upbeat note, and giving him a smile she hoped was reassuring as she turned and made her leave.

As Preston stood in the doorway, his eyes followed her down the front walk flagrantly noticing her tight, short skirt and visible panty line, certain he detected an increasing snap to the sway of her shapely derriere as she progressed toward the street.

* * *

35

Rachael had more to pack than just papers, and she was thinking about some of the other stuff as she hurried away, sexy things she hadn't used since her last trip to the Caribbean; uplift bras, thong panties, black lace bikinis, and, even a few little toys for added sexual pleasure and eroticism. She was really getting quite excited about the trip ahead. Thank heavens Barbados had a Club Med with all those delicious beach boys. Her womanhood was wet thinking about it.

Chapter Five

Secondhand Rose

Laura Hopkins changed her mind about the plane, as she was prone to do about many things since Jake died, and drove herself to Red Moon, a full day ahead of when Preston was to meet her at Flint's Bishop Airport.

She had learned that shaking up the schedule of a man, especially one as well organized as a Supreme Court Justice had to be, often cracked their outward facade of being in total control, allowing her a peek at the real person within.

She wanted desperately to find somebody, of the opposite sex, that was as much of a free spirit as she had become. And her lunch with Preston had gone a long way toward convincing her that he might just be the answer to her prayers.

Her spirits were soaring as she headed north in a white BMW convertible, with red genuine leather interior, its top down to allow her to feel the wind on her face, long black hair streaming out behind her.

Laura had found Lapeer on the road-map, now stashed on the floor in front of the passenger seat so it wouldn't fly out with her high-speed driving. She was surprised at how close it was to Detroit's affluent northern suburbs, where she lived in the summer months.

She knew more rich women in Bloomfield Hills than she wanted to know that would travel the mere hour and a half to flock to the prize rooster that was about to open the henhouse door. And she had already decided not to tell any of them about the pleasant opportunities that Red Moon may afford the well-heeled, attractive, widow, divorcee, or otherwise single woman.

Laura could barely stand the wait to reach her destination. She had mailed the $2500 charge for the weekend to Preston in advance, so there would be no need for either of them to mention money. From everything she had seen so far, it appeared to be a bargain. This would be the first time in her life that all she would have to do was lay down and say, "Do me."

* * *

37

Preston found that X-rated books and videos were harder to find than he thought they would be. He hadn't expected to discover any at Lapeer's library, of course, but was surprised to find that neither Borders Bookstore nor Blockbuster Video stocked any for sale. He had stopped at both those stores on his way back to Red Moon after seeing Laura for lunch.

It soon became apparent to him, after driving around Lapeer for five minutes, that his churchy hometown had been successful in keeping out any sort of business that would, at least openly, sell such things.

That left him to rummage through the sleaze shop he had just parked three blocks away from in Flint. Still safely in his locked car, he motivated himself to go forward with his quest by savoring the memory of their unforgettable conversation at Forte.

At first, Laura's unexpected suggestion that his proposed "establishment" needed erotic stuff like that had almost offended him. He had certainly never had any trouble getting it up.

They had been finishing off their lunch together with her favorite dessert, sipping Kahlua to keep their buzz going while sharing a single serving of Georgia pecan pie smothered in French vanilla ice cream, when she mentioned that maybe he should have a few sex toys available, catching him off guard.

"It's not for you, silly," she added quickly, sensing ruffled feathers, and then reaching across the table to take his hand, she continued, "Us girls sometimes need a little extra even with the best of men.

"If we were in Paris now," she said, abruptly changing the subject, "your waiter, without asking, would bring you and the beautiful coquette you're dining with tiny glasses of room-temperature Sauterne from the southern provinces, served with delicate pastries they call 'mille feuilles.' It is wonderful in the City of Light.

"We will see how our weekend goes," she said then, adding very softly for his ears alone, "Perhaps you would accompany me to Paris as my guest if your 'package' turns out to be as good as it sounds."

His vivid recollection of her extraordinary suggestion regarding a trip abroad at her expense energized him just enough to leave his car and walk quickly toward the Sittin' Purty, with its cheesy plywood cutout of a showgirl perched on the roof with one moving, neon-lighted leg forever kicking toward the street. But not before looking in all directions to make sure no one saw him.

* * *

38

Its tires squealed their protest as the BMW sped up the tightly-curved exit ramp from the I-75 expressway unto northbound M-24. Laura noted the rural towns, each one smaller than the last, that the black-topped state road led her through: Lake Orion, Oxford, and then folksy Lapeer. Much sooner than she had expected, she was on Shady Oaks, the gravel country road leading to Red Moon, a rooster tail of dust recording her passage.

Bobby Foster, who took it for granted, had not told her about the beauty of the countryside. Lakes, as blue as the clear sky reflected in them, were nestled among rolling hills embellished with emerald-green cornfields. Big white farmhouses with clusters of red barns behind them dotted the landscape. Clumps of white and yellow daisies brightened the overgrown roadside.

Slowing down and grasping the steering wheel tightly with one hand, Laura glanced quickly down at the Forte cocktail napkin she held in the other. Below Preston's scribbled directions, he had drawn the outline of an arrowhead around the words "new sign."

A quarter mile further down the road she saw it. A three-foot-long varnished birch wood board, cut the shape of his drawing, with the words "Red Moon Bed & Breakfast" darkly engraved upon it with a burning tool.

In contrast to the cheery greeting provided by a pail of red geraniums placed at the foot of the post holding the sign, a combination padlock, its chrome sides flashing in the hot sun, dangled from a chain connecting the two halves of the divided gate where they met in the center of the driveway. Laura hadn't counted on being locked out.

* * *

Foster decided not to hint at his destination by slowing the pace of his walking as he neared the small black-painted one-story cement block building. Twigs, scraps of paper, and an assortment of other debris, including a crushed red box with the word Trojan printed on it, littered the cracked and pot-holed parking lot.

A few new or late-model clean cars were parked in a row along the side of the building. A dirty, rusted-out Chevrolet Caprice from an earlier decade, looking twice as big as the others, sat tightly against a high wooden privacy fence in back that only partially concealed the junk yard behind it.

The Chevy's massive rear bumper was missing, revealing a bulky gas tank and its mud-caked fill pipe, a rather revolting sight that would have appalled the car's proud designers, akin to the experience, Foster supposed, of being able to see up an old lady's skirt and glimpse her soiled underwear. He figured the wreck of an automobile probably belonged to some wretch the owner of the place had scraped off the street to man the front counter.

Surveying his surroundings one last time, and relieved to see nobody was looking his way, he turned abruptly to the right, crossed some uneven squares of cement with weeds growing up between them that passed for a walkway, and quickly slipped inside the erotic sex store.

* * *

How long had it been, Laura asked herself, since she had walked a country lane alone, her footsteps barely audible upon the broken grass in the tire tracks she followed?

She was passing through a pasture that was a rolling sea colored in countless mixed shades of green and brown. Heat raised a scent of wild roses along the way that made her suddenly stop and inhale deeply. Had she ever known such quietude before, she wondered aloud.

Abruptly, the great silence that surrounded her was broken by the cry of a male bobolink springing up out of a nearby patch of tall, white Queen Anne's lace. Ten feet into the air, it wheeled to survey its territory, its repeated warning call, a beautiful melody to human ears, delighted Laura as she realized that the black-and-white-feathered sentinel was singing its own name in syllables.

She felt intuitively that Bobby Foster, in some seamless way, was a part of all this. Yet he seemed to know wines, and ballets, history, and symphonies just as well as the tractors, and weather patterns, and hunting rifles that she imagined were a part of country living.

The land was gradually rising toward wooded hills before her. She quickened her pace, curiosity building about what lay beyond them that she couldn't see yet. Partway up the first one, tiny beads of sweat dampening her forehead, she found herself welcomed by the cool shadows of towering oaks.

* * *

Once inside the Sittin' Purty, Preston was immediately drenched in visual sexual stimulation. Surrounding him were uncensored pornographic photographs on the covers of hundreds of magazines and video boxes displayed on the sharply tilted shelves of tall display racks that were lined up in several rows down the center of the large room and set against its four walls.

Battery-powered dildoes for women and complicated-looking male-masturbation devices, all priced for sale, dangled from the ceiling, presented in such an artful way that a more innocent generation might have mistaken them for futuristic mobiles.

For the browse fee of two dollars, collected at the door and applicable towards a purchase, a customer had the run of the place 24 hours a day. Preston decided he had figured right about who owned the decrepit car outside in the parking lot. It no doubt belonged to the world-weary-looking wreck of a woman, dressed in stained pink sweats, who was collecting the money.

She was the only one in sight who didn't appear to be a customer. A pale creature with stringy hair, that appeared to be somewhere in her early sixties, she struggled to hide bad front teeth by talking out of the corner of her mouth.

At one time 25 years ago, she could possibly have been attractive even with her protruding incisors.

But give her credit, Preston thought, *working here is better than turning cheap tricks in some abandoned house.* Then, of course, maybe she had resorted to that and found out that nobody wanted her.

Already uneasy about being recognized, Preston became even more fearful of being spotted by someone from his judicial past when he saw that the other patrons, all middle-aged men, wore suits and ties. In an effort to go unnoticed, he had dressed down, putting on the Levi's and red plaid shirt getup he had bought at the feed store in Lapeer which now made him stand out, enough so as to temporarily distract the admission-taker from the worn, dog-eared paperback she had been reading to ease her tedium. His casual dress had set the war-horse-put-to-pasture at such ease that she volunteered a friendly comment when she noticed him concentrating on a photograph on a video box that showed a white woman bestowing oral sexual favors on a black man.

"That one's all blowjobs, you'll like it," she announced loudly enough to be heard from across the room where she sat, her flabby buttocks overflowing the bar stool she was balanced upon, behind the cash register.

Preston was relieved to see that the other men in the place, avidly perusing the merchandise, didn't look around at the sound of her voice. They were apparently as intent on remaining anonymous as he was.

His fear of being spotted by someone who knew him was quickly being crowded out of his mind, anyway, by another, even more pressing worry: In spite of his brain being bombarded with enough eroticism to prod a dead man to immediate action, nothing was happening in his pants. Had Celexa already done a number on him?

41

"That one is running in booth six, maybe it will help you to watch it," the woman suggested as if reading his mind. Startled, he stared at her in embarrassment as she added, "To make up your mind about buying it, I mean." Then she added, helpfully, to possibly save him a wasted trip into the other room, "You'll need some quarters for the viewing machine."

Why not? Preston asked himself, maybe it was the stress of being in such a public place that was blocking his physical response. Going to an archway, she motioned for him to follow her through a flimsy partition. Passing under a sign that read "Only One Person per Booth," he found a row of cubicles, their door numbers barely visible in the gloom of the unlighted area.

As Preston gingerly opened the door marked "6" and looked inside, he heard hoarse breathing, its rhythm accelerating, the sound coming through the thin plywood that separated him from the excited customer in booth number 7. Littering the floor of the enclosure, between a small seat built into one side of it and what appeared to be a television screen protruding from the other, were crumpled Kleenexes amid puddles of liquid the color and consistency of thin wallpaper paste.

Without going inside, and suppressing a sudden craving for a shower, he quietly closed the door and returned to the front room. Still carrying the video box the haggard crone had commented on, he set it down in front of her on the counter. If she was surprised to see him back so soon, she didn't show it, continuing to read a moment before looking up at him and saying matter-of-factly, "Oh oh, don't tell me you're another one of those 'minute-men.'"

Setting her book aside, she reached toward a shelf behind her and picked up what could have been mistaken for toothpaste, and said, "Your wife's going to love me for selling you this salve, just put a little on the head of your trouser mouse beforehand, it'll slow you down some."

"No wife," Preston replied.

"Sorry, most of the guys that come in here are married and fantasizing about things their wives won't do. You must have a girlfriend then, nobody that looks like you wouldn't have one or the other, unless maybe you're gay."

"Forget the tube of Slow Poke," Preston said, adding, "I'm beginning to think I've got the opposite problem because of some medication I'm taking."

"I've heard about that stuff," she said, pleased with herself for knowing something about medical problems, but keeping her face as devoid of expression as ever, adding, "For high blood pressure, right?"

"Right," Preston echoed her monotone, then he gestured with his hand toward the video box he had just laid in front of her, and said, "Find one for me to buy like that, but only the kind that will excite my woman instead of me, I'll trust your judgment."

"You will?" she said, the first hint of a smile she had let appear playing for a moment around the down-turned corners of her mouth.

* * *

Laura studied the scene below her as she stood at the crest of the last of the wooded hills.

A sun-sparkled dark-blue lake lay crosswise in front of her in the bottom of a deep trough that looked like it might have been gouged out by the garden hoe of a giant. Running out into it was a small, forest-covered peninsula, with a red cottage with white shutters where the land ended. It glowed like a ruby in its green surroundings, clinging precariously to a sharply slanted grassy clearing where the gradually descending hillside that ran out before Laura made its final plunge into the clear, fresh water.

She could see the figure of a man and, though a long way away, recognized Preston's tall, slim build and his assertive gait as he moved back and forth loading a bright yellow pickup truck parked near the picturesque building.

Delighted, Laura reached quickly down to pull off her uncomfortable city shoes, then, holding them in one hand, she bounded downhill as lighthearted as a child just off the school bus.

She was once again following the tire tracks, as her intended destination was out of sight, her view temporarily blocked by a mixed grove of white pine and poplar trees she was sailing through in her dash toward the clearing on the point.

Proud of the country girl she had just discovered in herself, she began shouting Bobby's name so he would be sure to be looking her way when she burst out of the woods in full flight, an entrance she expected to make at any moment.

* * *

As Foster drove the twenty-five miles back to Red Moon from the smut emporium in Flint, he fretted about Laura's check he had found that morning in his box at the post office in Lapeer. What if he couldn't perform? Would she tell her friends, his future guests?

Maybe he should call her to say he was returning the money. Or maybe he should hold on to it but postpone the date of their tryst. After all, Rachael had explained that if he had negative sexual side effects from Celexa, they sometimes adapted out after several weeks of taking the drug.

A blazing red sky heralded the coming of darkness as he slowed the Jeep to make the turn off Shady Oaks. He put on his bright lights to better see the gate that was his landmark and was startled when they captured Laura's parked BMW convertible, its top down, in their glare. It was the same expensive-looking car he had walked her to when their lunch was finished at Forte.

Pulling in behind it, he hurried to get out and check the other car for occupants, surprised at the pleasure he was feeling at the sight of it, considering the complications Laura's far-too-early presence at the barely finished bed and breakfast would cause.

Now there would be no fresh-cut flowers in the parlor to greet her upon her arrival, no crystal dish of her favorite candy, either, waiting for her on the bedside stand to sample while she unpacked her bags, and so much for the antique cherry wood tray piled high with fruit for her to discover on the glass game table in the sun porch.

Confirming that her car was empty, as he had expected, he turned his attention to opening the gate, first reaching down inside the BMW to switch on its brightest headlights so he would be able to see the numbers on the padlock.

It was new and its combination barely committed to memory, and competing with his effort to recall the numbers were thoughts of a far more serious calamity that was almost sure to have resulted from Laura's unexpected appearance. She would have met Uncle Earl without Preston being there to civilize the introduction.

A sound reached his ears that confirmed that the dreaded event had almost certainly come to pass. Through the still night air, from the direction of the bed and breakfast, he heard his uncle's truck motor roaring to life with a rapid series of shotgun-like blasts since the muffler was long gone.

His hurrying of the spinning of the padlock's dial caused him to go beyond one of the needed settings, the hard jerk made on the lock achieved nothing but a feeble jingling sound from the chain it was attached to.

Uncle Earl was now negotiating the roller coaster ride through the hills in his usual wild style, Preston knew, from the sound of the straight-stick transmission being shifted into low for the roaring climb, then slipped into neutral to silently coast down the other side.

In the intermittent moments of quietude, the unmistakable sound of a woman, squealing either in agony or delight, came to Preston's ears, increasing in volume as the distance between him and the advancing pickup rapidly diminished.

44

He knew it was sort of a petty guy thing, but he had to get the gate open before they got to him. Cocky Uncle Earl would love to catch the-kid-with-too-much-college struggling unsuccessfully, jump out of the truck he rode to the rescue, and swagger to the gate and open it on the first try.

The woman, not too far away now, began to belt out a song, Broadway-style, à la Barbra Streisand, filling the silent countryside with a booming yet unmistakable throaty voice that Foster recognized at once as being Laura's.

To Preston's great relief, he got the combination right just as his uncle's yellow pickup bounced to a stop a few feet away. As he quickly threw open the two halves of the gate, he was astonished to see Laura on the truck's hood, where she apparently had ridden the whole distance from the bed and breakfast.

Ablaze in the BMW's high beam, with feet spread apart to steady herself, chin held high, one hand on her hip, the other held skywards to make a two-finger victory salute to the stars above, she punched out the ending lyrics to her song in a dazzling musical shout, "There's no business like show business...."

Chapter Six
Bass Rafting

Most August nights in Michigan have a velvet softness to them. Warm, dark air covered Laura's and Preston's nakedness like a weightless blanket of the swan's finest down as they lay side by side on their backs looking up at the Milky Way.

Their bed was a raft, 20 feet on a side, consisting of a sturdy frame made of thick oak planks that fitted down over a cluster of steel water-tight barrels like a huge shoe-box cover, and which was held there by gravity. All that was visible of the lake they were floating upon was a circle of flat black water that disappeared into darkness no more than fifteen feet in the distance.

Preston thought about the recent events leading up to what now appeared to him to be, almost certainly, the moment of truth.

* * *

After Laura's Southern Comfort-fueled singing performance at the gate, with Preston watching glumly from the sidelines, envying the great fun the inebriated new pals were having, Uncle Earl said he was leaving. Both of them had asked him to stay but he had held firm, still in a snit about Preston's broad hint earlier in the week that he stay clear of paying guests.

"No way, sweetheart, your boyfriend gave me my walking papers a few days ago," Uncle Earl huffed to Laura as she danced a few lively last steps with him in the headlights after she climbed down off the hood of his truck.

When Laura had burst out of the woods shouting Preston's name, Uncle Earl had turned in her direction to see "what in the Sam Hill was going on," as he put it. At that close range, she was able to see his beard for the first time and realized, of course, that she had mistaken him for Preston.

His astonishment at seeing a gorgeous barefoot woman bounding toward him out of the bushes moved him to slug down a sizable swallow out of the pint of "medicine" he kept in the leather nail pouch suspended from his carpenter's belt.

Without a word of greeting, he offered the bottle to Laura when she joined him by the backdoor of the cottage, and she gratefully nodded her acceptance, putting it to her lips after he performed the gentlemanly gesture of wiping its top off with his shirttail.

The chemistry of his surprise mixed with her embarrassment was an ice breaker, both their states of mind being eased considerably by the brown glass bottle they passed back and forth between them, and soon they were talking and laughing together, thoroughly enjoying each other's company.

When Laura and Preston were left alone together in silence after the sound of his uncle's truck had gradually faded into the distance, there was an awkwardness between them. They drove separately to the bed and breakfast, Preston locking the gate behind them.

He had first carried her bags into the dressing room adjacent to the bedroom in the guest suite and then given her a tour including her private, torch-lit deck.

She followed him around, politely acknowledging the special decorating touches and family heirlooms with the word "cute," which was not one of his favorite descriptions. When they reached the kitchen, she asked for another short drink of Southern Comfort but this time in a glass with some ice.

As he went upstairs to his living area to get the bottle, Laura gave in to the temptation to look into a paper bag, with "Borders Bookstore" printed on it, that was lying on the round oak table, to see how well Bobby knew her taste in books. She was pleased to find *Royal Invitation*, the latest bestseller by Julia Fenton, and one of the few of Harold Robbins books that she hadn't gotten to read yet, *The Dream Merchants*.

Preston looked at the orange plastic container of Celexa on his dresser and cringed. Should he skip the 40 milligrams that he should be taking and forestall sex with Laura until the drug in his system metabolized? That would take another 12 hours or so, roughly 24 of the 36 hour half-life of the drug having elapsed since he took his daily dosage the night before.

On the other hand, why pay all that money to Rachael and then ignore her suggestions? Even though she was brusque at times, he was convinced she had his best interests at heart.

And she had made it clear that he needed six weeks of uninterrupted use as a minimum "fair try" time to find out if Celexa would relieve him of his obsessions. No obsessions, no repetitious reading, and he would have his judicial career back again.

He decided to take the medication, washing it down with a small glass of orange juice, standing by the sink in the kitchen of his tiny second-floor innkeeper's quarters.

The distress of indecision now behind him, his zest for the pleasant duty at hand returned. What a great plan he had to make money! And his sensational-looking first client waited patiently downstairs, probably reading the adult fiction books he promised her at Forte and getting in the mood for some dynamite lovemaking.

He had intentionally left the Border's Bookstore bag where she would be sure to see it, expecting her to do some harmless snooping, paving the way for him to make his first move when he rejoined her.

Having placed only one captain's chair at the antique table for her to use, set in such a way that her back would be toward the stair door, he would be able to speak to her before she actually saw him. He would say something like, "Sorry I took so long, I've missed you terribly," and then walk up behind the chair, lean over, and kiss the back of her neck.

That done, he would put his arms under hers, to gently hold her breasts from underneath in the palms of his hands, using his index fingers to harden the nipples with tiny, circular caresses.

Emboldened, though to his disappointment not sexually aroused, by envisioning in his imagination what he was about to do, he returned downstairs, descending the old wooden staircase with great care, having learned through past years where to step so the worn, old steps wouldn't squeak. He didn't want the noise of his descent to intrude upon her quiet reading reverie before he interrupted it, as calculated, with his best bedroom voice.

Turning to the right when he reached the foot of the stairs, he tiptoed through the door that he had purposely left open leading to the first floor guest's kitchen. The room was empty.

His first thought was to charge through all five of the downstairs rooms and find her. But, no, he was in the bed and breakfast business now. The house was no longer entirely his to roam, not until the weekend she had paid for was over.

Calling her name brought no answer from inside the house, so he went to look for her outdoors.

"I went skinny-dipping to sober up," she called from the lake when she saw him appear in the yard light, adding, "it feels wonderful on my skin, why don't you join me?"

"You're full of surprises," he had called back, stepping out of the circle of light, into the darkness to slip off his clothes.

"Go back where you were, so I can watch you undress," Laura teased, "I want to see what I paid for."

Gamely, Preston laughed and edged his body sideways back into the "spotlight" as if coming on stage out of the wings of an old-time burlesque theater. He began to undress, imitating the only stripper he had seen, taking off one piece of clothing at a time and whirling it above his head before tossing it off into the surrounding darkness.

One night he had gone with some of his fraternity brothers from the Sigma Chi house in Ann Arbor to the Gayety Burlesque, one of the last of such places around, on Cadillac Square in downtown Detroit. It was a raucous, boisterous group of guys.

However, the row of beautiful girls he and his friends had expected to ogle turned out to be one heavily made up middle-aged woman with drooping boobs and stretch marks across her puffed-out abdomen. A creature that Woody had immediately deemed to be "disgusting."

Her act had consisted of slowly removing her clothes while making pelvic thrusts toward Preston and his companions, lined up like pigeons on a telephone line in the front row of an otherwise empty theater, her tired-looking movements made more or less in time with Ravel's monotonous Bolero.

The scratchy sound of the music was testimony to the countless times the classic piece had been played on the portable record player sitting on floor boards black with age a few feet from where she undulated on the ancient stage.

Running out of things to take off, Preston wanted something special for an ending. He realized that his role model's grand finale, elaborately guiding an imaginary penis into herself with a hand-over-hand procedure reminiscent of what you do to choose up sides or to decide who bats first, wasn't going to work for him.

Bending low as he stepped out of his boxer shorts, he dashed headlong down the grassy slope and shallow-dived into the lake, all without straightening up, as Laura yelled "chicken" from where she stood on the sandy lake-bottom, her firm breasts uplifted by the warm surface water that covered all but a sunrise-shaped sliver of their pinkish brown aureoleus.

Preston surfaced in front of her, kneeled in the water, and playfully flicked one nipple with the tip of his tongue.

"I'm not quite ready, besides, it would scare the fish," Laura said.

They swam to the raft then, Preston staying close to her side, a powerful, protective Adam to his adventurous Eve.

A hunting great horned owl, the pupils of its huge, round eyes dilated to the size of a dime, allowing it to find its prey in the dark, dropped silently down from high in the sky to determine what swam at the point of their V-shaped wake.

It saw a man and woman, gliding through the water side by side, as beautiful a matched pair as any of the wild things of the forest that come together for a time for sex, and broke its dive with silent wings spread wide, six feet from tip to tip, to sail on in search of weaker game.

Preston circled the raft a couple of times when they reached it, feeling full of life with strength to spare, while Laura climbed up the ladder hanging from its side.

The air was hot, but the evaporation of the lake water on her skin chilled her slightly and she shook herself, much like a dog, to get rid of the excess water. Preston had never seen anyone do that before and watched in fascination from his vantage point in the water, mesmerized by the shadowy figure of this beautiful, statuesque woman standing above him.

While he didn't feel any particular sexual urge at the moment—he chalked that up to the Celexa—something always seemed to start up with his privates every time that he was in Laura's presence. If he was falling in love with her, that didn't bode well for his new profession, in which he would be expected to perform on demand with lots of different women. He remembered how, when his first love, Anna Rose, was alive, the thought of having sex with anyone but her really turned him off.

He promptly shook off all thoughts on the matter by swimming down as far as he could go into the black depths, penetrating different temperature layers, each one cooler than the last as he came closer to the icy-cold springs on the bottom of the lake that were the source of its crystal-clear water.

When he returned to the surface next to the raft, he looked up to see Laura smiling down on him from the edge of it. She lay on her stomach, hands framing her lovely face, elbows on the planking that had been padded with a white canvass cover. "Let's pretend we're brother and sister for a while, I never had one," she said.

As he climbed up the ladder, she added enthusiastically, "I'll tell you everything I know about women, to help you with your new enterprise." Then, staring wide-eyed at Preston's mid-section as he stepped onto the water-soaked deck, she said with exaggerated concern in her voice, "We have to start with that, it's too, well, little."

Laughing, Preston said, "It's the cold water down deep, it will revive, I promise."

Then, lying down beside her on his side, he went on, "Tell me more, my new sex-business consultant, even experts can improve their game."

Laura rolled onto her side, so as to be facing him, and took his hand, "You're too direct, Bobby."

"Brothers and sisters aren't supposed to hold hands on rafts alone naked in the middle of the night," he teased, "I think it might lead to something called incest."

"Listen to me. Women, even pent-up ones like me, don't like to get it on right away. Know what I mean, bro?"

"Sure do. Then, sis, let's first go skinny fishing, since we've already been skinny dipping."

* * *

In daytime, during the hottest part of the summer, largemouth bass hang suspended far down in the cool depths, their shallow-water spawning rituals completed in mid-June. They rise to just below the surface during the steaming hot nights of late July and early August, to cruise silently back and forth in search of food.

Manufacturers of artificial baits knew about that and designed floating lures for fishermen to pull across the water which imitate small swimming animals ingenuously well.

Preston's favorite was called a jitterbug, and he kept several spinning rods on the raft rigged with them. Each had a different color treatment, several depicting mice and frogs, and one was solid black for moonless nights like the one at hand.

A concave, oval-shaped piece of metal on the front of each bait caused them to wiggle in a swimming motion, and make a bubbling sound, as they were reeled back in after a cast.

Laura had another surprise for him when he gave her the rod with the black lure on it. Without hesitation, she held it above her shoulder with the tip behind her, then, with an expert flip of her wrist, sent the bait sailing high out into the darkness.

"Jake taught me," she announced proudly, "we used to fly to Ireland to trout fish on weekends."

"This is pretty tame compared to that," Preston observed with an expression of mock humility. He was pleased to find out that she knew what she was doing so he could fish, too, without having to be constantly helping her with the tangled lines and equipment glitches that always seemed to be a part of fishing with a novice in the dark.

"Actually, this is pretty spooky compared to that," Laura said with a laugh. "At least we had our clothes on and it was daytime so we could see what we were doing."

"You know what they say," Preston said, "an ounce of different is worth a pound of same. By the way, we're fishing with our ears. When Mr. Bass

52

makes a splash out there, we both have to jerk our line hard to set the hook because we won't know which one of us he hit."

As if to demonstrate, the sharp crack of something smacking the water reached their ears, and Laura jerked so hard with her rod that her bait flew off the water and high over their heads to drop into the lake behind them.

"Don't tell me you thought that was a fish, wow, you really are a city kid," Preston teased, "that was just a mamma beaver using her tail to tell her kids to get the hell out of here so they don't get hooked."

They ate the fish they caught as the night progressed, Preston expertly filleting them and then broiling the boneless strips on a small, tray-style, charcoal grill he kept on the raft for such occasions.

Laura, "to be nearer to the stars," as she put it, sat ten feet above him, cross-legged on the flat top of a wooden diving tower that stood at one edge of the raft. An electric trolling motor barely moved the awkward craft along its silent way down the center of the long lake. Wisps of fog corkscrewed off the water with their passing.

She interrupted her casting to use her fingers to eat one of the delicious morsels Preston handed up to her, and then said, "It's like we are the only two people on the entire earth."

The owl that had seen them earlier hooted loudly from a tamarack swamp they were approaching at the south end of the lake, and the haunting sound made her shiver involuntarily. Climbing down the tower's ladder, she put her fishing rod in the storage box under the tower, then lay down on her back on the raft's deck with her knees up and said, "Come over here with me, Bobby, I want to talk some more."

He kneeled at the edge of the raft and reached down to wash his hands in the water, then turned off the motor and joined her, leaving the glowing-red charcoal to burn itself out in the cast iron hibachi next to them in the dark.

"Why do they call it a new moon when there isn't any?" she asked.

"I'm not an information bureau."

"In other words, you don't know."

"Nobody knows everything."

"It's a time to plant," she said, "I read that in your *Farmer's Almanac*."

Ignoring for a moment her comment that he took to be a thinly veiled green light, Preston said, "I've got a question for you. Looking straight up through that Milky Way, and if our eyes were able to see all there was to see, is there an end to the Universe?"

"Bobby, not only are you too direct sometimes, but you can get way too serious, like now. Get over here, and lighten up some."

Chapter Seven
Scaring Yourself

Six months of in-home therapy with Rachael, done three times a week at the rented house in Ann Arbor, had begun to pay off.

Preston was frequently besieged by the same obsessions at those times when he tried to read, since Celexa had not totally relieved him of the phenomenon as Rachael had said it might. However, the anxiety it caused in him was no longer at a panic level thanks to her behavioral approach to his treatment.

Just knowing that millions of other people in the United States and around the world suffered from OCD was greatly comforting and gave him a sense of community.

Far from being insane, he had learned that those who struggled with the disorder most often possessed well-above-average intelligence. They were usually college-educated, too, if the illness hadn't struck too early in their lives, and they often, in spite of their illness, became high achievers like the brilliant aeronautical engineer Howard Hughes, and Samuel Johnson, the early English writer who compiled the first dictionary.

Rachael had turned out to be a patient yet demanding taskmaster, working with Preston for the several weeks it required to painstakingly identify the triggering aspects of his reading, such as subject matter and environment, that seemed to bring on the unwanted mental image.

Most times there were no clearly identifiable ones, but, often enough to make their effort worthwhile, they could see a logical cause and effect connection, such as beginning to hear the dreaded organ prelude in his mind while reading about infant mortality or after looking up from his newspaper to see a hearse pass by the house.

While Rachael spurned psychoanalysis as a cure for OCD, she nonetheless demonstrated great respect for what a human brain did that was beyond its owner's control, such as signaling the heart to pump or, as in Preston's case, generating disturbing obsessions.

The big surprise to Preston came when their survey of triggers was completed. He had assumed that they were compiling a list of what to avoid. Instead, Rachael explained that he was to purposely expose himself daily to the triggers, one at a time for two weeks each, rewarding himself for his effort each time by placing a colorful paper star on a calendar.

Together, they chose to begin with one of the more obvious triggers on their list, obituaries in the daily *Ann Arbor News*. He was not to give in to the temptation to read them four times, instead engaging in what Rachael described as response prevention, steeling himself to tolerate the emotional pain of the organ music and the image of the casket, the newspaper rattling in his shaking hands as huge chunks of anxiety blew wildly through him.

* * *

Preston had decided not to tell Rachael about his method of financing his treatment. But it came out anyway, in fragments, over time as their sessions continued, mainly because the sexual side effect of Celexa was a legitimate medical issue that he felt she had a right to know about, but also because she kept pressing him for details.

The OCD drug had rendered him a sexual wunderkind from a woman's point of view. His ejaculations were blocked but nothing else was affected. His clients were pleasured for as many hours as they liked in any way they chose with nothing to douche, wipe off, spit out, or swallow.

While his travel agent contact in Toronto had yet to deliver one Red Moon customer, Grace Marvel, an agent from Chicago, had accepted his invitation to stay a night without charge, which she had informed him was her policy before recommending a bed and breakfast to her customers.

A member of Zonta International, a network of exclusive professional women's clubs, Grace put the whispered word out at the first meeting after her return to Chicago, generously sharing with her lady friends the titillating tidbits about her "discovery" in Michigan. The same experience could be properly accessed by the other ladies through her agency for her usual twenty-percent commission.

Preston had expected most of his clientele would come from Detroit's wealthy northern suburbs, but Chicago far exceeded metropolitan Detroit because of the successful promotion of Marvel Destinations. The reservations poured into Preston's Red Moon office. The greater distance, he supposed, also made his customers' sexual forays seem more advertursome and made it easier for them to keep their clandestine junkets a secret.

* * *

56

One day, while Rachael helped him work on his exposure and response-prevention exercises that desensitized him to anxiety, Preston complained to her that his new business had grown to the point where he needed a short break. He told her of his plan to devote a long weekend for visiting art museums in New York City, catching an intriguing show opening at the Guggenheim consisting of Egyptian tomb paintings, and to include a collection of works by the modernist sensation, García Sánchez, hanging in the Museum of Modern Art.

"What a lovely place to recharge your battery," she said with a trace of a smile. "You'll be traveling alone, I presume?"

Her question hung in the air for a moment, Preston silently straining to find the best response to her question from the possible ones flashing through his mind.

He had eventually told Rachael about his trip to France with Laura that September, describing their stay at the George V Hotel in Paris, from which they were able to visit the sights of the city on foot in the warm, afternoon sun, and their leisurely road trip through La Côte d'Or, the narrow strip of hillside vineyards that stretches from Dijon to Beaune in Burgundy.

His story of one stop they made on that excursion, at Saint-Jacques, the three-star restaurant in Joigny, for a glorious seven-course meal, featuring an entree of truffle-stuffed beef tenderloin, brought an exaggerated gasp of surprise from Rachael when she heard the steep price of 100 Euros per person, which converted to 108 American dollars.

He didn't tell her that Laura had presented him with a $20,000 bonus check, along with her proposal of marriage, upon their return to Michigan. Laura told him that she had become convinced that they were kindred spirits, even suggesting that she would finance his political comeback, and that perhaps, in the meantime, he should consider moving into her magnificent Tudor-style home in Bloomfield Hills.

He had been pleasantly shocked when Laura confessed to him then that she had taken it upon herself to begin to research his reinstatement to the Michigan Supreme Court, already partnering with Woody in the effort, whom she had sworn to secrecy.

He hadn't known how to respond to either Laura's invitation to move in with her or marriage, and now he seemed to be in the same sort of speechless mode with Rachael, although the stakes were much smaller. Or were they? Was she also interested in something more meaningful than recreational sex?

If he had learned anything about women, it was that they were much less direct than men in discussing anything involving sex, and yet he was convinced that they attached far greater significance to that perfectly natural

57

function than most men did.

He felt sure that Rachael was waiting for him to invite her to New York, and just as certain that she would never ask him directly to join him on his jaunt to the Big Apple.

"I didn't think I was supposed to fraternize with my professional caregiver," he said, putting up a test balloon that she might choose to take aim at, hoping that in her response she would more fully reveal her true intentions.

"Pretend you're in the grocery business and I've happened into your store, not realizing until now that it was in my neighborhood," Rachael said immediately, displaying her usual quickness of mind.

"Well, hello, Doctor," Preston replied without hesitation, making himself wide-eyed in mock surprise, "I didn't know you lived around here. Would you be interested, by chance, in the special on standing rib, or perhaps the lamb chops?"

"I wouldn't expect a little shop like yours to have a large variety of other cuts for me to chose from."

"Oh, you're quite wrong, it's my specialty. You might have to pay a little more, but I'm sure I'll come up with something that will please you. All our meats are first cut and prime, only the best for our customers."

"But I lean toward the spicy side of things," Rachael said, unable to maintain a straight face.

They laughed together over their silliness. And Preston, turning more serious, explained that she was more than welcome to go but that she would be paying the trip expenses in addition to his customary weekend fee of $2500.

"Throw in ice-skating with me at Rockefeller Center and it's a deal," Rachael said with a firm, businesslike tone to her voice, but the hand she extended for a shake, to seal the bargain in response to the nod of his head, felt soft and warm in his. Surprisingly, it turned him on.

Chapter Eight
You Don't Look Crazy

The deceased Justice Fredrick Walberg had had a paramour for almost 25 years, and she was still trim with more than a trace of her youthful exotic beauty. The woman, Mame Fleming, sat next to the wall in the back row of Grosse Pointe's St. Paul's Cathedral, dressed in widow's weeds, her face heavily shadowed by a densely meshed black veil.

Preston spoke to the overflow crowd from the front of the sanctuary. The podium before him was touched in red and blue hues by rays of sunlight streaming through the stained glass windows.

When he finished his eulogy to the 80-year-old man she had loved unconditionally, he saw Mame touch the brim of her black hat with a black-gloved hand and nod her head in approval. Preston's gentle words of bereavement had included his first, public mention in passing of his OCD, and he returned to his seat feeling that a great weight had been lifted from his shoulders.

Widow Walberg, a handsome, queen-sized woman, sat in the customary place of honor in the front row on the aisle. She looked dowdy in her black mourning dress, loosely fitted to conceal her thirty extra pounds.

She held her head high, maintaining an expression of calm stoicism, expertly playing the role of the dearly beloved spouse holding up reasonably well under the circumstances. Mildred Walberg had plenty of practice in acting out the rigid social conventions of the Pointes. Getting through this final day of sham was made easier for her by the knowledge that her ordeal of keeping up appearances for so many years had at last come to an end.

Mildred would have preferred someone else other than Preston for the eulogy, but she had no say in the matter. It was a decision made by her husband and his lover, the lady in the back row, just months before his death caused by prostate cancer.

Mame was paying for the funeral, the burial, and the luncheon at the Country Club of Detroit following the church service, a meal which promised to be a mammoth expense judging by the number of mourners crowding the chapel. Many of the well-heeled and expensively dressed attendees had to settle for watching the service on closed-circuit television in the vestibule.

Fredrick had arranged for Mame to pay all the expenses because she was his primary beneficiary. The entire residue of his considerable estate was to be hers after generous testamentary trusts were funded out of it for the lifetime support of his wife and their two adult children.

Mildred had made up her mind that she wasn't going to like the eulogy before it began, but Preston's masterful way with words, spoken with his sonorous baritone voice, had touched her. Especially after he had finished with the standard recital of the deceased's many accomplishments and began to speak of his mutually supportive personal relationship with her husband.

Preston revealed to the attendees that he and Frederick were the youngest and oldest members, respectively, on the Court before Preston's medical leave. He noted that in families, and other human groupings, the youngest and oldest members were often drawn to each other and formed a special bond, perhaps because of the commonality they shared of neither one being in their prime of life.

The funeral, as a whole, was a rather theatrical affair, reflecting Mame's flair for the dramatic.

A sort of souvenir program was handed out at the entry door, that included a two-page biography of the deceased, with a large head-and-shoulders photograph of him in color on its cover.

Mame's niece, an attractive woman with a dynamite voice, who still performed for a living as a cruise ship headliner, sang "Amazing Grace" cabaret style, over and over again, until the very last person in the long, winding lines of communion seekers had taken their wafer and optional wine.

Those touches fit together well with the pageantry of the high Catholic mass, which included Cardinal Adam Maida, several archbishops, and the parish priests, replete with robes made of the finest embroidered fabrics, marching slowly up the center aisle with colorful flags and a gold Christian cross on long wooden poles held high above their heads, like crusaders heading into battle.

* * *

"How are things at Big Sky?" Preston asked as he kissed Mame's cheek. She had lifted her veil up onto the wide brim of her hat as they walked out of the church together to stand by themselves to one side, at the top of the series of wide front steps leading down to the street. Family members, well below them on the sidewalk, were being loaded by assistant funeral directors into limousines for the ride to the country club.

Three decades before, Daimler Chrysler AG, then known as Chrysler Corporation, through its subsidiary Chrysler Realty, had partnered with Chet Huntley, the legendary television commentator, to develop Big Sky as an expensive retreat for the wealthy in the Montana Rockies. Fredrick, who had helped put the partnership together as the house counsel for Chrysler Realty, had expected, correctly, that it would succeed.

After Fredrick had moved on from Chrysler Realty's legal department, where he had spent the middle years of his legal career, he invested heavily in Big Sky stock when the original partnership was incorporated and made its first public offering on Wall Street. And he made a fortune.

Mame made her home at Big Sky in a posh condominium that Frederick had provided for her. Her penthouse view was so spectacular that it had once been photographed by the famous Irving Penn, using a wide-angled lens, and the picture served as the backdrop for a Marlboro advertisement.

"As beautiful as ever," she replied to Preston's inquiry, adding, "The Rockies are everlastingly gorgeous. Remember when you and your lovely wife, Anna Rose, used to visit Fred and me? How the four of us would drive up into the foothills to ski or horseback ride together, depending on the season? I just wish our loved ones would stay put the same way the mountains do instead of dying out on us."

Preston was startled at the bird-like boniness to her once voluptuous frame when he put his arms around her to follow up the kiss with a long, gentle hug. How had this previously bodacious woman shrunk so as to have the body of a starved street waif?

Then he remembered the double mastectomy that had saved her from the breast cancer that had threatened her life five years before. It had been a terrible ordeal, both physically and emotionally, for Mame, the woman Fred had always said was the love of his life. But somehow they got through it together. The nightmare of her devastating illness served to draw them together even closer than before.

"Your eulogy was lovely, Bobby. What you said about Fred being the only Justice that remained friendly to you during that terrible period when you were hanging on to your Justice robes without a diagnosis, just before you took a leave, was that true? What about Woody?"

"Woody was under a lot of pressure, as Chief Justice, to get rid of me," Preston replied, and added, "I guess he figured defending me against the bitter complaints of some of the other judges was effort enough for him.

"But it's true what I said about Fred. All through that whole terrible time, including the day I left, he asked me, every time he saw me, 'How's it going,

Bobby?'" Blinking back tears, Preston continued, "It seems to you, I suppose, like a small thing, but it meant the world to me when I was bumping along on the bottom of the ladder.

"Do you want to ride with me to the club?" he asked her then, smiling in an effort to lighten things up.

"No, this is all I wanted to see, to make sure he got the church service that was so important to him. He was very religious, you know?

"That's why he never divorced her," Mame said, adding, "they were from a different era, when divorce was considered morally wrong, a scandalous thing, especially in this place, where the pillars of the community, like old Henry Ford, got the kind of sex they really wanted outside the sheets and then went home to mama and the kids.

"Anyway, enough of that," she said, sighing. Then she smiled, showing a flash of her former sparkling beauty, and continued in a livelier manner, "Get Woody to fly you out to see me sometime, I miss you, dear. I'd say bring your girlfriend, but I don't think Montana is big enough for them all."

Her comment made Preston wonder if Woody had told her what he was doing for a living, but he decided to let it pass as the sort of teasing compliment Mame would make, anyway. She knew just what to say to make a guy feel great.

* * *

As he drove from St. Paul's, on Lake Shore Road, to the Country Club of Detroit, Preston thought about what lay just ahead. All of the Justices would probably be there, including his replacement. It would be the first time that he'd seen any of them, except Woody, since leaving the Bench.

He felt resentment welling up inside himself as he entered the club's parking lot. Why hadn't he gotten the understanding and support he had expected from them in his time of adversity?

Walking across the parking lot jammed with freshly washed, expensive cars, he tried to reason with himself, knowing he shouldn't go inside feeling the way he did. His anger against the other Justices was so strong within him that he had been involuntarily clenching his fists. He told himself that attitudes, unlike emotions, are a matter of choice, and that he had better pick a more positive one in the few minutes that remained before he would be face to face with his former colleagues.

He composed himself before going inside by standing for a time in the club's beautiful portico, pretending to look at the flowers that had been planted too early in the season in extensive beds on both sides of the club's impressive entrance.

Pink begonias and purple impatiens were arranged in alternating rows. Forced to bloom months before their time in a heated greenhouse, they were at the mercy of the biting April wind. Of course the gardener would know they would never survive, but he had to provide flower color for club members who demanded it look like summer regardless of cost.

* * *

Through a seemingly undivided wall of window glass along one side of the tastefully decorated dining room, the golf course looked cold and gray, like winter had hung it up by its neck until dead. The sight of it, to those in the noisy crowd who happened to notice, made one appreciate all the more the warm room and the buffet table heaped with the highly paid chef's creations.

Prime Rib of Beef, Lamb Wellington, Hawaiian Crusted Chicken and Cajun Blackened Swordfish were the entrees, while enormous sweet potatoes baked in a thick butter and brown sugar glaze stole the show in the side dish department.

After the large round tables were cleared of used dishes, uniformed waiters with red jackets, white shirts, and black bow ties circulated among them, bending low to offer the selection of gourmet desserts they carried on their oval-shaped aluminum trays.

The delightful concoctions were displayed on a white cloth liner to better show them off, trimmed in lengthy lace that hung down over the sides of the trays to swing with the carriers' movements.

"More coffee, sir?" a waitress outfitted in a floor-length floral-print dress said to Preston as she stood by his right shoulder. He nodded and she poured it skillfully into the flowered English bone china cup set upon a matching saucer before him on a white linen tablecloth slightly soiled with spills.

Savoring the moment, Preston looked about him. Three of the Justices and their wives sat at his table. The others were scattered about the room. He had made it a point to have a few words with each of them, and to try to gauge their reaction to his resurfacing here.

Most had commented on how well he looked, as they would if he had a physical rather than a mental illness. He figured that was all they could think of to say when confronted with someone suffering from a psychiatric disorder. Maybe they were afraid he would have grown horns, or perhaps fangs from his mouth, by this time.

He watched them talking and occasionally laughing, and thought about how harmless they looked now that they were no longer shunning him like a pariah. Even the ones who wouldn't return Preston's simplest spoken greeting during that awful period chatted happily at some length with him here. A major improvement in his opinion of the Justices was this day's gift.

Most important to his tranquility, Preston concluded, was the passing of the corrosive hostility he had felt toward the other Justices ever since he was forced to leave the Bench. They were just people after all ... that had defended their own interests against the threat that they perceived him to be and the adverse publicity which would undoubtedly follow. Truly, he had expected too much of them.

Chapter Nine
Out of Here

When the pillared facade of Chicago's Union Station was viewed across the broad tiled plaza lying between the building and the street, the massive structure looked more like the Lincoln Memorial than the train depot that it was.

Inside the enormous lobby, huge wall murals and towering frescoed ceilings combined to create an ambiance of grandeur, though that was quickly dispelled with one's first escalator ride down into its rumbling bowels, where the trains parked briefly between their continuous arrivals and departures.

Lacey Lee wouldn't be noticing any of that stuff, anyway. Always in a hurry, which was her way of life, she tipped her cab driver as they stood together a moment by the open trunk of his vehicle, then she turned and stepped quickly up on the sidewalk, where he had placed her two pieces of Christian Dior luggage.

Carrying the smaller of the two black leather bags with her left hand, Lacey used her right to tow the heavier one along on wheels with its extended pull. She crossed the plaza on the nearest thing to a run that her tight skirt would allow, almost stepping on a fat, soot-stained gray pigeon. It was one of a resting flock she charged through, sending them all skyward on clattering wings, swirling like leaves caught in a circular updraft.

Lacey was born Mildred O'Rourke, but she had chosen to go by what she thought was the zippier, more fashionable name. In her highly competitive field, she figured, a person had to give themselves every edge possible, and the advertising business, like every other business, after all, was about making the best possible impression.

Only five feet two inches tall, she was dubbed "small but mighty" at McMannis Mann, the public relations firm she had chosen from several offers she received as a senior student in business administration at the University of Wisconsin.

With long, thick titian-colored hair that cascaded down to the middle of her back inherited from her Irish ancestors who settled in Wisconsin's famed dairy country in the 1800s, her family background only aided in her rapid rise in the advertising business.

With her flaming tresses piled high on her head, and her slim, well-turned legs, she had no difficulty getting client companies' predominantly male executives' attention as she began her presentations in their conference rooms across America.

They were mature, older men mostly, who had spent years reaching the top echelons of management. Many of them saw in her their own daughters, especially when she blessed them with her impish smile as her deep dimples glowed in both lightly rouged cheeks.

Not a few of the dignified gentlemen in attendance thought about what it would be like to have sex with her, one lascivious rascal imagined her astride his manhood, her lengthy locks unpinned to flow down upon his gray-haired chest, a 21st century Godiva bouncing along on a midnight ride.

Her well-prepared pitches were winners, her artistic skills and creative mind almost never failed to impress her audiences and, remarkably, at only 25 years old, she was the account executive for five of her firm's second-tier corporate clients.

The coveted handful of first-level accounts were reserved for vice-presidents, a title she was rumored to be receiving favorable consideration for in a few years when she began to look a little older. It was a business in which a person's appearance counted for a lot, with age being equated, sometimes mistakenly, for wisdom.

Once inside the cavernous station, Lacey took the only escalator going down to the lower level, speeding the process by descending the moving steps at a fast clip. All of the escalators were reversible, their direction determined by the time of day. As Lacey's moved downward, the other six were lifting to street level the thousands of rail commuters from the suburbs in a typical Friday morning rush hour.

Those people would be fanning out across the heart of the city on their way to their various places of employment. Lacey experienced a natural high at being on her way out of town just as everybody else in the world, it seemed, was going to work.

Her total commitment to the success of her career had deprived her of the time and energy necessary to the encouragement of any kind of lasting relationship with a man. She thought about that as she sipped a Sloe Screw, orange juice and sloe gin, at a table in the club car of the Amtrak International.

The shabby tenements and run-down single-family homes of south

Chicago were flashing by outside the large, rectangular window with rounded corners. It occurred to her as she looked at them that it was similar to watching an old-time silent movie, and that the screen was the thick glass pane.

On the street, there were overweight women, some carrying babies, with half-grown children in tow. They wore drab-colored shawls and nondescript clothes that were rags compared to what hung in the walk-in closet of Lacey's stylish town house in the north shore district of the city.

Occasionally, she saw men, skinny-looking alongside the women, that she figured were the husbands, the expression on their lean faces made hard, Lacey supposed, by work in the nearby slaughterhouses and steel mills; men of a sort who would never be allowed to touch her precious body that she had sculptured to perfection at Bally's.

Yes, her approach to satisfying her sexual cravings was the superior one, keeping her mercifully free of a husband, children, and marital obligations that she was sure would hold her back from achieving her dream of success. Lacey knew that she had a tough-broad, Grace Marvel-attitude, to thank for coming up with the delightful, no-strings-attached solution to every career woman's dilemma.

Lacey had always heard that older men were better in bed than young guys because their blood had cooled some with age, allowing them to last longer before they, as Grace, her travel agent, put it, "broke their nut." Well, Bobby Foster had far exceeded Lacey's cautiously optimistic expectations in that regard.

She had been skeptical when Grace had gushed about him at Zonta. According to Grace, not only did her "find" look like a "mature Adonis" naked, but he could "fuck like a race horse" until you lost count of your orgasms and begged him to let you rest a few minutes.

Now on her fourth trip to Red Moon, Lacey would be the first to agree that he was not only gorgeous to look at, but that he also knew how to give a willing woman every pleasurable sensation possible, all delivered nonstop until she signaled him that she was exhausted and was finally satiated, perhaps for the first time in her life.

Lacey drained her glass and rose to her feet, a slight unsteadiness was a small price to pay for the warm glow the alcohol provided. Passing the bar on her way out, she placed a folded ten-dollar bill into the homely bartender's tip jar, noticing how much more lovable he and everyone else in the room looked after three drinks.

After using the rest room, Lacey returned to her seat in the first class car. She raised the foot rest as high as it would go, to accommodate her shapely legs, fully reclined the back, placing the fresh pillow on it that the porter had provided upon boarding, and then settled comfortably down upon the soft upholstery.

She turned her head lazily toward the window and saw that the International was racing by the warehouses and coal yards of Gary, Indiana, completing its 80-miles-per-hour sweep around the southern tip of Lake Michigan.

Lacy hoped she could stay awake awhile, for she knew that beyond this steel town, with its buildings stained red from the smoke of smelting iron ore, lay the broad grain fields of western Michigan. Their vast expanse, reaching unbroken to the horizon, always gave her the same feeling of serenity that she got from looking at the sea.

But it was not to be. Her energy drained by a just-ended promotional campaign across California for one of her clients, the murmur of the turning wheels and the gentle swaying of the car lulled her quickly into slumber.

She slept all the way to Lapeer except for a moment of wakefulness when a change occurred in the sound of the wheels against the tracks. Without raising her head, her face still turned toward the window, she had briefly opened her eyes. The sound was different because the train was on a wooden trestle built across a small river.

It was the Flint, a small but lovely watercourse that meandered through the countryside for a hundred miles before reaching the town of the same name, which had been a fur-trading post two hundred years before.

Lacey saw it flowed through a shadowy tunnel formed by mighty oaks heavy with lush green foliage that arched far out over the water from either side in their search for nourishing sunlight.

A whitetail deer was standing in the shallows, shaded by the trees, a vision of loveliness framed by water and leaves. It lifted its head, its drinking interrupted, water dripping from its mouth, to idly watch the train go by. It knew that there was no need for flight, its acute senses long since conditioned to the daily passing of the noisy, man-made nuisance that caused the ground to shake.

In an instant, the idyllic scene was gone, but Lacey had glimpsed a tiny spotted fawn that butted its head against its mother's hind legs as it tried to reach the milk-filled bag between them.

Just as she drifted back to sleep, it occurred to the exhausted urban warrior that it must be spring. Preston had told her that the does had their babies then. She had been too busy to notice the change of seasons.

Chapter Ten
Looks Old to Me

"I'm glad that bastard's gone," Wanda Applegate announced loudly to an empty waiting room in the Lapeer train depot. In an effort to convince herself of the truth of her statement, she often found it necessary to hear it and not just think it.

Her missing husband usually came to mind when the International was about to arrive because he was supposed to help her get the mailbags and suitcases out on the platform ahead of time. That way, they were in a pile ready for the hasty on-load during what could best be described as the sleek cross-country train's "pause" at the Amtrak station the couple managed.

Not that Wanda wasn't able to do it without him. A big-boned six-footer, had she been a man, she could have been a professional linebacker. Bib overalls worn over a long-sleeved denim work shirt added to her imposing bulk. She wore her thick, auburn hair pulled back from her plain face into a ponytail held in place by a rubber band.

Besides her philandering spouse, her only other major complaint in life was the "hysterical society," as she called the organization in town that fought to preserve historic sites, often using stirring, emotionally charged rhetoric in the process. It owned the old depot and refused to upgrade it on the grounds that it would compromise the town's prized lumber-era heritage.

The Greek Revival-style building had been constructed in the late 1800s by the white pine baron, William Peters. It was the bait he used to lure the New York Central Railroad into laying its rails through Lapeer so he could transport to market his lumber milled in the town from the thousands of trees his crews were cutting in the surrounding forest.

If Wanda had her way, their precious, old-fashioned wooden depot would be demolished and a tidy cement block structure put in its place, one that wouldn't rattle so that her teeth chattered each time a freight train blew through town. It would be wired decently, too, with an outlet on every wall so she wouldn't have a myriad of extension cords running everywhere.

She had improvised, converting the light bulb hanging from the ceiling of the stationmaster's tiny office, on its brown cloth-covered wire, into multiple outlets with an adapter she screwed into the socket. A maypole of power cords dropped to a desk lamp, telephone answering machine, coffeepot, facsimile, and computer.

At the sound of the International's thunderous air-horn in the distance, she rose from the antique roll-top desk where she was working, having completed the manifest in which all passengers arriving and departing were listed by name and address as required by Homeland Security.

They could have their frigging desk, too, she thought as she headed for the door leading to the platform where the train would pull in. A piece of cherry wood furniture built for people much smaller than Wanda, she had to sit sideways to do her paperwork, since the desk was too low-slung to accommodate her knees.

*　*　*

"Handsome ain't here yet," Wanda said to Lacey as the International pulled away, leaving the two of them, looking like a female version of Mutt and Jeff, alone together on the platform. "You might as well come on in for a coffee."

When they were settled inside the waiting room, seated facing each other on hard, wooden benches that looked like church pews, Amtrak mugs in hand, Wanda opened the conversation in her usual way with an observation about men. "They all want the same thing. You know what they call a little bitty gal like you?"

"I'm afraid to ask," Lacey said with a smile. She had gotten to know the station manager somewhat from her previous visits to Red Moon and found her to be a real hoot.

"A spinner, and you know why? Because they can lay on their back and spin little ones like you around on their cock. Whenever Richey and me fight, he always says he's going to the Hitchin' Post for a beer and a spinner to go with it."

"I saw him here once, he's pretty small himself," Lacey said. "Do you think he could really do that with a woman?"

"Hell no, I spin him!" Wanda answered with a chuckle.

Lacey made a mental note to tell that one to the Zonta girls.

Then the big woman's face took on a more serious expression, and she added, "Seriously, honey, don't fall for that jerk you're here to see."

Startled at the turn the conversation had taken, Lacey asked in some confusion, "What are you talking about?"

70

"He sends 'em all back to the big city with Monday-morning smiles."

"Of course he does."

Now it was the older woman that was surprised. "But doesn't that bother you? When Richey's out tomcattin' around, like he is right now, I can hardly stand it."

Seeing Preston entering the waiting room, Wanda's tone of voice changed. "Good afternoon, Judge," she cooed, "we were just talking about your lovely place on the lake."

Chapter Eleven
Return to Health

It was a little over two years since Preston, discouraged and depressed, had taken his medical leave and retreated in despair to Red Moon. But things had changed for the better. Spring of 2003 found a man whose mental acuity had caught up again with his always-superb physical condition.

Days were becoming longer, and the sun was shining from a different position in the sky as it returned to warm the Northern Hemisphere. Preston noticed, constantly observing the natural world around them is the way of most people raised in a rural environment, but he no longer desperately looked to such life forces outside himself for inspiration.

He didn't need to. With each dawn, he felt delighted in receiving another precious day of life. He had an eagerness to get outside the house for his morning run, knowing he would return to Red Moon energized by it and ready for whatever the day would bring.

This morning he had chosen a circular route through the nearby Lapeer State Game Area, a 10,000-acre wilderness tract containing small freshwater lakes and streams, hidden deep in a dense second-growth hardwood forest consisting mostly of maple, oak, and birch trees.

As new growth, they had taken over the hilly landscape in abundance. This was after Michigan's white pine primeval forest had been stripped away by the nonstop logging operations that took place between the time of the Civil War and the beginning of the twentieth century.

Reveling in a sense of being in perfect harmony with his natural surroundings, Preston loped down the same long-abandoned trails that teams of oxen had once pulled sleighs piled high with the trunks of forest giants.

Great in diameter but soft, as wood goes, they had been felled with a two-man crosscut saw, then trimmed free of branches with a double-bitted axe, all done by men who smelled like mountain goats in clothes they put on in the fall and didn't take off until the following spring.

Preston easily pictured the scene in his vivid imagination, almost hearing the shouts of the drivers, the crack of their bull-whips, and the jingle of the chains that held their precarious loads together.

In order to keep his Nike Air running shoes relatively dry, Preston avoided the long grass that grew on the mound between the wheel tracks. It was heavy with dew from the lower nocturnal temperatures. The coolness remained and would keep the mosquitoes dormant for a precious hour or so until the rays of the morning sun found the crevices through the umbrella of trees overhead and comfortably warmed the pests into action.

He couldn't think as he jogged along through the woods the way he was able to when driving his Jeep down these identical trails. The effort of remembering to put his feet down toe first, and to lift his knees as high as possible, in order to get the best exercise, not to mention watching out for rocks and other obstacles, required his full attention.

It was a blessed, necessary concentration that broke the bonds of one's self-absorption, similar to the intense focus required to make music. The same freedom from personal cares occurred when he played the guitar to accompany Laura Hopkins' talented vocal attributes. She did, in fact, sound like a Barbra Streisand clone.

With her infatuation for everything French, she used that country's lyrical language to describe his rejuvenated mental state as "joie de vivre" which, when translated into English, meant "a delight in being alive." And she rejoiced with him in his recovery.

Preston experienced a near ecstasy sometimes on his early outings, the runner's high caused when naturally produced endorphins in the blood lock into receptors in the brain the same way cocaine does. The rush he experienced at those times came close to sexual orgasm in the intensity of the pleasure it provided him.

He appreciated it more than he ordinarily would, like an alcoholic relishes beer when hard liquor isn't obtainable, because Celexa continued to prevent the bird from flying. All the other aspects of his active sex life, such as desire and his sense of touch, had returned to normal.

As Rachael had predicted, most side effects of the drug had adapted out within a week or so, with the exception of his persistent anorgasmia. But even she came to agree that it was among his best assets while on their trip together the previous winter.

His fear that taking Rachael with him to New York would adversely affect their doctor-and-patient relationship had proven to be unfounded. She had resumed her role of being the consummate professional upon their return to Ann Arbor.

It appeared to have been a transaction of little significance to her. As if she had merely stopped by a market of his and bought a filet mignon she cooked for dinner, exactly like they had joked about before they embarked upon their brief tryst, to her a totally pleasant and satisfying one, in a metropolis 600 miles away.

* * *

The artesian spring was on a hillside overlooking a tiny round lake that gleamed like a newly minted silver dollar in the morning sun. All around the natural fountain grew the flowers of the season, white trilliums on foot-long stems, purple violets half-hidden in the grass, and, in the soggy ground below the spring, a half-acre of yellow marsh-marigolds.

It was here that Preston came to make some of the most important decisions in his life. He maintained the spring, keeping it free of leaves and dirt, and repairing its rope-handled circular wooden cover when necessary, as a memorial to his late father, who had first led him to it on horseback when he was a young boy. Its remote location, deeply buried in the forest and well away from any sort of path, was their secret.

Icy cold water welled up in a clay tile that was two feet across, set vertically into the ground. It spilled over the rim and down into an oxen watering trough made of thick wooden planks held together with square iron nails. The overflow from that ancient receptacle made a bubbling sound as it struck the ground and began its winding, downward course to the distant lake.

This wasn't the first time he had interrupted a run through the state land to have a quick drink, using the long-handled speckled-blue-enamel dipper that hung on a forked stick driven into the soft earth. A coffeepot of the same material was suspended on an iron tripod over a fire pit enclosed with a circle of stones. He left both utensils there for himself to use, as well as the rare passersby who stumbled upon the delightful place by accident.

He lingered longer than usual this time, after noticing a peculiar-looking flower growing apart from the rest. It had five cream-colored petals, the traditional number for wildflowers, but that was its only similarity to the others that grew around the spring. Its small bloom adorned the top of a delicately shaped but oddly leafless stalk, about a foot and a half in height.

The lovely flower's isolation, and its lack of leaves for the photosynthesis it needed to survive, reminded him of Rachael and her quest to prove the efficacy of her treatment methods without the support of her peers.

She was beautiful, like the flower, and would need acceptance by the mainstream of her profession for her career to truly flourish, just as the plant would have to grow some leaves in order to live. Maybe, he thought, her successful treatment of himself, being a high-profile patient, would be her first leaf.

He would take the strange flower to Rachael for identification. She had once mentioned that her hobby was horticulture, describing to him a tiny greenhouse attached to the back of her home.

Reminding himself that it was probably an endangered species—after all, he had not seen one in all his years in the out-of-doors—he resisted the temptation to simply snap if off halfway to the ground and take it with him.

Instead, he took a loose scrap of bark from a fallen birch tree and, using a shard of charcoal from the fire pit, skillfully sketched a picture of the rare flower to give to her, all the while sitting on a log with the coffeepot gripped upside down between his knees, the bottom of it serving as his portable desk.

His art project was brought hurriedly to completion by a mosquito that was drilling into a patch of bare skin where his baggy sweat pants didn't quite reach his crew socks, a gap created by his bent knees.

As Preston smacked the insect pest with the fingers of his right hand held together to form an efficient bug-swatter, a thought came to mind with startling clarity. While it had already been quietly swirling around in his mind, he finally realized with certainty that the time had come to close Red Moon Bed and Breakfast, he no longer needed it. He was going to be a fine jurist again.

Chapter Twelve
Gentlemen's Club

It had been almost a year since Preston had been in the Detroit Athletic Club when he and Woody decided to meet there for lunch.

He had forgotten how unattractive it was. Even though it had been designed in 1915 by the renowned architect Albert Kahn, his lovely, richly detailed exterior treatment, perceived as being dated, had recently received an ill-advised facelift that failed, at least in Preston's opinion.

With its new, plain facade, dismally gray in color, the building now resembled a huge block of poured cement that somebody had carved windows in after the forms had been torn away. Seven stories high, it provided a forbidding barricade for Detroit's two new stadiums it was adjacent to, Comerica Park and Ford Field, against the decayed city to the south of them.

Rows of once-elegant buildings, their windows now broken or entirely missing, lined Madison Street, which ran in front of the club. Directly across the street from its varnished oak and polished brass front door attended by a strapping uniformed black man, the delicately arched entrance of one of the derelict buildings, the Madison Lenox Hotel, was sealed from top to bottom with cement blocks.

Once inside the DAC, if a person was not so busy socializing or deal-making to notice, the building was an even stranger bird, looking as if an interior decorator had strained without success to convert a sterile, character-less office building into a medieval castle.

On the main floor, massive chandeliers, with a coarse, Bavarian look, as opposed to the traditional delicate French or Italian designs, were suspended from high ceilings. Large tapestries depicting a boar hunt, designed by Gobelin in 1587, and plundered from Sans Souci, the German Imperial Palace, at the end of World War I, concealed a relatively small part of the plain walls.

Woody had joined the DAC a few years before, in order to better network with the business people that constituted his political base. But he preferred

77

the more prestigious and intimate Detroit Club across town, on the corner of Cass Avenue and Fort Street in the financial district, where Detroit's old-money families, including the banking Thurbers and the automobile Fords, as well as the Woodwards, enjoyed each other's company in a much smaller and more exclusive setting.

"There's just too many faces I don't recognize, it's a circus atmosphere here," Woody groused over his Chivas Regal scotch whiskey on the rocks.

He wasn't complaining to Preston, but instead to John Engler, who was standing by their table after greeting them with a warm, "Hello, Chief Justice Woodward and Justice Foster."

"You'll get used to it," the former Governor consoled Woody with a friendly smile. "If farm boys like Preston and I can get used to city crowds like we have, you can learn to deal with having a few more people around at lunch," he added before he moved on to another table, shaking hands with everyone who extended a greeting.

"I'm glad he doesn't know how I made the money to pay for this lunch," Preston said when Engler was out of earshot.

"Second thoughts, Romeo?" Woody asked dourly, still discontented with his surroundings, the manicured fingernails of one hand tapping the white, linen tablecloth restlessly, as if playing a piano.

"We can go elsewhere, like Roma Cafe," Preston offered, knowing from what seemed to him like a hundred lunches in the past that his friend would say, "Let's make the best of it, we'll just waste more time changing restaurants now."

Woody glanced at his gold Patek Phillipe watch and then replied as expected, adding, "I'm glad that one of your johnettes finally owned up to you that she had called me."

"Laura Hopkins is far more to me than that, Woody. She happens to be a good friend that wants to help me get my job back, a pursuit I'm expecting you to join in wholeheartedly."

"Wait just a minute," Woody said with a scowl, "I don't control the new Governor, and in case you have lost touch completely, Jennifer Granholm is a Democrat."

"But she will be consulting with you soon. I've let her know by letter that I'm interested in an interim appointment to fill the vacancy created by Fred Walberg's death and included my doctor's written statement that I've improved to the point where I can again handle the responsibilities."

"Are you sure it's good to subject yourself to that sort of pressure so soon?" Woody asked, his expression changing from surprise to concern. "And Jennifer and her husband, Dan Mulhern, are friends of mine from

Harvard Law School. I don't want her to be criticized later in the media, just in case she returns you to the Bench and you fall back on your butt."

"You never have understood my OCD, Woody. It's a disease. You get sick, take off work to get treated, then go back to work when you're well. If it was cancer and I told you it was in remission and I was ready to come back, you wouldn't have any misgivings."

They talked of other things then, Preston steering the conversation in the direction of Woody's interests to achieve more of a balance to their lunch conversation. Nonetheless, Woody's comment when they parted made it clear that he had been thinking about what Preston had said.

"I'll talk to Sandra Wells, our Supreme Court Administrator, I think she can tell me exactly how the wind is blowing so far on the search for Walberg's replacement. And incidentally, don't be so touchy about what I said about Laura Hopkins, I think she's great."

Chapter Thirteen
Request for Investigation

"Do you know someone by the name of Barbara Hemion?"

"What happened to 'hello'? Have we now dispensed with the customary amenities?" Preston good-naturedly chided Woody after taking his friend's call in his Jeep on his Nextel cell phone.

"H-E-M-I-O-N," Woody spelled the name, ignoring Preston's question.

"Are you trying to get a date with her, or something?" Preston teased, continuing to disregard the serious tone he heard in Woody's voice.

Annoyed, Woody demanded: "I hear car traffic noises instead of cows mooing, where the hell are you?"

"House hunting in Lansing, in preparation for my triumphant return to this capital city founded in 1835 on the banks of the Grand River so Governor Mason could canoe to work from his log cabin in Grand Rapids.... What else would you like to know?

"Sorry, Woody, for the diatribe, but it's just wonderful to feel good again; I'm never going to let myself get so far down again. What can I do for you?"

"I'm not calling for me, I'm trying to help you, you turkey. I checked with our Court Administrator, Sandra Wells, as promised. Sure enough, you are on Granholm's shortlist for an appointment, although I still think it's going to be a near miss."

"Don't be so negative about my prospects, Woody," Preston said, feeling his natural high starting to slip away as Woody continued on with his assessment of Preston's chances.

"Sure, it makes the Governor look bipartisan for her to even consider a Republican, Preston Foster, for the Supreme Court since she needs the support of the Republican-controlled legislature for her state budget cuts.

"And she has asked the Attorney General, Mike Cox, for an opinion on your eligibility, Bobby, to serve again on the Court, which means that she is seriously considering appointing you. But she probably has already made her mind up to choose someone from her own party if Cox has the slightest reservation about your appointment."

"He won't, Mike's a Republican, too."

"It's not that simple," Woody said, pausing to control his growing impatience, then continuing, "That's where Barbara Hemion comes in, she is an attorney serving on the Attorney General's staff."

"As usual, Woody, you keep forgetting the mental health angle. And apparently, you haven't seen the front page of this morning's *Detroit News*. Michigan ranks at the bottom of a national evaluation of mental health care by a highly respected watchdog organization."

"Which one?"

"The National Mental Health Association, it's the oldest and largest group in America that represents the mentally ill. Stretch your brain, Woody, and try to imagine the political impact of Governor Granholm giving a second chance to someone like me who uninformed people like you have dismissed as a total nutcase. It would save face for Michigan nationally, and help her get reelected next time around. Do you have any idea how many voters in this state are on Prozac, or have kids on Ritalin, or—"

"Spare me your wishful thinking, pal," Woody said, cutting him off.

"Excuse me, Woody, for interrupting your interruption, but here's something else to consider. Everybody loves a comeback from almost anything. It's sort of like a happy ending in a movie, you know what I mean?"

"Oh, please, spare me the theatrics."

"Your problem is," Preston persisted, "you don't believe that what I'm overcoming is real. You and your ilk will probably forever cling to the bigoted notion that psychiatric disorders were invented by psychiatrists so they could make a decent living. That's an ignorant assumption often made by lucky ones like you that didn't happen to get sick with one."

"Your ridiculous rationale is making me sorry I called," Woody snapped impatiently and he hung up.

Preston struggled to push away his anger in order to remember what Woody said he was calling about. Something about a woman, with an unusual last name that he had never heard before, who worked in the Attorney General's office.

A squeal of tires on blacktop, followed immediately by the blast of a car horn, distracted him from his thoughts just in time to swerve to the left so as to barely avoid an accident.

As Preston drove on, he caught a glimpse of the lady driver of the other vehicle, a Saturn, shaking her head in disgust, and realized he had blown through a four-way stop without even slowing down.

82

* * *

Woody expertly brought down his Mooney M20J, a single-engine four-seater, onto the runway of Bishop International Airport in Flint. It had been an uneventful flight from his family's summer home in Harbor Springs, and he was anxious to talk to Preston, who he expected would be waiting for him inside the newly completed, grandiose terminal.

The vast open spaces of the building's magnificent design were wasted upon only the handful of people who now used the facility. It was as if its planners thought they were in another city, perhaps Cincinnati or Tampa, instead of a medium-sized factory town, one that had been economically devastated by the closing of the General Motors' Buick Division plant, referred to locally as "Buick City."

"Our phone conversations don't seem to go well these days, Bobby," Woody had observed when Preston called him back to apologize for getting on a soapbox about mental illness.

When Preston asked Woody to repeat the mystery woman's name, all he got in the way of reply was: "I'm not saying any more about her or what she's doing until we talk in person."

* * *

Preston watched Woody taxi his fast, high performance plane to the area reserved for private aircraft. He knew it would take a while for his friend to make the necessary entries in his flight and maintenance logs, take care of registration with Homeland Security, and order refueling and tie-down services.

He appreciated the fact that Woody had interrupted his vacation week "up north," as Michigan people call the portion of the state that lies above Bay City, to meet with him to discuss Preston's hoped-for appointment to the Court by the Governor.

The "serious threat," which is how Woody referred to the change of circumstances that moved him to fly to Flint, had to be, in Woody's words, "addressed immediately and aggressively." According to him, there was now more at stake than just the appointment.

From his vantage point in a seat next to a tall window in the airport's coffee shop, Preston could easily distinguish Woody from the other men around him down on the tarmac due to his friend's stocky figure and shiny pate. The onset of male patent baldness in Woody's early twenties had left just a fringe of dark hair around the sides of his large head.

He had gotten his commercial pilot's license six years before, and his flying provided some balance to a bachelor's life dedicated primarily to the reading of legal tomes, not just in his judicial work but also pursuant to his avocation of researching the origins of constitutional law.

When Preston noticed Woody start to walk briskly toward the terminal, he went to the cash register and bought his friend the customary large black coffee and peanut donut. He returned with them to his window table, sitting down in time to see Woody enter the room and start walking toward him, weaving between the mostly empty tables.

* * *

Laura Hopkins parked her BMW next to the robin's egg blue caboose. She had some time to spare before Preston would return from Flint with Woody and the three of them would start their drive together to nearby Frankenmuth for dinner.

By now, she had made numerous trips through Lapeer on her way to Red Moon and had noticed the old wooden train depot, but she had never gone inside. A double set of steel tracks passed in front of it, with three out-of-service train cars on public exhibition some distance behind the building.

Each was freshly painted in a different bright hue, the other two being red and yellow. Set about the now-vacant parking lot, they looked like colorful toys left behind by a giant's child.

They once served as crews' quarters at the end of freight trains. The county's historical society had arranged for their restoration and display, remnants of the vital role played by railroads in the region's history.

Laura had something decidedly more current on her mind, however. It wasn't as if Preston was trying to cover anything up. He had told her that most of his "lady guests," as he called his Red Moon clients, came to Lapeer on Amtrak's sleek, cross-country train from Chicago.

Since the International didn't arrive for several hours yet, she figured there might be an Amtrak employee available to answer her questions. She walked briskly toward the quaint building, knowing that what she expected to learn inside might not seem as pretty to her as the cabooses had. She pressed the button on the remote device in her hand that doubled as a key chain and heard the BMW's doors lock decisively behind her.

* * *

84

"This Barbara Hemion person has filed a document called 'Request For Investigation Form' with the Michigan Judicial Tenure Commission," Woody said as he sipped his coffee. "It concerns you." The donut had been consumed, with a few small crumbs of peanut remaining on the waxed paper in front of him.

"I thought the Commission was supposed to keep matters that come before it confidential," Preston replied.

"That's right."

"I still don't get it," Preston admitted with a puzzled expression on his face, then continued, "they shouldn't be sending you anything about it."

"It's because Ms. Hemion is unhappy with me, too. I'm being called to task before the frigging Commission myself, and I've received a letter summoning me to testify before it. As Chief Justice, I was the one who granted your request for a medical leave of absence.

"Michigan statutes and case law are silent as to medical leaves for Supreme Court Justices. I suppose I should have asked the Attorney General's office for an opinion on the matter, but that would have delayed your leave for six months while we waited for them to get off their asses over there."

Now Preston understood. To help a desperate friend, Woody had taken the risk of granting him a medical leave with not a trace of legal authority to support it.

Preston stared at Woody for a long moment, taking in his close-set eyes, thin lips, and extra-large nose, a face that not even its merciful symmetry could save from homeliness.

It occurred to Preston that by an accident of birth he had gotten the great looks but that Woody was blessed with a good and courageous heart.

It crossed Preston's mind, then, how at Lapeer High School when he was a student, especially pretty girls often paired up with very unattractive ones to hang out together.

He guessed that the two women who had been glancing in his direction from a table at the other side of the coffee shop might be noticing that same sort of contrast in appearance in Woody and himself.

Whoever had coined the phrase "looks are only skin deep" had it right, Preston acknowledged to himself; for example, take Abraham Lincoln. He wondered how many good, maybe even great, people he had deprived himself of over the years, by judging their desirableness in terms of good looks.

Preston reflected upon how so many of the women drawn to Red Moon for sex were plain, yet he had to admit that he had learned something

85

worthwhile about life from almost every one of them. When they left him at the end of their experience, Preston thought each one was very special and beautiful in their own way.

Woody's voice broke the pattern of silence that had become typical of their more recent conversations. "We had to find a replacement for you when your leave dragged on longer than a month because there are some judicial functions that require a full, nine-member Court. That, and because somebody had to get your frigging work done."

"Would you believe," Woody rambled on, "within three weeks after Bill Miller was appointed and took over your cases, he was complaining about not having enough to do?"

Again Preston stared at Woody, wondering if his friend had made that dig for the purpose of ending the warm, fuzzy moment they had just shared. He knew that revealing emotion of any kind was not Woody's style.

"Bill got what he wanted—in spades," Woody said, chuckling. "I gave him back your Mester Oil case. Remember? That's the one I had been writing the majority opinion for, to help you out just before you left."

"That shut him up, I bet," Preston observed, forcing himself with difficulty to paste on a smile, hiding his growing discomfort. He continued to search Woody's countenance without success for the slightest trace of rancor.

Finally, to change the direction of the discussion that was making him increasingly uncomfortable, Preston suggested, "Let's get back to Barbara Hemion."

"OK," Woody agreed, but with a frown. "There is only one more thing I've been able to find out about her that I haven't told you yet."

"Tell me."

"She's the Chairperson of the Judicial Tenure Commission."

* * *

"There is one little chicky from Chicago that goes out there quite a bit more often than the others...." Wanda Applegate responded carefully to Laura Hopkins' inquiry about Preston's bed and breakfast guests. The arrival of a waitress with menus and a pot of coffee interrupted their conversation, to Wanda's immense relief.

They were seated in a booth facing each other over a Formica-topped table with a wide, vertical band of chrome around the edges. Luckily, it turned out to be movable, otherwise Wanda would never have gotten her bulky figure between it and the bench-style, stationary seat.

Laura was treating the train station manager to lunch at the Country Kitchen. It was a favorite hangout for the people who worked in Lapeer as well as farmers who came there in their pickup trucks from all directions, filling its parking lot with Dodge Rams, Chevrolet S-10s, and Ford 150s.

Varnished wooden shelves attached to the wallpaper-covered walls were crowded with trinkets and gewgaws, all with paper price tags dangling on white strings. They were for city people passing through the area.

Knowing looks were exchanged by the local residents when they saw a stranger heading for the cash register with a cement wren house embedded with colorful buttons that country people knew no bird would use, or a coffee mug decorated with hand-painted clusters of blue morning glories that probably would run together with their first trip into a microwave oven.

"This is still partly a farm town, honey," Wanda said with a chuckle when she noticed Laura look away from her menu to eye the breakfast food on other tables. "Most of these folks have been working in their barns and fields since daybreak. It's part of their traditional fun to come in here for a whopping big breakfast at noon."

Wanda ordered the "Sunrise Steak Special," which came with a small T-bone steak and a heap of potatoes that had been boiled in their skins and then thick-sliced and fried in bacon fat with sweet onions and green peppers.

Their waitress brought it to their table on an oval platter made of white earthenware with a green trim-line around the outer edge. Piled on top like a roof were four triangular pieces of one-and-a-half-inch-thick sour dough toast.

Wanda suggested a strawberry waffle to Laura since the fruit was at its peak, it being the second week in June. "I happen to know," she confided in a whisper, "that this place buys their strawberries right from Rupert's Berry Farm on the edge of town. They pick 'em fresh out there every morning."

"Is anything a secret around here?" Laura asked, with her distinctive, throaty laugh. She used long, beautifully tapered fingers to brush her shining black hair away from her exquisite, angular face, basking in the stimulating attention she was getting from the predominantly male diners, most of whom had never seen anything like her except at the movies.

The undeniable physical appeal of one particularly handsome man, wearing a leather hat that made her think of Crocodile Dundee, was starting to get to her. Under his unabashed, admiring gaze, the mounting excitement in her body made her feel like dancing on a tabletop.

He sat alone at a counter that projected out from the rear wall near the kitchen door. His dark tan, she supposed, came from many days in the sun doing farm work, and he was dressed in a blue denim shirt and Levi's that appeared to confirm that occupation.

"That's my cousin you're staring at over my shoulder," Wanda announced, between mouthfuls of food. Then she added, "Cute, ain't he?"

"Don't tell me, Wanda, let me guess. He married his high school sweetheart. They have a boy, eight, and a girl, six. And the four of them live happily together in a white house on a hill. Oh, I forgot their Golden Retriever and picket fence."

"Are you telling me that's what you want, honey?"

Before Laura could answer, she saw the man stand, towering up so high it looked for a moment like he might hit his head on a low ceiling fan turning slowly above the aisle. Then he started to walk toward their table.

Laura struggled to remember what she had intended to ask Wanda in her effort to gauge the depth of Preston's involvement with his customers. But every one of her questions seemed to vanish from her mind as the tall, lean man approached. It was as if the issue of competition for Preston's affection didn't matter anymore.

Chapter Fourteen
Entertainment Business

White wooden carriages, trimmed in polished brass, moved slowly along Frankenmuth's Main Street, carrying tourists from mainly Michigan but others from all parts of the world. Each elegant conveyance was under the command of a woman outfitted in a white coachman's uniform with matching top hat and gloves. Perched high up on elevated drivers' benches, and holding leather reins used to steer their horses, with eight-foot-long whips close at hand pointing skyward from metal holders, the ladies were imposing to behold.

All dignity was lost, however, when one of the massive black Percherons pulling the carriages found it necessary to dump a cluster of horse puckey on the street. Then its unlucky master had to hurriedly scramble down from her high seat, change gloves, and deal with the droppings, sweeping them quickly out of sight into an oversize pooper-scooper.

The horse-drawn carriages were a grandiloquent remembrance of the splendor of the past. Their rather peculiar blend of elegance tempered by necessity was evident as well in the sprawling white frame restaurant just beyond the carriage stand where passengers were taken aboard.

A pillared veranda, about half a football field in length, was all that could be seen of the structure from the street, giving the appearance that a plantation's main house had been transported from the Mississippi Delta in the late 1800s.

White-painted cement urns, set at 15-foot intervals on a knee-high brick wall that ran between the sidewalk and Main Street, were filled with luxuriant masses of vivid red geraniums to accent the white building behind them.

Most of those brilliantly colored annuals, too, were the old-fashioned, upright variety, placed in the center of each of the planters for height, with some of the new, hybrid vine type trailing their blooms down over the rims to create an overflow effect.

A peek around either end of the splendiferous edifice, however, revealed an architect's nightmare. Built upon the Cass River flats in 1856, the building had been repeatedly damaged by floodwaters, some parts being demolished, and multiple rooms added on through the years, creating a maze of connected structures of assorted shapes, sizes, and heights.

The flooding ended in 1966 when the Army Corps of Engineers completed its ten-year-long project of building a flood control dike on the river a short distance upstream. But the popularity of the eating place continued to grow, resulting in the addition of even more rooms to house a bakery, gift shop, and food store.

It had become the largest family restaurant in America, catering to 875,000 patrons a year, and serving them 950,000 pounds of chicken. Not to mention side dishes including 750,000 pounds of cabbage, 100,000 of squash, and 47,000 of cranberry relish. All washed down with 26,000 pounds of coffee.

Clearly, the business no longer needed to borrow the ambiance of another time and place for its success. So, instead of displaying an old antebellum name from the South to go with its facade, a sign in front read "Zehnder's Famous Chicken Dinners" in red neon with the word "Frankenmuth" done in blue. Its steady light glowed in the warm, soft dusk of summer, as dozens of people strolled about the tree-lined walks or lounged on the comfortable benches set upon the broad porch.

* * *

Inside the main dining room, Woody had just finished his dessert. Touching a napkin to his lips, he said, "Unless we can resolve this on an informal basis before the Judicial Tenure Commission, an interim appointment for you by the Governor is practically dead."

His pronouncement was directed to Preston, but only Laura was paying attention. In fact, just as Woody finished delivering his warning of the adverse consequences of inaction, Preston excused himself from the table. Quickly standing up, he announced, "I want to speak to Banjo before he goes on, I'll be back before the show begins."

"He said to wear something red," Laura observed to no one in particular as they watched Preston disappear into the crowded hallway, where some of the other diners were taking a stretch break, shaking off the numbing effects of eating too much chicken, mashed potatoes, and gravy.

Woody looked perplexed. "His judicial career is at stake and he won't sit still long enough to talk about how to save it, and all you can think about is clothes. Why are we here?"

90

"I think for me," Laura replied with a smile, adding, "I really do appreciate your support, Woody."

"For what?"

They sat at a table just large enough to hold a hodgepodge of empty serving bowls, a bubble-shaped plastic bread holder, heavy-duty plates, and stainless steel silverware, far different than the Royal Doulton china and Rogers Brothers sterling silver eating utensils Woody was accustomed to.

Two plastic containers of seasonings, with labels that read "Zehnder's World Famous Quality," placed in the middle of the table, one in green marked "All Purpose," and the other orange for "Chicken," added to the family-style look of things, as did the paper packets of cream and sugar that had been piled into sauce dishes for convenience.

Frankenmuth had achieved the enviable position of being Michigan's number-one tourist attraction with over 100 specialty shops and attractions, including St. Julian's Winery, the formidable Fortress golf course, and a 150-passenger paddle wheeler, the Bavarian Belle, for dinner cruises on the Cass River.

Had Woody known the city's distinction of being the target of over 2200 bus tours a year, that alone would have been enough to keep him away. Zehnder's, as just one of the many albeit the largest of the restaurants in the town, daily served 6500 people home-style meals during its peak, summer season.

Their chicken had been brought to them on loaded-to-capacity platters to be passed around the table, along with heaping bowls of mashed potatoes with giblet gravy, creamy coleslaw, butter noodles called "spaetzle," sauerkraut, green beans, and Wiener schnitzel. Generous helpings of apple strudel à la mode had topped off the scrumptious dinner.

"Bobby went to high school with Banjo Harris in Lapeer," Laura explained. "Now though, when he's not on tour, he lives on his cattle ranch near Kissimmee, Florida where he raises prize Herefords and Black Angus. He's even got a few of those weird-looking Brahmans that are sacred to the Hindus."

Rattling on, Laura lowered her voice as if saying something for Woody's ears alone, "See those three people to the right of the stage standing next to the big camera on a boom? That's the crew from *20/20*. They're following him around the country filming a segment for ABC."

"You mean those young women in baggy sweats, with ponytails and earrings?"

"Yes, but they're guys."

"Whatever," Woody replied with a shrug. Then with a sudden expression of surprise on his face he added, "Do I detect in you a certain fascination with the heady scent of show business?" He raised his eyebrows.

"Bobby is trying to get me a tiny bit of stage time with Banjo ... and I already know I'm going to get it."

"So that's it!" Woody exclaimed. Then with a stern look on his face he added emphatically, "Forget it, lady, it's a tough, often unfair business in which talent, and I'm only assuming you have some, simply isn't enough. They say that half the time it's nothing but sheer luck that pries that supposedly golden door open a crack for wannabes like you to try to squeeze through.

"Which leads me to my next question. How do you know so much about this Banjo person and what's going on here even before our Bobby Prince Charming gets around to dragging the guy to our table for introductions, in order to give you your first so-called 'break'?"

"I met him already, today, at the Country Kitchen in Lapeer, but please don't tell Bobby. I made Banjo promise not to. I don't want to risk putting a damper on Bobby's really sweet gesture, he's so excited about all of this."

"Now I'm getting really confused," Woody said, shaking his head. Then he continued grumpily, "But I guess I'd better try to show some interest in this silliness.... Who told you to wear red?"

"Come to think of it, they both did."

* * *

Banjo Harris was a musical genius, able to play any instrument that made music, and it was happy sounds that he produced. Before very long, an audience began to sing and their feet started tapping in time to the music.

He could even coax a tune out of a makeshift bass consisting of a broom attached by a long piece of fishing line to the center of an upside-down washtub, making different notes by changing the string's tightness as he plucked away at it with his fingers.

Trained on a full scholarship at the Juilliard School of Music in New York, he was comfortable playing classical music such as Mozart and Beethoven on the piano, but his first love was bluegrass, performed on a violin, or sometimes by playing two instruments at once, a guitar or banjo with both hands and a harmonica held to his lips by a wire frame resting on his chest.

His music carried an audience back to an earlier time in America, when people looked to the sky for their weather report instead of a television set, and the sight of a freshly plowed field made its owner's eyes tear up at the

92

beauty of it.

Banjo knew that nobody really wanted to go back again to live in those hardscrabble days, but his discovery that they surely loved to return to them now and then, even if only for a musical visit, had made him rich.

His rural background allowed him to give his distinctive brand of bluegrass music an authenticity that his competitors lacked. During a 30-minute television interview earlier that year with Barbara Walters, he had credited that advantage to growing up in the farm country around Lapeer.

Banjo had made the point with her that putting a straw hat and blue jeans on a singer raised on city streets and giving him a country-sounding name didn't fool bluegrass aficionados at all. He asserted that they were picky audiences that would quickly determine that the entertainer was a real phony.

Banjo compared it to hunting and fishing stories a guy was subjected to while getting a haircut at Wes Felton's barber shop in downtown Lapeer, telling Walters that you knew after about the first ten words whether the customer in the next chair was a true outdoorsman or merely a windbag.

* * *

At the close of his first set, Banjo took the two steps down off the carpeted riser where his piano and various other instruments were placed and walked across a small, open area to sit down next to Preston. Even seated, his height put his head well above everybody else's at the table.

"This must be our guest soloist," he said in Laura's direction, smiling. Then he added, winking, "I'm afraid the folks will be too busy lookin' at you to listen good when you get up there."

"Thank you. Yes, I'm Laura Hopkins, and I'm looking forward to it. This is Chief Justice Woodward."

"I hope you do more on that wonderful Steinway piano in your next set," Woody said with a sincere tone in his voice. "Preston tells me it belongs to you and goes where you go. You pleasantly surprised me with that little piece from the Rachmaninoff Second Piano Concerto, and I understand that is one of his most difficult pieces to play well. I could listen to you perform that kind of music all night."

"With this crowd, Justice, you probably wouldn't be able to hear it over the snoring," Banjo said, laughing. Then turning his attention back to Laura, he asked, "What are you going to sing?"

"Oh, I don't know."

"I suggest you choose something you've always dreamed of performing in public," Banjo advised. "Living that dream just this once may be the only

93

thing you accomplish tonight, and you will at least have a memory that nobody can take away from you." Then he added gently, "Unfortunately, Laura, we never know how a crowd will react to a particular performer, no matter how talented they may be."

"Well, that little speech makes it easy for me," Laura said. "Do you know Sammy Fain's 'Love Is a Many Splendored Thing'?"

"Of course. But please don't start singing the first verse until I nod to you, there's a gorgeous, piano-only opening I'd hate to leave out. It's one of my favorite songs, too."

Getting to his feet, Banjo said, "It's nice to meet both of you, and keep in touch, Bobby, we probably won't get a chance to talk much after the show, it's a mob scene since my bluegrass song 'Last Chance' crossed over into Billboard's pop chart."

"That must be a real ego builder," Preston observed, using some of the psychology talk he had picked up from his psychiatrist, Rachael Childs.

"Yeah, lucky me. But now there is a complete lack of privacy. I usually try to sign autographs but keep moving toward the door at the same time, just to get back to my motel room and lay down, right on top of the bed spread, and enjoy the quiet time for a while."

"It does seem that every one of us has some unique behavior to cope with the stress of our work," Woody observed as he shook Banjo's hand, adding, "I fly through the clouds to get away from law books now and then."

"Well, I have to make a quick change of clothes before I go back on," Banjo said as he pulled himself away from a conversation he was starting to enjoy. "It's goodbye to my Levi's and snakeskin boots.

"And I want to alert the *20/20* folks that you'll be coming on stage soon, Laura. They'll welcome the easiness on the eyes that you'll provide them, I'm certain of that, and it will add variety to the video tape for television they are filming. You know what they say, 'an ounce of difference is worth a pound of the same.'"

As Banjo left them, Preston turned to Laura with a worried look on his face and said, "You've gotten awfully quiet. I hope he hasn't caused you to have a bad case of stage fright."

"Hell no," she said with a confident smile, "he's lucky to have me sing with him, I can hardly wait."

* * *

Like the outside of the building, the interior of Zehnder's was a study in contrasts. The central performance room did double duty, serving as the largest of several dining rooms, reflecting the reality that the dominant function of the eatery was to sell chicken dinners.

The room's decorating theme was the Black Forest of the Bavarian Alps, testimony to the German heritage of the restaurant's owners, as well as that of the founders of the city of Frankenmuth. It was in 1845 that 15 German-Lutheran missionaries settled there for the purpose of teaching Christianity to the Chippewa Indians.

A massive wooden beam divided the room's ceiling into two vaulted sections. From each, there were suspended three plain brass chandeliers. Half a dozen frosted, flame-shaped electric bulbs on each one of them gave off just enough light for the skilled waitresses, dressed in German peasant-girl pinafores called "dirndls," to attend the closely packed rows of white cloth-covered tables.

The window treatments consisted of colorfully stenciled wooden boxes, with the centers cut out to reveal eight-pane wooden-framed windows covered with cream-colored sheer curtains. Probably few of the diners noticed that out of the nine such windows in the room, the three on the inside wall that separated one room from the next were clever fakes.

The same see-through fabric as the curtains were made of was used in small lamp shades set atop single-bulb wall sconces. They were placed near the top of vertically applied rectangular pieces of wallpaper outlined in mitered wooden molding, with three wood-framed pictures hung within the same border.

The decorating touches broke up the monotony of the rose-color-painted walls, and the little shaded lights contributed their gentle glow to the edges of the room, the same soft quality of light provided to its center by the chandeliers.

At the moment, however, none of the motionless, quietly entralled customers at the tables were noticing such amenities. Instead, their eyes were riveted upon a magnificent woman filling every inch of the place with an incredible voice.

* * *

The trio of *20/20* technicians in sweat suits were lulled into a near-stupor by boredom and what they had been smoking in their van and had been expecting just one more desperate, hopeful local singing her heart out for fame and fortune. Suddenly they were electrified by Laura's immense, soaring, yet restrained contralto, the lowest female voice.

Seasoned veterans in the business of video-taping entertainers, they had their job made more complicated by the need not only to record the performance but often to make rather homely singers like Celine Dion and Barbra Streisand look good so as to curry their favor for future business. This new talent was a stunner from any angle or distance, without any special enhancement effort needed on their part.

Sensing an opportunity to add greatly to the probability that their documentary would be chosen for broadcast by the producers of *20/20*, they quickly took up positions about the room to meticulously record every detail of Laura's performance.

The crew's sound man, wearing earphones to monitor the recording mix, and not trusting Zehnder's pickup system, held a foot-and-a-half-long fuzzy-appearing cylindrical microphone on a long boom several feet above Laura's head.

Striving for what movie people call a "surround," another of the crew slowly moved the largest of their cameras, about five feet in length and mounted on a dolly, in a circle around Laura just off the small stage, its wheels rolling smoothly on the hardwood floor of the dining room.

A "reveal" was the goal of the other cameraman. It is commonly used in advertising, first picturing a distant, unclear object, like a speeding vehicle at the head of a cloud of desert dust, and then moving rapidly toward it to clarify what exactly it was, such as a certain brand and model of automobile.

Hurrying out into the hallway with a second camera on a shoulder mount, he propped open the dining room's double doors. The resulting burst of glorious sound made almost everyone in the distant lobby turn their heads in his direction.

Walking gingerly backward down the hall until the door frame began to intrude on the outer edge of his camera's viewfinder, he stopped and stood still, adjusting the framing function so that the indistinct red object on the distant stage was in the center of his composition.

Slowly, the preset, computerized panning device did the move in on Laura for him as he stood so rigidly in place that he might as well have been crazy-glued to the carpeting. A crowd grew steadily behind him, jostling quietly with each other to see past him into the dining room for a glimpse of the woman with the breathtaking voice.

Many of the curious had already noticed the van in the restaurant's parking lot bearing the ABC logo, and they knew from Zehnder's promotional blitz that Banjo Harris, the famous bluegrass singer with local roots, was trying out his new material there as had become his custom once each week, generally on Friday nights.

Only the cameraman could see clearly what was going on from that distance as he monitored the digital image display screen with his well-trained eyes: A glistening black 10-foot-long concert grand piano, played by a tall, handsome man in a black tuxedo with velvet lapels of the same color, were the showcase for a slender, yet curvy, raven-haired beauty that was doing the Barbra Streisand-type singing. Her crimson low-cut gown of simple, classic design touched the floor. One smooth white hand and forearm rested casually on the top of the stool that she had been sitting on when first coming on stage.

Instead of straining to put a loud, dramatic ending on her rendition of the Sammy Fain movie-soundtrack classic, she slowed her delivery of the lyrics, mindful that Banjo's set was just beginning and that it was a professional courtesy to leave grand finales to him. Her gradual, perfectly controlled tapering down of volume as she approached the song's end culminated with the last word being sung in a near-whisper.

The audience was silent for a long moment as if spellbound, then vigorous applause rippled through the room with a sound like a breaking ocean wave. Many of the listeners at the tables stood up, calling for an encore. Laura nodded to Banjo, mouthing a "thank you" over the din, and then returned quickly to her table and sat down.

Not yet satisfied, the crowd began a thunderous stamping on the oak planking beneath their feet. Thrilled, but determined not to grandstand, she had rehearsed just such a moment mentally beforehand, she stood up briefly to acknowledge the amazing response to her song with a smile and a wave before sitting down again for good.

* * *

"It was your night, my dear," Woody said to Laura as they stood together on Zehnder's front steps waiting for Preston to return from the parking lot with the Jeep.

"Thanks," Laura replied, taking his hand for a moment and squeezing it as a gesture of appreciation for his words.

Then she changed the subject, saying, "Now that we have a minute or two alone, I want to speak with you about Bobby's lackadaisical attitude toward the meeting he has next week with the Judicial Tenure Commission."

"If you remember, I'm the one who started this conversation about two hours ago," Woody replied sarcastically with a wry smile. Then he quickly added, "Don't mind me, Laura, I guess I'm just a born grump. But it bothers me that Bobby is fiddling with distractions like the business here tonight while Rome appears to be burning. This Hemion character, for instance...."

97

His voice trailed into silence as he and Laura stared at one another, searching each other's faces for clues, each one trying to take the measure of the other's commitment to help their mutual friend, Preston.

"You should call her," they both blurted out at the same time after a long moment of quiet.

Without another word, they solemnly hooked pinky fingers to commemorate their unplanned duet, chanting the timeworn saying together, both amazed that the other knew it: "Needles, pins, when a man marries his troubles begin."

"OK, we'll both call her," Woody said, as they laughed together for the first time.

It had been a childlike, rather silly experience that they had just shared, and it was over in a minute or so, but it marked a change for the better in their relationship. They had finally become a team.

Chapter Fifteen
Sharing a Personal Triumph

"Why am I feeling so good about a meeting when it concerns a buddy that may be in deep shit just for helping me out?" Preston asked himself as he eased up on the Jeep's gas pedal and let gravity do the braking on the tight, rising curve of the ramp from southbound I-75 to West Grand Boulevard.

He thought about what was about to transpire. The Judicial Tenure Commission's investigation of Woody, or of anybody for that matter, was serious business. Even though the Commission's actions so far remained informal, not yet declaring a formal, public hearing to be necessary, it had the bad smell of a witch hunt to it, possibly a political one.

How could this Barbara Hemion woman, Preston wondered, serve on the Attorney General's staff and at the same time be Chairperson of the Judicial Tenure Commission, on the one hand advising the Governor on Preston's current fitness for office while at the same time looking into a claim of Woody's misconduct in the way he handled Preston's disability a couple of years back. It didn't strike him as a clear conflict of interests, but he knew something was wrong, like seeing a red flag go down on a play in a football game without knowing what it was for.

Yet, Preston couldn't wait to get into the meeting and start talking. He had been annoyed by every delay, and morning rush hour traffic coming into the city had begun to slow him down once he had reached its northern suburbs toward the end of his drive from Lapeer.

* * *

Nine in the morning in July of 2003 found Detroit's New Center Area vigorously alive. Cars and trucks jammed Grand Boulevard. And the sidewalks in front of the Fisher Building and an equally magnificent building across the street that had once been the headquarters of General Motors, the world's largest corporation, were filled with pedestrians hurrying to work.

But all the noisy hustle bustle between seven thirty and nine thirty each morning here during the workweek was like a brief flashback to better days, only temporarily masking the sad decline of this former epicenter of business and entertainment in the Detroit metropolitan area. Venturing two blocks in any direction from the two majestic but isolated office towers found the same depressing inner city decay prevalent in many American cities.

Radio station WJR remained with the region's most powerful transmitter, "Coming to you from the golden tower of the Fisher Building," as an announcer's sonorous voice had been saying to its hundreds of thousands of listeners all throughout the Midwest for decades. As did the renowned Fisher Theater, a prime venue for nationally touring theatrical productions, and the last tryout stop on the way to New York for some of Broadway's greatest hits like *Hello Dolly*.

But General Motors had departed several years earlier to its newer, gleaming World Headquarters Building by the Detroit River. Now its former home on the Boulevard contained state offices, and it was there that Preston was to testify as a witness at the Judicial Tenure Commission's monthly meeting.

What a triumphant tale he had to tell, he thought, as he circled the building looking for one of the scarce street parking spots. After only two years or so in treatment with his psychiatrist, Rachael Childs, his OCD was contained so successfully that he was reading as fast as he did before the devastating illness struck him.

Under her guidance, he had discovered that the anxiety he had been a slave to would crumble of its own accord as long as he used all his will power and tolerated it for a time. These days he did just that, instead of rereading four times whatever he had before him at the time of an anxiety attack which had been self-defeating in its enormous consumption of time and only provided temporary relief.

Expecting a short stay at the meeting, he knew he could crow about his recovery only so long before people got bored, he pulled into a one-hour parking zone on the street that ran behind the building. He turned the motor off and sat quietly for a moment, engaging in self-analysis.

Probably, he supposed, straining to be honest with himself, his eagerness for the meeting to begin reflected a deep desire for redemption in the eyes of his peers. Lawyers and judges and politicians were a gossipy bunch. He was sure stories of his "breakdown" had made the rounds. Today he had an opportunity to make some progress toward bringing back into balance his personal history book.

* * *

Ornate bronze doors, with the word "Pull" cast deeply into the burnished metal, gleamed in the morning sun. Preston was amused to discover that they only opened when pushed, a contradiction aggravating to people in a hurry. He knew that the management of the modernized General Motors would have done something about that if they were still here, intent as they were on impressing the public with the giant corporation's newly found efficiency.

Now that the building was owned and run by the State of Michigan, quite a few changes in the building's operation were in evidence, most noticeably heightened security.

Uniformed guards were everywhere in the huge first-floor lobby, where the car company had once displayed its latest models, and you couldn't get to the elevators without first registering at one of the several attended checkpoints.

Upon reaching the eighth floor, where the Judicial Tenure Commission's offices were located, Preston encountered restrictions upon entry that seemed to him to border on the paranoid.

A red stop sign, clearly meant to emulate those at highway intersections, though not quite as large, was attached to the wall next to the Judicial Tenure Commission's door, along with printed directions that forbid going further until ringing a bell to alert those inside to a visitor's presence.

As Preston was looking about unsuccessfully for a button to push to activate the bell, an unseen woman who must have already been made aware of his presence by a surveillance camera, asked, without expression, "May I help you?" her mechanical-sounding voice coming from a nearby speaker.

"Preston Foster," he said, announcing himself, "I have a nine thirty appointment."

There was a buzzing sound as the lock on the door was released, and Preston entered an unusually small, empty waiting room. Through a reception window made of three-quarter-inch-thick bulletproof glass, with a narrow opening at the bottom to pass items through, he was able to look into another room but still saw no one.

By a door to the left of the glass, another red stop sign had more extensive directions on the wall beside it, "No service, contract, security, or building personnel permitted beyond this point. Return to front door and ring bell."

A chair and one *National Geographic* on a lamp table were the only amenities provided to those awaiting admittance. It occurred to Preston that it was fortunate that he was looking forward to his time inside, because there wasn't even pacing room for those not so lucky as he, who might have a bad experience waiting in store for them.

Both the *Detroit News* and the *Detroit Free Press* every so often carried stories about judges from Michigan's various courts who had been accused by their own Barbara Hemions of acting wrongfully or becoming incompetent, including a recent spate of articles about a Municipal Judge who claimed a mental disability.

Many of them were required to appear before the Commission to explain themselves, risking official censure, suspension with or without salary, or even removal from office. Preston thought about all the others before him that had sat waiting for who knows what in this tiny, almost claustrophobic room, unable to see another living soul to exchange tidbits of small talk with.

Reminding himself that he wasn't the accused in this case, the Commission's jurisdiction was limited to sitting judges, Preston thought about what he could say to help Woody. There just was no way such a dedicated jurist could be faulted for his handling of "the Justice Foster matter" as the request for investigation had described Preston's leave of absence. Woody had consulted with the other Justices before granting the leave, which he didn't have to do, considering that such leaves were at the sole discretion of the Chief Justice.

Preston struggled to remember the details of what had happened back then, but his memory was blurred by the tremendous stress he was under at the time. Was there something important he had forgotten, or, perhaps, never knew?

"You can come into our conference room now, Judge Foster," the receptionist, a black, heavyset woman said, interrupting his thinking with a start. He looked up to see her leaning against the heavy door to keep it open as she waited for him.

"Another beautiful summer day for us," Preston said with a smile as he followed her inside. Her lack of a reply made him wonder if she mistakenly thought he was merely attempting to ingratiate himself with her by speaking. He supposed that plenty of others waiting to be called into the inner sanctum, people who really had something to be nervous about, had made nice with her in an attempt to gain an ally.

* * *

"I guess you could say I took the bull by the horns and choked it to death," Preston said, concluding his almost exuberant presentation that had centered upon his triumph over OCD. Only one of the Judicial Tenure Commission members seated before him around the table smiled, a dark-haired person who appeared barely old enough to be out of law school.

That young man, a female Probate Judge, and Barbara Hemion were elected to the Commission by the State Bar of Michigan, a professional organization all three belonged to as a condition of being allowed to practice law in the state. Two non-lawyers, an insurance executive and a car dealer, had been appointed to the Commission by the former Governor, John Engler. The other four members at the table were judges from various state courts who had been elected by the judiciary.

Barbara Hemion's appearance was a surprise to Preston. Expecting a command profile, he saw instead what some not as kind as he might describe as a library mouse.

He couldn't know that her short, unflattering haircut camouflaged blond, natural curls. Or that her loose, Mother Hubbard-style work outfit covered a slim, five-foot-six-inch-tall 10+ figure.

At 38, her position as Assistant Attorney General was, to her, a stepping stone to greater things. Her heroes were the women on the United States Supreme Court, and her dream was to get there some day.

Pleased with himself for keeping to about ten minutes what he could have talked excitedly about for an hour, Preston asked if there were questions from the Commission, continuing to stand by his place at the plain Formica-inlaid, wooden table.

In the long silence following his invitation, Preston was surprised to hear a clap of thunder through the windowless walls. More than a few of the Commission members glanced toward Hemion as if waiting for some sort of signal from her as to how to proceed.

She finally finished writing on a yellow legal pad and looked up to gaze directly at Preston, her emerald-green eyes hidden behind reading glasses with thick brown plastic frames.

She nodded at him pleasantly, her face completely non-committal, and said, "Yes, I have a question for you, Mr. Foster." He noticed she hadn't extended him any courtesies regarding the title of "judge."

Preston noticed a firmness in her tone that hadn't been there during the customary small talk that precedes most business meetings, when she had chatted with the others around the table about her plans for a canoe trip down the Flint River the following week, a yearly thing she said she did as a sort of reunion with a few high school chums.

Now she spoke more slowly as well, giving him the impression that she was thinking about each word before she spoke it. "But first, Mr. Foster, I want to point out to you that the Commission was created by constitutional amendment in 1968 to review alleged judicial misconduct or disability.

"After our informal investigation of the claim against Chief Justice Woodward is concluded by our meeting here today, we will vote on filing a formal complaint against him, which might require further testimony from you.

"Now, this DCO, or whatever it is, Mr. Preston ... was the Chief Justice informed of a diagnosis and prognosis by a properly licensed psychiatrist before he began his alleged cover-up of your lack of mental competence?"

"How dare you suggest such a thing, Ms. Hemion. Woody, I mean Chief Justice Woodward, is the most honest person I have ever known," Preston said quietly, feeling anger well up in him, making his face flush.

"Was he privy to a legitimate diagnosis? Just answer my question, Mr. Preston."

"Not until you retract the suggestion of subterfuge, Ms. Hemion."

"The complainant made that allegation to us," Barbara Hemion replied.

"Don't waste your cloak and dagger act on me, Ms. Hemion, I happen to know that you are the complainant."

"All of that honesty apparently didn't get in the way of Chief Justice Woodward giving you that piece of confidential information, Mr. Preston."

After a pause, while he struggled to get his growing rage under control, Preston said evenly, "The Judicial Tenure Commission has the obligation to maintain confidentiality prior to a public hearing, whereas the parties to a complaint before it can discuss the matter with anybody they want to at any time."

"Another witness," Barbara Hemion pressed on, undeterred, "has told us that upon being appointed as your replacement on the Supreme Court Bench, he quickly became bored with how little you had to do, tasks that were so overwhelming to you that you consistently missed deadlines for filing written hearing decisions.

"And isn't it true, Mr. Preston, that Chief Justice Woodward farmed out your cases to the other Justices to write opinions for you, and even penned some of your decisions himself, to prevent the Court as a whole from looking bad because of your mental disability?"

Feeling an adrenalin rush, Preston gripped his hands together until they hurt, out of sight under the conference table. He could have choked her skinny little neck, as she had grown more belligerent with each of her questions.

Glancing around the table, he saw the facial expressions of the other members of the Commission becoming more firm as they caught a first scent of blood. "I want an adjournment to get an attorney," he managed to stammer, straining to keep the anger from his voice.

"Does that mean you will not respond to our further questions?" Barbara Hemion asked, unable to completely suppress a little smile that played at the corners of her full lips.

"Not without the advice of counsel."

"In that case, you are excused to return to the reception area, Mr. Preston, while the Commission discusses this matter in private."

* * *

Unable to tolerate the confines of the tiny waiting room a second time in his highly agitated state, Preston had told the receptionist that he would await the Commission's decision in the outside hallway.

It was far more spacious than necessary, and Preston doubted that even "Generous Motors," as some of its white-collar workers called their company, would have designed it so, had the building been constructed in the current, more cost-conscious era of American big business.

Totally void of people at the moment, even though at least a dozen office suites appeared to have access to it, judging by the number of doors Preston could see, it gave him plenty of room to walk about as thoughts raced through his mind.

The place looked as dead as his career seemed to be, he thought, wryly. To distract himself, he tried to imagine what this eighth-floor corridor would have been like when General Motors occupied the building.

He envisioned secretaries scurrying across the wide, open space, on their way from one office to another, papers in their hands, while men in conservative suits with striped ties and blow-dried hair talked car business as they waited for an elevator.

But the image that had besieged him in the conference room kept returning to mind uninvited. He could visualize the demise of Ms. Hemion with amazing clarity. It was as if he had turned into a mob hit man, intent on whacking the woman who threatened both himself and his best friend, Woody. With a rush of satisfaction, he allowed himself to imagine grasping her neck with both hands, like the handle of a baseball bat, and slowly squeezing life out of her.

Hearing a door open behind him, he turned quickly around to see Barbara Hemion walking briskly toward him. Taking a few steps in her direction, he met up with her 20 feet or so from the door to the Commission's suite of offices.

It occurred to him that she had hurried to meet him more than halfway not for his convenience, but rather to make sure that their images and words would be out of range of the security devices that had previously signaled his arrival to the receptionist.

105

Without hesitation, she began, "The Commission has decided by a vote of eight to one that a formal complaint of misconduct will be filed against Chief Justice Woodward. Notice of the public hearing on the matter, including time and place, will be published in the newspapers when we secure a hearing room. "We are not going to let taxpayers unknowingly foot the bill for his betrayal of public trust in keeping you on far too long as a charity case two years ago."

* * *

"Mr. Foster, wait just a minute."

Preston was in the process of attempting to read the sign-out instructions at the top of the signature sheet before him, a task made next to impossible by the fit of rage that consumed him.

He had been halted at a security check point on the first floor, having walked away from Barbara Hemion without a word and taken the elevator down, afraid to speak to her for fear of saying things he might regret later.

Turning around at the sound of his name being called, which came from the direction of the bank of elevators he had just left, he saw that the young lawyer who had been the only halfway-friendly face at the Judicial Tenure Commission meeting was running after him.

"Our seven-year-old daughter was diagnosed with OCD only last week," the man said upon catching up to Preston. "Can you help us?"

The buxom security guard, in a blue uniform with a billy club and pistol on her belt, was annoyed with Preston's slowness, and seeing him glancing about for a clock, reached impatiently over his arm and scribbled the exit time in the appropriate blank.

Surprised to learn that it was already eleven o'clock, Preston hurriedly signed his name to the visitors' log and reached into the back pocket of his suit pants for his billfold. Taking out Rachael Child's business card, he handed it quickly to the young man who was waiting for a reply, then hurried away toward the door leading to the street, not yet trusting himself to speak.

* * *

Thunder rumbled through mountains of steel-gray clouds filling the sky to the northeast, where the fast-moving summer storm continued, having been pushed out of the New Center Area only minutes earlier by Michigan's prevailing southwesterly winds.

Dazed by what had happened, Preston was barely aware of leaving the

106

building, even though it took him two frustrating attempts to get the door open, having made the mistake once again of following the decades-old operating instructions.

Although the cloudburst was over, his shoes became soaked through by puddles of rainwater he didn't try to avoid, as he walked ever more slowly along the sidewalk to his parking spot.

His terrible rage had ebbed away and been replaced by disbelief. "How could they do this, so quickly return me to hopelessness, after all those months of hard work with Rachael?" he asked himself. He felt totally drained of all emotion.

Through sudden, unexpected tears, he saw a parking ticket drooped over the Jeep's windshield wiper, soddened by the recent downpour.

Chapter Sixteen
Turning Point

Dr. Rachael Childs had a most interesting background that significantly contributed to her successful psychiatric medical practice.

The retirement of Rabbi Sherwin Wine on June 26, 2003, was a milestone for her. It helped make up her mind to finally end the extensive volunteer work she had been doing for his non-profit, religious organization.

He was the reason she had chosen the University of Michigan Medical Center in Ann Arbor for her psychiatric residency over three other teaching hospital positions offered to her.

The Humanistic Judaism movement Wine founded in Detroit in 1963 was as radical in the field of religion as her own behavioral treatment of OCD was in the practice of medicine. He inspired her to move forward with her own original thinking.

Wine's willingness to move out of the confines of the Torah in his spiritual quest mirrored her own determination to shake free of the restraints of the Freudian psychoanalytic treatment for OCD that was so widely accepted in psychiatry.

While Sigmund Freud was certain OCD could be cured by psychoanalysis, and even though two of the famous case studies about the illness were written up by him in his wonderfully articulate way, "Rat Man" and "Wolf Man," Rachael still did not totally share his beliefs.

Her mother was murdered at the Mauthausen Concentration Camp established in Austria in 1938. Though more than 150,000 people were killed at the camp before the U.S. 11th Armored Division liberated its captives in 1945, most of them Jews, her father survived it.

Rachael first became interested in OCD as a specialty after listening to her father's accounts of inmates with the illness who had managed to stop their repetition and other strange rituals in order to save themselves from torture or death at the hands of the SS guards. Not surprisingly, the mysterious OCD behaviors returned full force after the prisoners had been set free by the Americans.

She began to record the oral histories of her father and other, more distant relatives who had spent time in the Holocaust's concentration camps during World War II. The old stories corroborated the phenomenon of suppression of OCD for survival and relapse upon release. Over a period of time, she came to believe that the collection of stories held the secret of the disorder's cure.

But Wine's new theology appealed to Rachael beyond its renegade quality. The fact that it was based upon human achievement rather than the Old Testament miracles augmented Rachael's pride in the history of the Jewish people, and it soothed the uneasiness she felt at her inability to accept the existence of a supernatural higher power.

The problem was that she was giving so much of her limited time and energy to the survival and growth of Humanistic Judaism that her medical career had suffered, especially the publish-a-book-or-perish part, delaying the achievement of her goal of economic self-sufficiency.

Now that Wine and his considerable charisma were out of the picture, her interest in continuing to contribute hundreds of pro bono hours to the cause had evaporated.

Instead, she would redirect all her time outside the confines of her psychiatric practice to the completion of her second book, with which there was a reasonable expectation of earning significant money since Harper & Collins had already expressed considerable interest in its publication.

Early in her medical career, she had begun her intense examination of the relationship between OCD and religion.

Her first book on the close tie between the two had been well received, a study of the Catholic icon Saint Theresa, entitled *Little Flower's Illness.*

In it, Rachael had first presented her now-widely-known hypothesis that the creatively gifted youngster had suffered from OCD, known for centuries in the Catholic Church as "Scrupulosity," growing out of damage to her brain caused by a bout with strep throat in pre-puberty.

Rachael suggested in her book that Theresa, as a determined teenager, fought a losing battle against repetition and other common manifestations of OCD while struggling to write her delightful little plays. She finally gave up hope and came to choose her famous "little way." Those were the words the sweet girl, who died in her early twenties, chose to describe her decision to turn the whole seemingly hopeless war with her self-defeating rituals over to God.

Rachael in her book had used word for word the saint's expression of immense relief at her profound self-delivery from personal responsibility: "From now on I'm going to say and do all the stupid things I want to and not worry about it."

Rachael had found the quote in the ancient archives of the European nunnery where the saint lived out her brief life, but the words were so fresh they could have just as well have been said by Rachael's teenage niece.

Both religious and medical scholars had lauded Rachael's exhaustive research. Fortuitously for book sales, Rachael's treatise was published the same summer that the National Institute of Health confirmed that overzealous antibodies manufactured by the body to fight the streptococcus bacteria did brain damage, causing OCD.

The Institute confirmed to the media that they were in fact "straining out" the antibodies from the blood of their teenage patients from around the country and sending them home OCD-free as a result of the relatively simple procedure.

Rachael's second book was an as-yet-untitled study of OCD sufferers persecuted by the Catholic Church during the Spanish Inquisition. Instituted in 1480 at the request of the rulers of Spain and not finally abolished until 1834, it was a court set up by the Catholic Church to seek out and punish heresy.

The Inquisitor held power direct from the Pope to take testimony, question witnesses and those others accused of heresy, and decide their guilt or innocence. The accused had none of the rights expected in a democratic system of law and sometimes were questioned under torture and forced to confess heretic beliefs when the same was not true.

Punishments for the guilty ranged from penances and fines to banishment, imprisonment, and death by fire. Kings and nobles supported what amounted to organized persecution of Jews, Protestants, and others considered enemies of church and state, including those charged with witchcraft.

The repetition and other strange behaviors engaged in by OCD sufferers to quiet the anxiety aroused by their often sacrilegious, sexual and violent obsessions were deemed by the Catholic Church to be conclusive evidence that the sufferer was possessed by the devil or was a witch.

To Rachael's astonishment, her research trail led to the University of Michigan Library in Ann Arbor, which owned one of the few remaining copies in existence of the dreadful, bloodstained Mada, the checklist circulated by the Catholic Church setting out the signs to look for when searching for those who should be brought before the Inquisitor. Prominent on the list was the repetition of behaviors, a hallmark of clinical OCD.

Rachael was thinking about all these things as she waited in her office for the arrival of Preston. He had called earlier in the day and asked for an emergency appointment due to a crisis resulting from some sort of meeting he had attended that morning. The regular business hours of the Anxiety Disorders Clinic were over, and its suite of offices surrounding hers were empty and eerily silent.

His brand of OCD was not unique or even unusually severe. Many of her clients' obsessions involved unwanted sounds and images that they tried to drive away with rituals that were both compulsive and self-defeating.

"Yes," she admitted to herself half aloud, "the trip to New York just about did in our professional relationship." Her infatuation with him had clouded her judgment just long enough to invite herself along.

Once she had made that fatally unprofessional suggestion to him, she had instantly regretted it, but her lust drove her on. She had never had such a magnificent man as a lover, and the thought of him made her weak.

The man sitting before her that day of her "big slip," as she now called her broad hint that he take her with him, looked like a movie star. For one thing, there was none of that bald business that begins with a receding hairline when some men turn forty as he had. Preston had a full head of blond hair with a little gray mixed in at the temples that made him look only more distinguished.

Rachael felt her breathing quicken as she relived the trip in her mind. She remembered him holding his perfectly maintained 6'2" muscled physique over her in the Plaza Hotel bed on his outstretched arms, as he let himself finally come, content that her multiple orgasms had run their course.

His Hollywood-good-looks, including a slightly aquiline nose and straight-line mouth with full lips, so close above her face during the pleasure-seizure they shared, was frosting on the cake. The pupils of his widely spaced blue eyes dilated in ecstasy during the near loss of consciousness that men experience at the instant of release.

She had considered graciously declining sex for the rest of the weekend after that first intimacy that occurred immediately upon their Friday late-afternoon arrival in Manhattan. She was fearful that in a moment of physical passion she would confess her love for him, and she was determined to wait to tell him about that until she had accomplished his cure with cognitive behavior therapy.

She was convinced that her professional effectiveness would be compromised by revealing her love for him. Ordinarily, she could withdraw and refer him to a colleague, but CBT was so groundbreaking in its concept that there were no other therapists in the Midwest that she would trust with his care.

And face it, she told herself, it wasn't entirely altruistic on her part, he was a big fish. Her unqualified success with the CBT treatment of someone as well known as he would enforce her reputation as a world-class behaviorist.

All those things made perfect sense until her desire welled up again that evening when he slowly moved his hand over hers as they watched a Broadway musical, *Rent*, at the Nederlander Theater. Suddenly, all that mattered was returning to the privacy of their room, and she could barely wait for the final curtain, and the bows of the youthful cast to be over.

She did manage to find the strength to resist crossing the line she had drawn for herself, by thinking of Preston at times as a sex robot she had rented, and at others a beach boy like all the others she had used for sexual relief, just smarter and more sophisticated.

The sex was great, and she restrained herself from expressing her true feelings. She did things with Preston she had never done to any man before. On Sunday afternoon, which they spent in bed, she had dared to let herself be transported by lust into a new realm of physical abandon, cupping his balls with her left hand while she used her right to grip a buttock and draw his hard, thick penis deep into her mouth.

* * *

Preston had apologized for the short notice for the appointment, but she had told him not to worry, that she had intended to spend the evening at her office anyway, working on a grant proposal after getting some dinner at the hospital cafeteria.

"Don't kid me, you were watching the boob tube, not sweating over a grant proposal," Preston teased as he opened their session with small talk in spite of being visibly upset, continuing with, "I recognize this week's *Detroit Free Press TV Book*."

Rachael explained, "Actually, I'm using it for an exhibit to be attached to my proposal. Monk's on the cover, the obsessive-compulsive detective played by Tony Shalhoub. A hit show like his on the USA Network does wonders in getting grant money.

"So does something like this," Rachael added, holding up a picture of Jack Nicholson holding the Oscar he won for his portrayal of a novelist with OCD in the movie *As Good as It Gets*.

"I don't see the connection," Preston admitted, rather abruptly, growing impatient with the subject matter of their conversation.

"Nervous grantors are reassured when they learn of the commercial success of OCD-themed entertainment because it proves that not only is OCD real, but that huge numbers of people find it interesting. Just telling them that five million people in the United States alone suffer from the strange illness, and that a like number of the victims' significant others are impacted by it, isn't quite enough."

"But it's very private, it doesn't affect those around me all that much."

"Dream on," Rachael laughed. "I tell my OCD patients to see how long their happy home stays that way when they continue to take two-hour showers and the other people in the house getting ready for work don't have any hot water."

"Those must be OCD people with the fear of contamination," Preston noted, "lucky for me I don't have to deal with that too."

"I'm glad to hear you acknowledge that you could be worse off," Rachael said with a smile, "but don't forget how angry the other Justices got at you when OCD prevented you from meeting case opinion deadlines. None of us live in a vacuum."

"What are you requesting funds for?" Preston asked politely.

"Special Education advocacy, for students whose OCD repetition rituals are viewed as punishable rebellion against authority by ignorant teachers and school administrators. They're no better than the German guards who did the same thing to concentration camp prisoners with OCD."

"Whoa ... I must of pulled your chain on that one ... obviously a worthy cause that is important to you ... but I'm just too distracted to give it the attention it deserves."

* * *

Rachael sat silently through Preston's detailed account of his appearance before the Judicial Tenure Commission that morning.

She had learned that clients felt an obligation to fill up silences between them and herself, maybe because of the money they were spending to see her. Whatever the reason, she knew if she could remain silent long enough, clients would usually blurt something out to break the tension of the quietness, and sometimes it was the truth.

But when Preston reached the part about his plan to intercept Barbara Hemion at Oxbow Landing, a canoe camp next to rapids on the Flint River, in order to talk to her alone, she decided it was time for her to initiate some rather strong dialogue to dissuade him from it.

"Sitting on stumps and asking her, 'Why do you hate me?' is quaint, but why don't you just pick up the phone and call her?" Rachael asked.

"She doesn't return my calls, and the two friends that I told you about who are trying to help me, Woody Woodward and Laura Hopkins, can't get her to talk to them either."

"But what I'm hearing is wishful thinking," Rachael persisted, "something you and millions of other people are very good at. This whole river thing sounds like Little Red Riding Hood conveniently coming into the forest to visit the Big Bad Wolf.

"After all, Preston, she just mentioned her canoe trip with high school chums in passing before the meeting started. She was only making small talk to relax the people around the conference table, basic Dale Carnegie, for heaven's sake. She may never take that trip."

"But she said they were putting in at Millville Landing just upstream from the Lapeer State Game Area. If she was just making small talk, the plans wouldn't be so specific. It's a go, I just know it."

"Does she know that you grew up hunting and fishing that section of the river and could probably navigate it in your sleep?"

"You've just made my point," Preston said with a smile of satisfaction.

"I hate lawyers," Rachael said loudly to exaggerate her feigned disgust. "Just kidding, of course. Ha, ha. What do you mean, I've just made your point?"

"She would never share those specifics if she had any inkling that was my territory, her knowing what she planned to do to me in the next half hour at the meeting. She's not stupid."

"Your violent obsessions that were playing in your head during that meeting may be causing you to make false assumptions about her behavior," Rachael said in a more serious tone of voice.

"I don't understand," Preston said.

"You must keep constantly in mind when you are interacting with others," Rachael continued patiently, "that they can't read your mind. Barbara Hemion knows nothing about OCD and the violent, intrusive images that are a common occurrence to those who suffer from it. She had no way of knowing at the meeting that you were chopping her up into little pieces mentally.

"She wouldn't in her wildest dreams see Preston Foster as a potential source of personal harm to her," Rachael continued earnestly. "She would expect a former Supreme Court Justice to be furious at what she was about to do but wouldn't expect you to go berserk and start stalking her in revenge."

"But the mental images are so clear … are so bloody that I'm embarrassed to tell even you, though you certainly have shown yourself to be non-judgmental. I wouldn't want anybody to know what they are."

"You realize by now that they signify nothing, that they are meaningless tricks of the mind, the OCD knocking on your door, wanting you to let it back in," Rachael said gently.

"I have given you the tools to deal with threatened relapses, use them," she continued in a firmer voice. "You must steel yourself and use all your strength to resist opening that door again. Starve the beast to death with total non-response to the anxiety that the images cause in you, tolerating it until it decays on its own because it can't survive without your help."

"So you don't think I'm going to kill her on the river, even though my brain has been bombarded with a dozen different ways to do it?"

For a long moment Rachael stared at him in silence, surprised again at the very real fear of themselves that almost all of her OCD patients exhibited in stressful situations, regardless of their cultural background or education. She then told Foster what she had always explained to all her OCD patients.

"You stand on the shoulders of giants and are the culmination of centuries of civilization, you're not going to hurt her. We have hundreds of OCD patients besieged by violent obsessions that we treat each year here at the University of Michigan Anxiety Disorders Clinic, and not one of them has ever hurt anybody."

* * *

Rachael waited a few moments until after Preston left at a brisk walk, heading in the direction of the elevators, before she stepped back inside her office and slid the noisy deadbolt into place. She didn't want him to hear her do so and think she was locking him out. He had had enough rejection.

Pressing her back against the door, she slipped one hand down inside her skirt under her panties to the warm, moist folds of her vulva, while she moved the other under her blouse, her first two fingers firm against the sides of her large nipple coming to a full erection between them.

He had asked her about the mysterious flower. "No, I don't know the name of it yet," she had replied, complaining about the hindrance of his crude sketch not being in color, done at the Lumberman's Spring on bark with charcoal.

"You're absolutely sure it had cream-colored petals and no leaves?" she had teased him, reminding him that OCD was called the "doubting disease" in France and questioning the reliability of an OCD patient as a witness. "But yes, she would continue her search for its name," she had assured him, smiling at his boyish enthusiasm over something many men wouldn't give a thought to.

She wondered if he had any idea of how attractive to women he really was. Someday she would, indeed, confess her love for him. Until then, except for the occasional weekend getaway, she would use her hands and pretend they were his.

* * *

"Coming here today was a godsend," Preston said aloud in the empty elevator as it lowered him rapidly from the ninth floor to the first, where he would walk to the parking structure.

Although he wasn't as confident as she seemed to be about restraining himself from acting on his violent obsessions toward Barbara Hemion, Rachael always seemed to come up with something to say that gave him strength.

He remembered some other good stuff she had said during one of their first appointments when he had half-seriously mentioned suicide, almost as if a dark part of him was testing her. Rachael's reply had moved him deeply.

"First floor," the talking-elevator announced, distracting him.

After stepping out, he changed his mind about heading for his Jeep and walked instead to one of the nearby twenty-foot-tall windows with its view of the hospital's tree-filled atrium, with pleasant walkways and benches surrounded with flowerbeds alive with summer colors.

Staring out at the lovely sight, he thought once again about what it was she had said that time, those many months ago, that had eased his almost-suicidal despair.

"You weren't born to die, you were born to live and then die," she had announced matter-of-factly, as if it was something she had just read in the day's newspaper and wanted him know. Then, taking his hand and giving it a quick squeeze, she had smiled broadly and added, "And this is still your living time."

He stared out at the trees that strained upward to catch a little of the sun's energy before the ball of fire crossed the square of sky framed by the surrounding hospital towers. They were certainly doing their living.

As he watched, a Medivac helicopter settled down onto the roof of the east tower as if its arrival had been cued by an unseen director to fit precisely the progress of Preston's thinking. The pilots, and nurses, even the unknown patient on board, were all busy doing their living too.

What right did he, Preston Foster, have to even consider dropping out of life's ball game?

117

Chapter Seventeen
River of Herons

Locals call them "the high banks" and don't offer strangers any further explanation, as if the name should be warning enough.

They are the steep sides of canyons, really, cut by the Flint River through massive gravel deposits, some rising nearly vertically 100 feet or more above the swiftly moving water.

Rushing torrents from melting ice carried the gravel, known as "glacial outwash" in geology jargon, out of the receding Port Huron Glacier 10,000 years before, dropping it where the currents ebbed, a valuable gift to man from the departing mile-high giant.

Preston was looking for the perfect campsite for his purposes, skillfully threading his small fiberglass canoe between glacial boulders scattered haphazardly in the river at the foot of one of the cliffs. A lifetime student of this section of the high banks, only a mile from Red Moon, he knew that the course the river presently chose in 2003 was not ordinary.

He had seen the satellite photos taken from the joint Russian and American space station Mir, part of a mapping project done of the entire United States from one hundred miles above the Earth. The computerized camera aboard the orbiting, manned spacecraft confirmed what the well-drillers of Lapeer County could have told Uncle Sam for a lot less money, that an unusual dome formation of Pleistocene Era rock rose to within 140 feet of the surface of the rolling countryside.

It caused the unique, circular meanders in the river that turned the 15-mile drive by car from Lapeer to the city of Flint into a downstream canoe journey of over 80 miles. The stretch of the Flint River that Preston was riding flowed through the Lapeer State Game Area and was the destination of a small number of "weekend floaters" each summer.

That was the term canoe racers used to condescendingly describe those who merely drifted down the river, letting the current do the work, using their paddles almost exclusively as a rudder for steering.

A better word for them would be sightseers, who came not only for the experience of traveling the river through the spectacular scenery provided by the precipitous river banks, but also to encounter its famous great blue herons that had maintained the same treetop colonies for as long as old-timers in the area, who called the birds "shitpokes," could remember.

The name they gave the stately birds, pronounced with a long "i" to make it more family oriented, was never adopted by the somewhat stuffy Audubon Society. But the expression could still be heard at the crossroads stores and small-town bars where country people gathered.

It stuck, probably because of the birds' long, narrow bills and their habit of suddenly arching their long necks to dart their heads down to pick up things from the ground at their feet.

The large bluish gray creatures' hoarse, guttural squawk quickly attracted the attention of approaching canoeists, who almost always went into a freeze mode to see how close the moving water could get them for a photograph of the majestic birds.

The 52-inch-tall bird would remain standing at the water's edge, watching for fish or frogs, which are its principal food, until the intruding craft, with it passengers still as stone statues, was almost upon it, then it would spring into the air.

Needing only a flap or two of wings measuring 70 inches from tip to tip in order to pick up speed, it would glide silently away only a foot or so from the surface of the water, to disappear down the dark tunnel formed by tree branches arched over the river.

* * *

Preston put his tent up on a grassy bank that was near to the water so he could easily see the passing of Hemion's party on their way downstream. He was pretty sure he would hear them go through, day or night, because it was here that an old, now-submerged bridge made of foot-square oak barn beams lay crosswise the channel, just beneath the surface of the noisy rapids it created.

The sunken bridge presented an obstacle that had to be portaged around or dragged across. He figured the women would probably engage in a lot of talking and laughing in the process, before continuing downstream the mile remaining to Oxbow Landing, a canoe camp built and maintained by Lapeer County, with a hand-pumped well and a cement block outhouse.

Preston didn't need any of those frills at his camp, but Oxbow had an important role in his plan. He intended to be there when they arrived, hidden out of sight but close by, where he would step out and quickly identify himself to Hemion and talk to her as soon as she split off from her companions, for any reason.

The riverside tent site at Oxbow was some distance downhill from its well and privy, and screened from them by trees and thick underbrush, so he expected that an opportunity to speak privately with Hemion would soon present itself once she and her friends were settled in.

* * *

Getting to Oxbow first would be easy for Preston thanks to the meander that gave the county's canoe camp its name; it was only a 5-minute walk to the north for him. It would take the women about 20 to reach the same place by canoe.

Oxen used in the area in the 1800s for lumbering were harnessed in twos, with a heavy wooden yoke across both their necks, notched to ride in place just behind the ears. It was held there by bows of wood, one for each animal, attached to the yoke, made from a bent sapling, that looped under their throats.

On the map, the river at this point looked like such a bow, and imagining an ox wearing it, Preston noted that he, figuratively, would be walking the short distance between the animal's ears while they were canoeing the bow around its neck to get from one ear to the other.

* * *

Light from the campfire danced on the nylon walls of the 4-person-size tent. Like a kaleidoscope, it created everchanging patterns of light and shadows around Preston, who lay naked on an air-mattress. He was on his side, an un-needed, rolled-up sleeping bag under one armpit, reading *Social Anticipations*, a book of essays by H.G. Wells.

He had rigged up the light overhead before he turned in for the night. Removing a shoelace from one of his Dockers, he had tied it around a flashlight which now hung from the convenient light-loop sewn into the tent's 7-foot-high ceiling.

Slowly cooling, nighttime air entered through the open door and three large windows, all mercifully screened over to keep out mosquitoes. The gently moving air caressed Preston's skin delightfully, still damp with sweat from the effort of setting up camp in the 90-degree heat.

He smelled the rank summer odor of the water and heard the steady bubbling noise it made as it slid across the half dozen squared logs that lay

121

side by side on the river bottom. He paused in his reading for a moment to savor both the scent and the sound.

Was Rachael Childs, his psychiatrist, right about his being able to think one way and act another when Hemion's group arrived? He certainly hoped so!

Shortly after putting his canoe in the river, he had remotely checked his messages on the answering machine at Red Moon and found he had one from New York. It was Banjo Harris telling him that he had fallen in love with Laura Hopkins, and that together they had received rave reviews for their appearance in the Rainbow Room at the top of Rockefeller Plaza.

Without waiting to think about Banjo's message, which had left him with a rather bittersweet feeling, he went quickly on to make a final call to Hemion's office in Lansing and, as with all his previous attempts to talk with her by phone, got only her voice mail.

This time though, it said she was on vacation until the following Monday, confirming to a large extent what he had heard her say at the meeting of the Judicial Tenure Commission. He had ignored her recorded invitation to leave a message and impulsively threw his cell phone into the deepest part of the channel.

Why had he just done such a wasteful, polluting thing, he asked himself. Was it to ensure his solitude? Or did he do it so the police wouldn't find the device to use for evidence against him later? He wasn't sure he knew the answer to that question.

Preston was certain of one thing, that he had not come here to this beautiful riverside knoll, where he had camped in his youth with his father, merely to wait for the river to deliver Hemion to him for a talk about why she hated him so.

More than that, he hoped that when she finally arrived, he would be able to prove to himself that he could, indeed, find the strength to disregard his violent obsessions about killing her, thoughts that a Supreme Court Justice shouldn't be having.

If he had his way, Barbara Hemion, someone who had a mysterious vendetta against him, would find waiting for her a charming, brilliant, and medically cured Preston Foster.

Chapter Eighteen
Firewater Willie's

It was no coincidence that Barbara Hemion was about to canoe the Flint River through the Lapeer State Game Area as one of the "Scraggs," as her group of five, all life-long friends, called themselves.

It was rather selfish on her part, she admitted to herself, to have insisted that they change rivers and gather here for their annual canoe trip for a long weekend, in order to accommodate her undercover work in the area. She would return the favor in the future.

Her assignment was the investigation of a Citizen's Complaint filed with the Michigan Attorney General concerning a large real estate development eleven miles outside Lapeer, Michigan, the booming former country town that was rapidly morphing into a suburb. And her work on the case had reached a critical phase.

As an Assistant Michigan Attorney General, Hemion was trying to operate quietly in the area since experience had taught her that more doors opened to her when she wasn't being perceived as an out-of-town threat from state government.

She had set up an office of sorts in the Lapeer Best Western Motel. Since the town was the seat of the county's government, it was the location of the land records she had been examining over the last several days in her effort to independently verify what the complaining party, Matthew Pitt, had been asserting.

He farmed 260 acres that adjoined the proposed construction site for the 100-million-dollar complex his Citizen's Complaint was about. He certainly seemed to be an honest person. But you could never be too careful with a complainant, let alone a man you were about to get in bed with, in the figurative sense of course.

Not when the two of you were about to go up against Melvin Peebles, who had the reputation of being the smartest, quickest, and most articulate Township Attorney in the state. Especially since, according to Pitt, Peebles concealed the fact that he had a big piece of the action in the real estate development deal.

Now she was alone at midnight, propped up in the motel bed, her back against two extra pillows. Hemion was alternately thinking about what had transpired at the Deep Creek Township Zoning Board of Appeals meeting that had just ended 2 hours before, and jotting notes into a secretary's notebook with a brightly-flowered cover. She was writing with a flamboyantly oversized white Mont Blanc pen with gold trim, an expensive law school graduation gift from her parents that she ordinarily didn't use for fear she would lose it or someone with "light fingers" would pocket it.

The choice of note-taking paraphernalia had been part of her disguise at the meeting. She had augmented her suburban-lady-learning-about-local-government look with a flowered sundress and white-dyed straw hat. She had considered sunshine-yellow gardening gloves but decided that was going a little overboard.

Pausing upon a sudden impulse to check her phone calls, she carefully laid her notebook down on the pale green top sheet, which she had folded neatly back over the rust-colored bedspread to protect herself from previous occupants' bodily fluids. She knew motels washed their spreads infrequently, like once a month if you're lucky, but under law must change their linen daily.

Reaching with her right hand across in front of her ample bosom to the bedside table at her left, she picked up the beige motel phone and placed it beside the notebook on her lap. Using a prepaid phone card provided by her boss to save money, she speed-dialed her office voice mail in Lansing, the state capital, and forced a wry smile as she listened to her prerecorded message, telling her that she was on vacation.

Touch-toning in first a "6" and then a "7," her remote message code, she heard a mechanical-sounding woman's voice which came on after a long pause, "You have a collect call from an inmate at Jackson State Prison whose first name is...." followed by the word "Danny" said in the voice of a young-sounding male.

The computer-generated operator then instructed, "Press '2' if you will accept the charges." An even longer silence followed, until finally Hemion heard the click of the phone company's automated disconnect because there was the lack of an acceptance of the collect call.

Hemion felt her heart sink a little. She would have eagerly agreed to pay for the call had she been there to pick up the phone in person. She was disappointed, because she really wanted to talk with her brother.

Then she heard a connection completed, but no message was left, and she made a mental note to check the caller ID record when she got back to her office. She hated it when people did that, at least she hadn't heard heavy breathing on the line like she sometimes did.

"Francine here," a Scragg's voice chirped next, "you owe me one, sweetie, I had my heart set on Michigan's beautiful Au Sable, and last-minute changes in plans do cause travel problems for us anal retentive types." Three beeps indicated that all the messages had been played, so Hemion hung up.

It was so typical of free-spirited Francine, Hemion observed, not to leave a number where she could be reached. Too confining, Hemion supposed. It didn't matter anyway, because her friend had left a more recent message for Hemion with the Best Western bartender. The desk, of course, would have been far too conventional for Francine.

Fortunately, the hunky guy, sensing possibilities, Hemion guessed, jotted down the information on a drink napkin and slipped it forcefully under Hemion's room door. She figured he probably was hoping to be asked inside to be given a tip, or more.

She had peered out at him through the safety-peek-hole and then continued to stand silently behind her door until his aggressive knocking ceased and a neat, orange-colored paper skidded to a stop at her feet. It suggested that she should meet Francine in the motel bar for last call.

Nothing from former Justice Robert Preston Foster on her voice mail this time, Hemion noted to herself with some delighted surprise. Nor was there anything from the dreadfully persistent twosome trying to talk to her on Foster's behalf, that Laura Hopkins person, who kept calling from New York, and Chief Justice Woodward. It would be good politics to return a non-committal call to Woodward in a week or so. Hemion figured his sidekick, Hopkins, was safe to ignore indefinitely.

Yes, she would go downstairs to meet Francine for a drink, but not until a few minutes before the 2:00 a.m. cutoff. There was a lot of preparing left for her to do tonight for her surprise call on Pitt at his farmhouse tomorrow, after which the Scraggs would put in their canoes at Millville Landing.

Perhaps the single most important thing she had to do now was make up her own mind about what had really happened at the Appeal Board meeting. The Board had granted the Guililand Group's requested variance, but there was something that instinctively bothered her about Peebles' advice to the Board as they considered the Guililand petition.

Hemion thought about the recent meeting at the Deep Creek Township Hall.

* * *

She had parked her rented Geo Metro in the Township's lot and hurriedly distanced herself from the inexpensive vehicle, one that probably would not be the choice of the upper-middle-class suburbanite she was portraying. Then she paused to consider the view.

Set atop one of the highest hills in the vicinity, the meeting hall overlooked a rolling countryside covered with a patchwork quilt of farm fields and an occasional clump of woods. Well below her and to the south, a cornflower-blue lake was nestled in a valley. She wondered if the people of the area truly appreciated the great natural beauty that surrounded them.

Hemion then checked her typographical map that she had borrowed from the local Department of Natural Resources' officer and realized that the picturesque body of water was not what it appeared to be.

Rather than a natural, self-enclosed inland lake, it was merely a tiny arm of the sprawling Holloway Reservoir, the water source created by damming the Flint River to serve the burgeoning population in the region.

In fact, when examined more closely, this wasn't really country out here anymore, she concluded to herself. Where the farmers' fields ended at the roadsides, the frontage had been parceled off and now formed the lawns of very large single-family homes, many with swimming pools. They lined the once-gravel roads that appeared to have been blacktopped in the near past to accommodate a substantial growth in the car-count.

A castle for two, Hemion observed to herself, with both husband and wife working their butts off to meet the mortgage payments. These were big-foot homes on the march with little visible governmental restraint, forever compromising the stunning rural vistas that once swept away unbroken to the horizon.

She knew it was the same story all over America, and it made her momentarily sad. Perhaps the worst part was that grand as the past might have been, and how glowing the future, you were forced to choose between them, because if you tried to hang on to both you would be torn apart.

Then she cheered herself up by imagining the little families that would spring into existence here when the wives were able to quit working long enough to have their babies. She pictured what this place would look like in 10 years, with dads in the backyard barbecuing while moms worked in their flowerbeds and kids played on elaborate swing sets and frolicked in swimming pools.

Would she ever have a rose garden? No way, her career was more than enough for her. She was exhilarated by her case load, not dragged down by it. Especially, the perplexing ones like Pitt's.

She remembered that when his complaint was first assigned to her, she had thought he was another crackpot, especially when he suggested collusion and payoffs. She went ahead, though, and took her customary first steps in investigating his story and, in fact, found nothing to substantiate any of the allegations … at first.

The Guililand Group had failed to register with Michigan's Better Business Bureau, a consumer protection organization. But that was not uncommon, since there was no statutory obligation to do so; and, in response to her inquiry, the BBB reported that they had received no complaints about the real estate development partnership.

It had properly filed its Assumed Name Certificate with the Lapeer County Clerk. In reviewing that document on her first trip to Lapeer, Hemion learned that the partnership's office was located in Southfield, Michigan, headquarters for many such real estate investment groups. The individual partners' home addresses were shown on the certificate as being in West Bloomfield, an affluent Detroit suburb not far from that office.

It was Deep Creek Township's representation by Melvin Peebles that brought her back to Lapeer a second time for the hearing on the variance request. She wanted to see him in action, but without disclosing her presence to him or to Matthew Pitt.

Peebles' name had come to her attention in connection with his representation of another township near Deep Creek several years before, and through discrete inquiries while at the Lapeer County Clerk's office, she was surprised to find that he represented eight different townships in Lapeer County at the same time.

Since townships frequently took legal positions that were adverse to each other, she wondered how he could not find himself in conflict-of-interest situations fairly often. Or, if not an actual conflict of interests, certainly a perception of one.

But she was determined to keep an open mind about Peebles, and to simply gather as many facts as possible about the Guililand Group's operation in Deep Creek Township, not unlike an investigative reporter does when first on the scent of an exposé to be written up for a newspaper piece.

Reminding herself that she had come to the Deep Creek Township's hall to do just that, she left the parking lot and went inside the small building.

It certainly looked to her like an average township Thursday night meeting about to begin. The members of the Board of Zoning Appeals were arrayed across the front of the room, seated on metal folding chairs behind four bridge tables set side by side.

Those were probably used sometimes to eat upon at township or social functions, Hemion supposed. She had noticed a sign on the door on her way in stating that the hall could be rented by township residents for wedding receptions, family reunions, and other such events.

A neatly dressed middle-aged woman, who identified herself as being the vice-chairperson, called the meeting to order. Motioning to a single empty chair at the center of the row of tables, she announced that the chairperson had another commitment that night, and that she would be the one conducting the hearing on the Guililand Group's request for a variance.

All the while, the same woman was nervously making excuses about her lack of experience, and she finally wound up her little speech with her best, ingratiating smile and a plea of, "So please, bear with me tonight and we'll do the best we can under the circumstances." Everyone silently nodded their assent.

Hemion was surprised by the Board's decision to go forward on such a big-money matter without having its regular chairperson, the well-thought-of Mason Ducker, at its helm. He was a man whose reputation for honesty, fair dealing, and conscientious attitude toward public service had spread all the way to her office at the state capital.

Melvin Peebles was then introduced by the vice-chairperson, and he sauntered confidently from the side of the room, where he had been waiting, and took Ducker's seat.

Hemion studied him intently, admiring his obvious enthusiasm about getting things done. She found herself amused by his couch potato appearance, which didn't fit at all with his energetic demeanor, and she smiled inwardly at the image her creative mind served up of a matzo-ball body with noodles for arms and legs.

The Guililand Group and their attorney, a cluster of men of various ages dressed in dark, expensive-looking suits, began a well-prepared presentation of their condominium proposal, complete with aerial photographs and multicolored charts displayed on aluminum tripods.

Hemion noticed that they had changed the word "Reservoir" to "Lake" on their flip-chart of glossy-paper drawings and site plans, and she figured that was planned to make the condominiums' setting more enticing to prospective buyers. She reminded herself that there was no law against a little prettifying.

A gaggle of onlookers filled about half the 40 or so folding chairs that had been set out in neat, crescent-shaped rows in the center of the room. Hemion, from her seat at one end of the back row, had noticed a number of men in farm clothes in attendance, but she had no idea which one was Matthew Pitt.

Nothing really unexpected occurred until questions from the audience were taken, and then a stocky man, one of those in farmer's attire, stood up and identified himself as Matthew Pitt. He then went into a long-winded

128

history of the purchase of his farm by his father in 1907 after the money for it was accumulated by working in the numerous lumber camps that were located throughout the region in the late 1800s.

The farmer rambled on from his main point to brag about how his dad had resisted going to the local houses of ill repute. In those days they were called "compounds," and many of the lumberjacks spent their entire wages on those establishments' painted ladies and watered-down whiskey.

Pitt, who had thick light brown hair, an erect posture, and vigorous body movements, looked to Hemion to be in his early sixties, but years of the sun's merciless rays had given the skin of his face and neck a deeply creased dark brown leathery look. Except for the color of his hair and his liveliness, she concluded, he could have passed for an elderly Native American Indian.

He went on to explain how his farm lay between the Guililand Group's newly purchased former farm property on the reservoir and the blacktopped county road, and how he had allowed its prior owner ingress and egress across his land, otherwise the other farmer would have been landlocked.

By this time, Peebles had fully assumed the duties of a chairperson without being asked to do so, and it was clear to Hemion that he had focused his full attention on Pitt, with more than a passing interest in what the weathered farmer was talking about.

The vice-chairperson, meanwhile, had meekly fallen silent, apparently content to simply listen and then vote, except for her occasional querulous request to Peebles for a legal opinion to help herself and the rest of the Board make up their minds.

No one on the Board appeared to doubt the validity of Peebles' confidently-delivered pronouncements of law. Hemion was sure that the quick thinking and verbally adept Peebles had picked up something of great significance in Pitt's rambling account of past history.

She listened carefully to the exchanges between the smooth-talking Township Attorney and the determined farmer who was so painfully outgunned in terms of speaking skills. Was Peebles showing favoritism to the Guililand Group, which now had nothing more to say, almost as if they were allowing Peebles to argue their case for them?

Hemion asked herself that hard question, knowing that much was at stake. She would file criminal conflict-of-interest charges against the colorful Township Attorney if she decided he was favoring the condominium developers in his legal advice to the Board for his own personal gain.

Pitt's Citizen's Complaint that brought her to Lapeer had boldly accused Peebles of accepting paybacks from the Guililand Group in exchange for his help in getting preferred treatment from Deep Creek Township. She doubted that Peebles was that dumb, but she suspected he might be a secret partner in the development deal, in which case he should abstain from participating in the hearing. Instead, he was running it.

The variance requested by the Guililand Group from the Board was to build condominiums, an apartment building, a shopping center, and single-family residences on land zoned A-1, which was an agricultural use category. A blowhard agent at the local Remax Real Estate Company had told her that a multimillion-dollar end mortgage commitment had already been obtained in addition to the construction loan by the partners.

She had gone to his office posing as a rich out-of-towner looking for an inactive farm to buy as an investment in land, and inquired specifically about the one the Guililand Group had bought, not letting on that she knew about their purchase. "Already taken," the salesman announced loudly, as if he got a kick out of hearing himself say it. Then lowering his voice so it couldn't be heard in the next low-walled cubicle, identical to his own and that passed for an office in the place, he added, "It's going to make a local man this town's first millionaire."

"Really?" she had replied, pretending to be awed.

"I can't name him, of course," the salesman said, making a praying gesture with his hands and rolling his eyes toward the ceiling.

"Of course," Hemion echoed.

"But I happen to know," the man continued, "that he got the land off that hayseed out there on the reservoir for 400 an acre. The re-zoning alone will jack it up to 1000, and when all is said and done he'll clear a cool million, maybe more for all I know."

And, indeed, Hemion's research at the Lapeer County Register of Deeds Office, which was her next stop after leaving Remax, had turned up an incriminating piece of evidence. In order for purchase deeds to be accepted for recording purposes, the name and address of the person preparing the document must appear on it's face. The deed from the farmer to the Guililand Group had been drafted by Peebles.

The driveway across Pitt's farm was being claimed by the Guililand Group as its property's only frontage on a public road. Such frontage was required by the township's zoning ordinance before the Board could even consider the question of giving a variance from the limitation of agricultural use only to allow the proposed multi-use development.

Pitt had refused the partnership's offer to purchase the driveway from him, so now it was claiming ownership under the theory of adverse possession; that the farmer they bought the property from had been crossing Pitt's land on the driveway for over fifteen years, which was long enough in

Michigan to transfer title to the user without the necessity of purchase for a valuable consideration.

Pitt was insisting that the use had not been adverse, that he had willingly allowed the crossing of his land and he explained why, his former neighbor's original driveway was some thirty feet under water in the Holloway Reservoir, a casualty of its birth. "Country people help each other," Pitt had observed in closing.

Title by adverse possession was a fairly obscure use of the law that Hemion recalled only vaguely from her three years at Notre Dame Law School. But she acknowledged to herself that this would not be the first time the success or failure of somebody's grand scheme rested upon a legal technicality. It occurred to her that might be why Peebles had taken such an intense interest in Matthew Pitt's little history lesson. If she had known before the meeting that adverse possession was going to be an issue, she would have refreshed her memory of the rarely used doctrine.

Hemion couldn't be sure that anything Melvin Peebles had said about it, or anything else for that matter, was legally incorrect; and furthermore, she found herself falling under the spell of his wonderful command of language. She laughed along with everyone else in the hall at his quick country brand of humor that he dispensed generously, like a gifted politician does in winning over a crowd of potential voters.

To her dismay, Hemion even caught herself smiling openly, once, when Peebles brought the house down by waving a hand at the petitioners for the variance and referring to the bunch of them as "these city slickers with their blow-dried hair, wing-tipped black shoes, and fifty-dollar ties."

She was ashamed of her display of pleasure at the expense of others, which was not her style, and she had been helped considerably in her effort to wipe her grin away by Pitt's serious response to Peebles' sarcasm, which was, "If so much as one load of their lumber for those stinking buildings starts across my land I'm getting out my shotgun."

The Board had unanimously approved the variance by a roll call vote. The part of the meeting that bothered Hemion most was Peebles' legal advice to the Board of Zoning Appeals that the petitioning Guililand Group had to have some frontage on a public road to qualify for the requested variance, but that it didn't matter how much.

She had almost had a fit when he said that and was tempted to jump to her feet and ask, "Would six inches be enough?" But she didn't. It would have drawn too much attention to herself, especially when the sexual innuendo made her blush, as she was sure it would the moment she threw out the challenge. Yes, it had been smart of her to hold her tongue, even though it had been awfully hard to do so. At least a few of those people in the hall would have begun to wonder who she was, and someone might make an effort to find out, and she had a gut feeling that most likely it would be Melvin Peebles.

* * *

She met Francine in Firewater Willie's around 1:00 a.m., just before last call, as they had planned. The cavernous place had a windowless warehouse ambiance to it, with heating and cooling ducts, two feet in diameter and painted dark green, hung on wires near the thirty-foot-high ceilings.

Nine television sets were placed on small platforms around the seating areas, suspended a few feet above a customer's usual line of vision. All were in operation, tuned to sporting events or CNN's continuous menu of news from around the world.

Large, stained-glass lamps dangled from even longer wires to within a couple of feet of the dozen or so matching oilcloth-covered tables. Each lampshade was different, their antique work-of art appearance sharply at odds with the modern look of everything else in sight.

Hemion had no problem spotting her friend, whose short, plump figure was perched on a bar stool. She was talking nonstop to the only bartender's back. He was rapidly washing dishes, turning toward her occasionally to set glasses upside down to dry on a white dish towel spread out between them on the bar.

"So what have you decided to do?" Francine asked, after they had moved to a table and she had heard Hemion's story of possible wrongdoing by Peebles and the Guililand Group.

"If it involves postponing the Scraggs' canoe trip, I might as well go home right now," Francine added, tossing her head with a threatening tone to her voice.

"I'm going out to Matthew Pitt's farm before we hit the river today," Hemion replied decisively. It was a relief to have finally made up her mind on a course of action after so many hours of exhausting indecision. And it felt good, as well, to be reinforcing her thinking by sharing her plan with a trusted friend who wouldn't hesitate to point out its weak spots.

She continued, "In order to drive the termites out of the woodwork, I'm going to ask Pitt to sue both the Guililand Group and Deep Creek Township for an injunction against using his farm to reach the condominium construction site, with me advising him secretly as his ghost attorney."

"Wow," Francine said, "sounds cool. But shouldn't you be consulting with Lapeer County's Prosecuting Attorney about now if you're that sure there's trouble in paradise. I mean, this place looks like the Garden of Eden, with its rolling fields, and trees, and rivers, and lakes, there can't be any bad people here."

Ignoring Francine's customary sarcasm, Hemion continued, "Lapeer hasn't been attracting new blood all that long with its newfound boomtown reputation, so who knows how many good-old-boy networks are still in place here from its old-boy-sleepy-farm-town days."

Francine made a face and said, "In other words, you don't know how far the impropriety extends?"

"You got it, pal, but I've had enough shop talk for now," Hemion said.

"Hey, big guy, my friend wants another one real quick, it's five minutes to two," Francine shouted to her new chum tending bar. It was the man Hemion had seen earlier through her peephole, now first beginning his closing chores behind the bar some twenty feet away.

Francine's voice became raspy with increased volume, as it always did, and her desperate-sounding call for a last drink turned heads in their direction, causing an embarrassed Hemion to put a menu up close to her face to hide her blushing.

* * *

They stayed well beyond closing, of course, catching up on each other's adventures experienced over the year since the Scraggs' annual canoe trip the previous summer. Now they were the last customers in the place.

The bartender, having again gotten a sense that other services might be wanted later by these two single women, was prompted to interrupt his cleaning up the place long enough to sit down with them. Francine told him that they were Scraggs and volunteered an explanation of the name.

"It's from the *Lil' Abner* comic strip," she told him, receiving a blank look from him in return. The two women exchanged glances, and then Francine continued in her best explaining-to-a-child fashion, "There was this hillbilly family, see, and all these tall women, called the Scraggs, lived over the hill from them."

At this point, the thirtyish bartender brightened and said, "Yes," emphatically, to show that he got it.

Fearing Francine was about to sarcastically compliment him on his accomplishment, Hemion quickly intervened to wrap up the story, "We all played basketball together on our high school team."

"So?" the bartender inquired politely, without a trace of comprehension

133

crossing his blue-eyed, even-featured, suntanned countenance.

"Trust me, you'll get it," Francine snapped. "Sometime while you're mopping, or wiping up a spill, it will suddenly come to you, right out of the blue."

"How did this place get its unusual name?" Hemion asked him perkily, sending the conversation off in another direction and, hopefully, one in which he was better informed.

"I really don't know since I've been working here for only about three years, and that's only in the summertime."

"Well, make something up," Francine snapped, her patience exhausted.

"Francine, please stop now," Hemion said firmly.

"If you ladies will excuse me, I've got to get back to locking up for the night," the bartender said with a smile as he got to his feet, not appearing to notice the looks of disdain that passed between the women.

When he had returned to the bar, Hemion said softly, "Francine, why were you putting him on so?"

"He failed my test, and he is such a perfect specimen physically," her friend wailed.

"What are you talking about? What test?"

"I want to have a baby," Francine said softly, tears welling up suddenly in her large brown eyes. "But only with the right man."

"Oh, my God, you weren't seriously … with that dim light? Don't even think…."

"I don't have my pick like you do," Francine interrupted her, "with your curvy figure and blond curls, and you know perfectly well why great-looking men like him work in hotels, they're all in it for one thing, that's why these places can get away with paying them so little."

"But Francine, this is a park-your-own-car motel in a town that's still relatively small. He's just a local yokel with a great build working for bar tips, his day job is probably at the car wash. Ten years from now he'll have a stomach on him the size of a Georgia watermelon. In the name of the great American gene pool, don't choose him."

"But did you see those pecs under that tight shirt, and you know what they say about men with prominent noses like he has, the guy's probably built like a bull."

"So we're talking lust now, instead of stud service," Hemion blurted out in annoyance, surprised that words she had never used before came to mind so readily.

Then she added, "Well, good night, Francine," and stood up abruptly, suddenly feeling exhausted on top of bad-tempered. "I've got an important meeting with Matthew Pitt in about five hours, so I need some sleep."

Heading for the door that separated the bar from the rest of the motel, Hemion said rather flippantly over her shoulder, attempting to end their heated conversation in a lighter vein,

"Don't do anything I wouldn't do."

"That's your problem," Francine yelled in a loud, raspy voice to Hemion's departing back, "you've never done anything, you don't even know what a man feels like inside you. Well, I'm not as stupid as you, I'm not going to miss out on anything, including a kid."

Then the stud-of-a-bartender watched Hemion leave for her room, having paused in his cleaning up the bar for the following day to listen to the women's angry exchange, and wondered if it was due to anything he had said.

Chapter Nineteen
Night Wings

A male great horned owl's hunting call was the last thing Preston heard before he fell asleep, the loudest one so far, this time coming directly from above his tent. It was as if the night flyer was extending to Preston a personal invitation to follow him along on a search for dinner.

It was a primitive sound that often seemed to stir something hidden deep within a human listener's psyche. Something which ordinarily lay dormant, a power that had atrophied perhaps, from lack of use. And Preston was no exception, since this night he had felt the call's primeval pull more than once.

The series of low, sonorous, far-carrying hoots, sounding like a musical giant tooting on a wooden flute the size of a lumber mill log, had been coming from different directions in varying volumes while he was still able to read by his flashlight suspended from the nylon roof.

Preston figured it was an organized hunting party of the night raptors, communicating with each other as they glided above the dark forest on silent wings. He knew it was their grisly custom that the lucky hunter among them share what it was able to swoop down silently and catch with its razor-sharp hooked beak and large claws.

The hapless rabbit or other small creature was torn apart by the pack of powerful birds, sometimes while it was still alive. Preston had interrupted his reading to make a grateful mental note that human beings, for all their faults, at least killed the steer before they ate the steak.

As he drifted into slumber, Preston's book slipped from his grasp and fell to the tent floor. And though he continued to lie on his side, he snuggled downward toward the foot of his air mattress, so that now only his head rested on the rolled-up sleeping bag he had used to prop up his upper body so as to be able to read comfortably.

* * *

Preston in his dreams discovered much to his delight that he could fly. Soaring high above his campsite on the Flint River, he looked to where the horizon glowed from the lights of Lapeer, which was seven miles beyond the surrounding, wooded hills of the Lapeer State Game Area.

Then he playfully plunged downward, to glide swiftly, within inches of the river's surface that shimmered in the moonlight. He came so close to the noisy, splashing water of the rapids by his campsite that he felt a few drops of it hit his cheek, as if he was being christened by a priest whose parish was the outdoor world.

Why not join the winged hunters in their thrilling pursuit of food, he asked himself, the natural man within him lured by the siren song of Mother Nature's brutal ways. He could always back off when their evening meal began. Hadn't his psychiatrist, Rachael Childs, told him he should find strength from within to put on the brakes when he found himself in a fever to kill?

He decided then that he would fly above the birds of prey, so as not to scare them off, and enjoy their journey like a tourist following a guide. He would simply leave them when they gathered to feast upon their most recent victim.

* * *

At first, the dreaming Preston had to settle for following the great owls only by their sounds. But after a while, he caught a glimpse of them, flying far beneath his own chosen altitude. They were fast-moving, shadow-like objects, only slightly darker than the landscape they seemed, from his prospective, to be slowly moving across, ever alert in their pursuit of food.

To Preston's surprise, the powerful birds left the Lapeer State Game Area and moved swiftly northward toward the tip of Michigan's Thumb Region, sailing over towns of varying sizes, that sparkled with thousands of electric lights. Soon they passed over the sandy shores of Lake Huron and, after a long journey over open water, reached land again.

Here, Preston saw very little artificial lighting, which he looked for as the telltale sign of the presence of people. He knew then that they were over the northern portion of the Canadian province of Ontario, a vast wilderness region which he had once traversed by canoe with a college friend.

He remembered it as being a flat, desolate place, laced with countless string-shaped lakes. They all ran north and south, as if their basins had been clawed there by a gigantic clinging hand that had lost its grip on the North Pole.

Now he saw that the owls were heading downward, toward one of the many islands that seemed to sail upon the water like ships of stone with cedar groves for sails. Studying the island they apparently had chosen to land upon, he saw nothing special about it, no clue that might explain why the birds had singled it out for their destination.

As he drew closer, moonlight revealed it to consist of the typical dome-shaped basalt rock that rose from the depths with nothing resembling a beach at the water's edge. The usual cluster of storm-battered, straggly trees were perched on top, like a cheap toupee set artlessly down upon a bald man's head.

The owls were disappearing into that small patch of forestation, which Preston estimated to be only a couple of acres in extent. He continued to fly in high circles until the last of them were out of sight. Then he spiraled downward to land, feet first, on the convex surface of the gray monolith.

From the air, he had seen lights in the center of the island. And from his different perspective as he stood at the tree line on the curving rock face, he could see now that it was firelight, filtered through ragged, storm-stunted cedar conifers, many of which had been twisted and broken by savage winds and lightning strikes.

He stepped into the bedraggled woods, moving cautiously toward its center. Partway there, a great clamor reached his ears from ahead of him, but it was the sound of men shouting excitedly, not the cries of owls sharing a kill that he had expected to hear.

Seized by a sense of urgency at the unexpected sound, he tried to hurry but fell several times in the tangle of underbrush. But finally, he neared a lighted opening. Peering cautiously around the trunk of a tree, he looked out into a small, grass-covered clearing lit by a circle of torches set into the ground on its perimeter.

Instead of the great horned owls, a group of men stood in the center, crowded around something on the ground. They were naked except for feathered headdresses they wore that depicted the owls that had suddenly disappeared from sight, with the same terrible beaks for tearing apart their prey, and huge, luminous yellow eyes.

With a shout like that of a football team coming out of a huddle, they clustered upon whatever it was they had been looking at and at the same time seemed to fight for position with each other. They became so intertwined in their struggling that not one of their bodies was wholly visible.

Propelled forward by the screams of a woman that cut the humid night air like a razor, Preston ran out from his hiding place without thinking of possible consequences. Intending to pull the men off the object of their

139

frenzy, Preston grabbed a protruding shoulder with both hands, gripping it with all his strength.

Suddenly the masked ones were no longer there, evaporating into the air in response to his touch. But Barbara Hemion lay sprawled upon her back at his feet, apparently the prize the men had brawled over with one another.

She didn't appear at all unnerved, let alone injured, by what seemed to Preston should have been a horrendous ordeal. In fact, she smiled serenely, like a woman in the afterglow of orgasm.

He watched, transfixed by the sight of the golden beauty of her face and figure in the soft, caressing light of the torches, as she raised her knees with feet spread wide apart. Slowly, she reached between her legs to spread apart the lips of her vagina with two fingers. Looking to her face for a sign, he saw her beckon him down to her with the tip of her protruding tongue.

Lowering himself down upon his knees, Preston used his right hand to place the head of his erect penis where the sides of her smooth, inner labia came together to frame the darkness of a tiny entrance to a cave, no bigger around than a pencil. Then he reached upward with the index finger of his left hand to gently trace the rim of her ear that peeked through short but naturally curly blond hair.

The touch of her hardened nipple against his chest gave him an unexpected shock of pleasure as he lay forward upon her, taking some of his weight on his left hand, which he had moved from her ear to rest palm open on the grass. A month had passed since he closed Red Moon Bed and Breakfast, so the dam was already close to bursting.

With his face close to hers now, she whispered, "This is your reward for saving me."

He arched his back to pull his penis up into her, but even before it was fully encased in her satin tunnel, the uncontrollable pumping of a premature ejaculation began to flood his body with waves of physical ecstasy.

* * *

The force of his wet dream awakened him in cold darkness.

An Alberta clipper, as severe cold fronts are called in Midwestern America, had moved in during the many hours he had been sleeping. The temperature inside the tent had dropped to an unseasonable forty degrees Fahrenheit, its large screened windows having been left open to welcome the night air.

The once bright flashlight was now just a faintly glowing amber dot in the darkness above Preston, and no light came from outside the tent. The campfire that had put dancing shadows against its nylon walls while he had enjoyed his reading had long since burned itself out. The moon and stars were obscured by a thick blanket of dark clouds that hung so low in the sky that they magnified the sound of the nearby rapids.

He knew that his semen would have been splashed across the air mattress in front of him, and he slipped carefully off it in the opposite direction. The cold plastic squeaked its protest against the quick slide of his skin.

Groping hurriedly about in the dark for a moment, Preston found his packsack and removed two "D"-size flashlight batteries from it, which he used to get his improvised ceiling light on again. Now he could see his breath steaming in the still, chill air.

As he picked up the air mattress to take it to the river for rinsing off, he noticed a tiny wisp of steam above the largest of the half dozen whitish puddles on it. How many barrels of the stuff went to waste around the world each day, he wondered. He smiled then, amused at the direction his always-inquiring mind had taken him this time.

* * *

How silly all this would look in daylight, Preston thought, as he waded into the current. A naked man, shaking with the cold, taking to the river with his bright-yellow floating device. Hemion would be able to take it all in with one glance, too, were it a few hours later, and she suddenly rounded the bend a couple of hundred feet upstream.

The same river that had seemed refreshingly cool during the heat wave that had just ended now felt wonderfully warm as he sank down in it to his chin, letting the moving water wash away the sweat that had dried upon him as he put the tent up in the sweltering heat of the previous day.

He thought, then, of the sun-drenched miles the river water had traveled during the last several sweltering days on its journey here, the farmers' fields and country meadows it had passed through as it flowed toward this beautiful place where it now warmed him.

He held the mattress downstream from him and let the swift current cleanse it and afterwards waded over to a nearby sand bar, stashing the floating device there until retrieved after his swim.

Laughing happily, he acknowledged to himself that he was the last person that needed a swimming aid. Running across ten feet of firm sand, he shouted "hello" to let the other river creatures know he had arrived, then dove like an otter into the swirling pool on the other side of the bar.

His first memory of the dream, a recollection that had put him in a low mood when he first awoke, feeling guilty and ashamed about his failure to stay the course in servicing Hemion, now had faded completely away. He just felt glad to be alive in this little paradise.

He only hoped that his real confrontation with Hemion, which was bound to happen soon, would go reasonably well.

Chapter Twenty
Eat Our Dust

Barbara Hemion, alone in the Geo, rehearsed out loud the pitch she was about to make to Matthew Pitt as she drove the seven miles from the Lapeer Best Western Motel to his farmhouse in the country.

She wanted the feisty farmer to start a lawsuit against both the Guililand Group and Deep Creek Township, asking the court for an injunction to stop construction of the development on the reservoir. She felt, instinctively, that it might flush Peebles out into the open so she could get a clear legal shot at him.

"Mr. Pitt, if you really believe," she began her imaginary conversation, "that the Guililand Group is kicking back a profit share to Melvin Peebles in exchange for his help in getting preferential treatment from Deep Creek Township, there is something you can do to help me catch him."

No, that's too soft an approach, she told herself silently, *and this isn't a kickback situation, because the township isn't buying goods or services from a contractor.*

She started again, "You are the only person alive that knows the prior use of their driveway was permissive. They can't own it by adverse possession because it wasn't adverse. The old bachelor farmer they bought the land from who you generously let drive in and out for so many years can't confirm in a court of law that you told him it was *OK.*

"Why?" Hemion continued her monologue. "Because he's dead. You know that," she chided the invisible Matthew Pitt. "And I know it too, now, because his deed to the Guililand Group, recorded at the Register of Deeds Office, was issued out of his probate estate, signed on behalf of the deceased by the executor of his will."

Way too long and complicated, Hemion concluded silently after her third try. *I'll play it by ear when I get there,* she decided, with a sigh of relief. She had found that having an imaginary conversation with another party was hard work, even if you spoke your thoughts out loud.

143

* * *

Nearing Pitt's farm, she was struck again by the beauty of the area.

It was the morning of the Fourth of July, and American flags and matching bunting were on display at almost every home she passed. So much more so everywhere in the United States, she noted to herself, since 9/11, the World Trade Center tragedy, in New York two years before. The country's people were certainly more overt in their display of patriotism now than they had been previous to that terrible disaster.

The bright, uplifting national colors were sharply defined in the clear country air, and they favorably accented the greens and browns of the earth as well as the aquamarine of the cloudless sky.

Without warning, tears welled up in her eyes, and she pulled off on the gravel shoulder of the blacktop road, the rattle of pebbles loud against the underside of the Geo. Her crying spells had been happening more frequently since she had come here to this paradise-like place. And she knew the reason why; because these were beautiful sights her brother would probably never get to see.

It wasn't the end of the world that she had missed his collect call from prison, of course. But those conversations were so much better than letters because they were live. They were precious!

She had gone to Michigan's maximum-security prison in the city of Jackson only once to visit Danny, and it was so awful to see him trapped there, like a helpless animal, that she had been unable to bring herself to go back.

They had appealed his so-obviously-wrongful conviction for murder without success. She had handled each step in the process as his appellate counsel, absolutely certain she could win his freedom by reversing the lower court.

Would they have done better with a different attorney, she asked herself. Had her overconfidence been their Achilles heel? No, she had reasoned with herself to ease the pain of her searing guilt. It was the court system that she had taken an oath to uphold when she was sworn in as an active member of the bar that had failed her kid brother so terribly.

As Hemion composed herself and began again to be aware of her surroundings, it occurred to her that the parked Geo had been swaying several times due to gusts of wind from passing trucks.

Just then, a long, heavy eighteen-wheeler, designed for hauling gravel, roared by her lightweight vehicle, causing the Geo to shake again because of the blast of displaced air. It struck her as odd that its driver would be working

144

on a holiday. Pulling back onto the blacktop, she fell in behind the speeding behemoth, curious as to its destination. Attempting to catch up, she pushed the Geo's gas peddle to the floor, knowing that she was putting a strain on its engine.

To her relief, the thundering rig slowed down almost immediately. She was surprised to see it turn into a country lane marked by a mailbox with Matthew Pitt's house number on it.

Had this been the destination of all the trucks? And wasn't this the driveway in which the Guililand Group claimed a co-owner's right to share by virtue of their seller's adverse possession?

Pitt's threat—to use force against the Guililand Group if they went ahead with construction—made before the Board of Zoning Appeals at the Deep Creek Township Hall the previous evening came vividly to Hemion's mind. She half-expected to see the stocky farmer standing resolutely in the path of the truck, like the Chinese dissident shown blocking the way of a tank in the now-famous photograph from Beijing.

The truck ahead of her on the driveway to Pitt's house swung to the right, through an opening that had been cut in the six-foot-high wire fence, and rumbled down a long slope toward the blue water of the reservoir. Its apparent destination was what looked to Hemion to be a construction site in full swing.

Yellow-painted bulldozers crawled back and forth below her at the water's edge, moving the rich black dirt around like giant beetles building an earthen nest. A towering cloud of dark topsoil dust rose skyward around the huge machines, almost obscuring the drivers sitting atop them from Hemion's view.

* * *

While she waited for Pitt to respond to her knock on the screen door of his house, Hemion looked at a sign hanging on the wall beside it entitled "History of This Farm." She read,

Nameless tribes of prehistoric people camped here eight thousand years before Columbus discovered America. Many of their stone tools and weapons have been found and are on display inside this house. In more recent history, this land was part of a vast tract of white pine owned by William Peters, a lumber baron whose mansion still stands four miles away. Phineus Pitt purchased the property in 1907, after all the great trees had been lumbered off. He dug up their stumps and lined them up on edge for fences and began farming operations in the fields he created. The farm he founded remains in the Pitt family today.

Since no one had come to the door during the time she was reading the sign, she knocked again, more loudly than the first time. She recognized the battered, old truck in the yard as the one Mathew Pitt had climbed into after storming out of the township hall the evening before. It was a dark blue 1988 Chevy 1500 Cheyenne, with a missing right front fender.

Gingerly, she tried the screen door and found it unlocked. Pulling it open a few inches, she peered into what looked to her to be a living room. A large couch was against one wall, with a coffee table in front of it, upon which a small television set was placed. Pitt liked to watch it close up, Hemion concluded.

On the side of the room opposite from where Hemion stood, a square archway, trimmed in varnished oak, opened into a hallway leading through the center of the house. A gun case with its glass door standing open stood against the living room wall just to the left of the hall's entrance.

Hemion called out, "Mr. Pitt, it's Barbara Hemion, are you home?" This time she held the screen door partway open with one hand and, making a fist with the other, hammered on the inside of the door frame. She was halfway in the house, with one foot on the living room floor and the other on the porch.

Hearing nothing in response from inside the house, and unable any longer to resist the pull of her runaway curiosity about what might be missing from the open cabinet, she slipped inside and hurried across the room to stand before its open door.

One of four elliptical slots cut into its wooden bottom shelf, lined with green felt and designed to hold the butt of a shotgun, was empty.

Turning to look down the hall, she saw at the far end what she guessed to be a bedroom because of its location. Its door was open and, through what she figured was a sliding glass door wall on its far side, she could see the reservoir with the heavy equipment moving about on the shore.

Growing uneasy in the silent house, she decided to proceed with a check of that room, although she knew she would be terribly embarrassed if Pitt found her prowling around his home.

When she got to its door, Hemion paused a moment, her right hand against the varnished oak door frame, her forward motion halted by her first awareness of a bad odor.

By this time, she knew she had been right about it being a bedroom. From her new, closer prospective, she noticed the foot of a bed and one end of a dresser.

She was able to see more of the bed as she leaned further into the room. Then she saw a man's bare feet and the cuffs of chocolate-brown pajamas. Very loudly, then, she shouted, "Mr. Pitt?" and, when there was no reply and the feet didn't move, she stepped into the room.

Matthew Pitt was propped up against the headboard, the same way she liked to sit. She might have thought he had simply fallen back asleep, after enjoying the sight of one more glorious sunrise over the reservoir through the door wall in front of him, except for the shotgun barrel in his mouth.

Blood and other, thicker matter on the wall above the headboard glistened in the morning sun, sprayed out like a freshly painted abstract mural. The back of his head was missing.

* * *

"He took the Board's unanimous vote in favor of the variance personally, you know," the young, male deputy sheriff said to Hemion an hour later as they stood together on the porch of Pitt's home.

"They were all his lifetime neighbors, you know," he continued, "that he thought would be on his side. I can understand, you know, how he saw it as a shocking rejection of himself by his friends."

Hemion had called 911 on her cell phone and identified herself, including the fact that she was an Assistant Attorney General. She figured that any chance of preserving her anonymity would vanish with the media's scrutiny of her that was sure to follow, with her being alone in his house and the one who discovered the body.

The 911 dispatcher, after hearing the description of Pitt's condition, and verifying Hemion's credentials with the Michigan Attorney General's Office, decided to skip any kind of rescue effort. The Lapeer County Sheriff's Office was notified instead, to enable them to investigate the scene of the apparent suicide before anyone else got there.

"My father's a farmer here, too, you know," the deputy continued, "and though it may seem weird to you, Ms. Hemion, they are so tied to the land that has provided their livelihood all those years, you know, that after a while some of them come to regard it almost like family.

"The thought of those fields with their fine, rich soil being torn up by that heavy equipment down there at the reservoir was to Matthew Pitt, well, like you, Ms. Hemion, would feel seeing your child hit by a car."

"I just don't know if I can buy into that," Hemion said as she turned to go,

147

not bothering to tell him she wasn't a mother. "I'll be back on Monday," she continued, "and follow up with the sheriff's office's investigation at that time."

Then she added, "You will keep your investigating officer's report open as to the cause of death until all the laboratory reports from the autopsy are back, I presume?"

"Of course."

"And no speculating about how he died to the media, to get your name in the Lapeer County Press," Hemion said, managing a smile in an effort to change what sounded like an order into a lighthearted tease.

"No, ma'am," he replied, suddenly wondering what she would look like with her clothes off.

Chapter Twenty-One
An Intruder

Once she was far enough away, down Matthew Pitt's tree-lined driveway to be out of the line of sight of the young officer, Hemion braked the Geo to an abrupt stop.

She quickly got out of the car, took a few deep breaths and stood for a time with her back leaning against it, arms folded with hands firmly gripping her elbows, composing herself for the drive back to the Lapeer Best Western Motel.

Murders were nothing new to her in her work as an Assistant Attorney General, but this was her first up-close contact with an apparent suicide. It was a different sort of death totally beyond her understanding. The ending of one's own life on purpose confused her emotions.

Pitt had come across as such a determined fighter at the Deep Creek Township meeting, Hemion remembered, and he certainly exhibited an intense interest in the future of his neighborhood. Why wouldn't he at least want to stay around to see how it all turned out, she asked herself.

Perhaps, she speculated, he had a terminal illness that nobody knew about except him, and he didn't want to spend the money on hopeless treatment; maybe even losing his farm to medical bills, if he had inadequate health insurance.

A few years ago, she had heard about a farmer that hung himself when he was unable to pay his real estate taxes. Her impression was that Pitt was a strong enough person to push aside everyone's innate fear of pain and pull his shotgun's trigger once he had made up his mind that it was his best course of action.

She watched the heavy equipment move steadily about the construction site below her at the reservoir's edge. Why should they stop just because a man was dead in his farmhouse? Certainly not when it appeared that he had come to regard suicide as the solution for him, she silently noted in answer to her own question.

After all, the building project had a vibrant, exciting life of its own, she told herself, and Pitt was gone, passed into the ages, his life story was just part of the area's colorful history now. The new shopping center, surrounded with its luxury apartments and condominiums, would enhance the entire region's quality of life.

During his spirited attack on the Guililand Group at the meeting the previous night, she remembered, Pitt had cited as part of his credentials the fact that he had been born on the farm and spent fifty years of his life managing it. He felt strongly that this should count for something in the Board's deliberations.

If during her unannounced visit to his home this morning he had used advanced age as a reason for not involving himself in the rigors of a lawsuit to stop construction, Hemion had been prepared to remind him that only two Justices on the United States Supreme Court were younger than him.

Yes, Hemion was sure she would have been successful in convincing him to sue the Guililand Group with her legal coaching him along the way as his secret mentor; if only she had gotten to talk to him while he was still alive. And the prospect of a rousing legal battle might have been all that was needed to save him from his severe despondency.

She could see how Pitt might have been devastated by the Board's unanimous approval of the Guililand Group's request for a variance, one that he had so vehemently argued against.

It could have been Pitt's very first personal experience with elected officials and he might not have had any idea how devious politicians could be at times.

To him, it probably looked like everybody on the Board, all lifetime friends and neighbors, were turning against him. Or, at the very least, placed little value on his opinion.

Hemion recalled how that was the first of the two motives the deputy sheriff had suggested for Pitt's offing himself. Maybe, there was something to it!

But the young officer's other theory, that business about the cruel bulldozers, backhoes, and earthmovers rending the earth of his beloved fields that had become almost human to Pitt, was just plain cornball crap. Next, she told herself with her first smile in hours, she would be hearing a chorus of angels trilling "America the Beautiful."

Then a shudder passed through Hemion, as a different thought crossed her mind. What if this had happened a few weeks from now, after she had been successful today in convincing Pitt to sue the Guililand Group with her clandestine direction from behind the scenes? She would be riddled with guilt about his death, in that case, just as she blamed herself now for the failure of her brother Danny's court appeals.

Another one of the noisy diesel-powered gravel trucks from the construction site was moving rapidly up the hill toward Hemion. She was parked in its way, so she climbed back into the Geo, started the small motor, and continued on in the direction of the main road.

To help her decide ahead of time which way to turn when she got there, she glanced at her watch and saw that it was eleven o'clock in the forenoon. Her plan to return to the Lapeer Best Western Motel, to check out before she met up with the Scraggs, no longer made sense.

The women would have already begun to arrive at the hilltop parking area above Millville Landing, where they had agreed to meet. Hemion decided to go there first, explain that she wasn't quite ready on account of the unexpected turn of events, and then make a quick trip back to the motel to check out before rejoining her friends.

Now the truck loomed in her rearview mirror, and a blast from its compressed-air horn, a deafening sound at such close range, made her angry at the man she could see in the driver's seat. Her car had been moving forward, albeit slowly, she reasoned, and that should have been enough to satisfy him that she was getting out of his way.

Reluctantly, she decided not to stop and confront him to complain, only because of lack of time to do so.

* * *

Hemion followed a lavender Cadillac convertible, its top recessed to reveal a hot-pink interior, into Millville Landing's parking lot, their procession looking, she supposed, like a little brown bug tagging after a gorgeous rain forest butterfly. Only Scragg Mildred would drive such a wild creation, Hemion figured.

She saw that two other Scraggs, Janis and Paige, had already arrived and were standing next to their vehicles. Smiling broadly, they were motioning herself and the driver of the Caddy into spaces next to them, using the impatient gestures of parking lot attendants hurrying customers into place. Hemion looked about rather uneasily for Francine, unsure of how her volatile friend would behave in front of the assembled Scraggs after the harsh words the two of them had exchanged not that many hours before at Firewater Willie's.

This was the Scraggs' twentieth annual canoe rendezvous, and past experience had taught Hemion that the first moments together after a year's separation were the most delicious. There would be a short honeymoon period of pure joy at seeing each other again, with hugs and kisses all around.

Through a side window of the Geo, she could see Janis and Paige racing towards Mildred, who by now had gotten out of the luxury car and was leaning against it. Dressed in outrageously out-of-place white silk cocktail pajamas, she had struck a pose with one hand on her hip and the other behind her head.

"Oh my God, you can't wear that ridiculous get-up in the woods, you idiot!" Paige shouted, in a tone that was a mixture of exasperation and delight.

No, Hemion confirmed to herself as she watched, she didn't want these precious, first moments together spoiled this year by having another nasty scene now with Francine.

Hemion had never had a problem with her friend's promiscuity, but the fact that she had been willing to exploit that oaf of a bartender to make a beautiful baby had gotten to her. There hadn't been time for Hemion to think it through yet.

There would be plenty of chances, Hemion told herself hopefully, to walk the forest trails alone in order to sort it out, as well as the Pitt thing, too, after they had set up camp at Oxbow Landing.

* * *

After an excited exchange of the biggest news, stuff that simply had to be shared now or the person felt like she would burst—like Paige's promotion to Assistant Vice-President at Chase Manhattan Bank and the syndication of Janis' bi-weekly column in the Hearst newspapers—there was still no sign of Francine.

She had been late in past years, so they weren't too worried about her. Instead, with the excitement of first seeing each other having run its course, the Scraggs turned their attention to assembling their camping gear.

Duffels, backpacks, and sleeping bags were hauled out of cars and, with the women helping each other, heaped onto their backs for the quarter-mile trek by foot to Millville Landing. A wilderness two-track logging road connected the parking lot to the landing, located downhill at the water's edge.

Its rustic combination supply store and canoe storage shed took up most of the narrow riverside, with barely enough space left for the ranger to park his pickup. Only he was allowed to drive down to the building, the trail's entrance at the edge of the parking lot being blocked by a locked steel gate.

Just as the steam-powered noon whistle blew in Lapeer, affixed to the roof of the feed store, Mildred spotted a large bird in the very top of a distant ninety-toot-tall, dead pine and proudly announced to the group that it was an eastern wild turkey.

Gales of laughter followed Hemion's quick check with binoculars that revealed it to be a bald eagle. Her rather laconic reminder to Mildred that turkeys are in trees only at night, and ordinarily roost only in the lowest branches, just high enough to sleep safe from predators on the ground, didn't seem to hurt the budding ornithologist's feelings.

A year or so younger than the other Scraggs, having skipped the sixth grade of middle school by virtue of her high marks, Mildred was confident of her superior intelligence. Secure in the role she had assumed in the group as a super-smart person who constantly said dumb things, she really wasn't sensitive any longer to corrective comments the other Scraggs were only too willing to make.

And her lesbianism was a non-issue among the Scraggs. They knew only that she was the attractive, red-headed "mistress", as she called herself, of a wealthy bull dyke that owned a textile factory in Mobile, Alabama.

They had noticed, of course, that she didn't go out with boys in high school. She was certainly one of the better-looking girls in the class, so they had naïvely attributed it to shyness.

Another noise, from nearby this time, caught the women's attention. It was a high-pitched metallic scraping sound coming from the direction of the primitive road that led to the river.

All of them turned to look that way, but instead of seeing the metal gate being noisily opened by somebody for the Scraggs' convenience, which might have accounted for the strange sound, they saw a middle-aged man in a cluster of small trees that grew by one of the gateposts.

He was poised motionless on a bicycle with one foot on the ground to steady himself. It was a light blue World War II vintage Schwinn, complete with white-sidewall balloon tires, and festooned with small American flags that poked out in all directions from the bicycle's frame. It also had a wire basket on the front and bells on each of the handlebars for riding in traffic.

"I like my presence to be known," the man said gravely, in a loud, manly voice. Then he gave a push with his foot to gain momentum and weaved expertly between the trees and out onto the parking lot, appearing to be as much at ease with off-trail maneuvering as he was at riding in open spaces.

The Scraggs dropped their gear to the ground and watched in silence as he began riding in tight little figure eights before them, a feat which he accomplished without touching the widespread Texas-Longhorn-style handlebars, causing the bike to turn merely by leaning to one side and then

153

the other.

He held two larger flags out at arm's length, their bright colors flashing in the noonday sun as he flapped them up and down like chicken wings, all the while maintaining a fixed, serious expression on his face. After repeating his remarkable cycling drill half a dozen times, he rode away across the parking lot.

When he stopped before going out onto Plum Creek Road, the bike's sixty-year-old brakes were revealed to be the source of the mysterious metal-against-metal noise that had first announced his arrival. The man looked ever so carefully in both directions for traffic like a child would, as if his parents' firm orders to always take that precaution were still fresh in his mind.

When not a single vehicle had appeared during the several minutes he waited and watched, he pushed off again and pedaled down the blacktopped road, the handheld flags straight up this time, a one-man color guard proudly leading an invisible parade.

When he had disappeared around a bend in the road, the Scraggs looked at one another but didn't speak; well educated, so-called liberated women who, for once, found themselves at a loss for words. Finally, Hemion said, "I don't know whether to laugh or cry."

Janis broke her silent reverie with, "That was done for us, you know."

"Yes," Paige agreed, "a patriotic show because this is the Fourth."

"He's not right in the head," Janis said quietly, "did you see how long it took him to decide that the empty road was safe to use?"

"They call it developmentally disabled," Hemion corrected her. "A state institution for people handicapped that way used to be located near here," she continued, "called the Lapeer State Home and Training School. When it closed, many of the inmates were mainstreamed into this community."

"I hate to admit it, but he gives me the creeps," Mildred announced, "and now you tell us that he might live around here, getting around on that old bike of his."

"What are you saying, Mildred, scaredy-cat?" Paige suddenly demanded, so loudly that the startled Scraggs turned to look at her face. Paige's frightened eyes gave her away, being what people who work in stand-up comedy call a "tell."

She continued to deride Mildred to hide her own fear, adding in a voice that was still much louder than necessary, "And now, Mildred, I suppose you don't want to do this?"

Before Mildred could respond, Barbara Hemion quickly changed the subject by saying, "I'm going down to the ranger shack." Picking up her gear again, she headed for the gate. The other Scraggs quickly followed suit.

* * *

They were laughing together again, the flag man incident all but forgotten, by the time they drew near the weathered, unpainted building on the riverbank. And, to their surprise, saw Francine waving wildly at them with one hand while she clutched one of the ranger's arms with the other.

Tossing a serene smile in Hemion's direction, she explained when they reached her that a kindly bartender at the motel where she had stayed drove her out to the landing. Therefore, she wouldn't have to extend her car rental through the long weekend.

While the other Scraggs gathered excitedly around Francine, Hemion walked to the front of the small building and set her heavy camping things down on its porch. If any of them noticed she wasn't joining in their reunion ritual, they chose to ignore her actions.

She suggested to the ranger, who had reluctantly untangled himself from Francine and walked over to stand next to her, after giving several rather shy, admiring glances in her direction, that the canoes be loaded in her absence. She explained that it was necessary for her to leave so that she could check out of her motel, but that she would hurry back from town as soon as she had.

She estimated the ranger to be in his late twenties, and the fitted Lapeer County Parks and Recreation uniform he wore showed off his trim, well-muscled build to good advantage. Had Francine been interviewing him as a sperm donation candidate before they got here, Hemion wondered.

Leaving without interrupting the fun of the other Scraggs' happy reunion with Francine to say goodbye, she started the walk back uphill to where the Geo waited.

* * *

There were several piles of used linens and two cleaning carts, but no other motel guests in sight as Hemion walked briskly down the hall of the Lapeer Best Western Motel toward her room. She found its door propped open by a third such cart, which was being used to keep the heavy, spring-loaded door from slamming shut behind the young Mexican-appearing chambermaid tidying up inside.

Hemion took a five-dollar-bill from her purse and, with a smile, handed it to the dark-haired young woman, saying, "I got permission at the desk for a late, one-thirty checkout."

"Gracias. I'll come back later, señorita."

With the maid and her cart out of her way, Hemion hurriedly packed her things, leaving her clean clothes on hangers for traveling wrinkle-free. That way, she acknowledged to herself with satisfaction, she would have something to wear to work in Lansing on the coming Monday.

The Scraggs were being met by the ranger at the other side of the Lapeer State Game Area on Sunday afternoon, where the Flint River passed under a bridge on Norway Lake Road. He would drive them back to their parked cars, where they would then individually return to their everyday lives for another twelve months of separation.

Taking one last quick glance around the place to make sure she had everything, it occurred to Hemion that she hadn't looked in the drawer of the small table by the head of the bed.

Pulling it open, she saw her paperback, *Lazy B*, lying next to a free hardcover Bible placed in the room by the Gideons.

Thankful to have found her book where she had been leaving it after reading a few pages almost every night to relax, she tucked it gratefully into her purse.

It was written by one of her heroes, Justice Sandra Day O'Connor, the first woman appointed to the United States Supreme Court. The author had penned her autobiography about growing up on a cattle ranch in the American Southwest.

As Hemion started toward the door, it occurred to her that there was something about the book that had been different than when she had last seen it. She sat down on the end of the bed, carefully laying the hangered clothes out flat next to her, and setting her luggage on the floor at her feet.

Then Hemion opened her purse and removed the book to get a second, better look at it.

She had the habit of turning page corners down; the dog-ears serving to mark her reading progress. Several times she had tried to stop doing it, but sooner or later she would forget a bookmark and would slip back into to her old ways.

But now there was a bookmark, its white end protruding from the top of the book's spine, that she was certain she hadn't placed there. She paused a moment and tried to shrug off the uneasiness that had come over her. A lot had happened in a short time, so it was no wonder that she was a little jumpy, she reasoned, and she cautioned herself not to let her imagination go wild. Yet, somehow, when she finally opened the book, she wasn't entirely surprised to find that the scrap of paper had a message hand-printed upon it.

She had not touched the paper, and she let it rest against the opened pages as she read, so that her fingerprints would not cover someone's that might already be on it.

156

Hemion took in all the note's words in one glance,

You're not fooling anybody, Blondie

and then carefully closed the book upon it.

She let the book rest on her lap for a time, gripped firmly with both hands while she waited for her racing thoughts to slow down a little.

Chapter Twenty-Two
Finding Someone to Trust

Mason Ducker was the first black man to establish a solid reputation as a business person in Lapeer County.

He and his wife, Daphne, now a County Commissioner, referred to as "Daffy" with varying degrees of both affection and disdain by her constituents, came to live in the county in 1947 when they had bought a farm near Matthew Pitt's and made it their home.

They were both 25-years-old at the time, and newlyweds. President Truman's decision to drop the atomic bomb on the Japanese cities of Hiroshima and Nagasaki had led to the conclusion of the Pacific phase of World War II.

Mason's tour of duty as a Navy-enlisted man aboard an aircraft carrier based in the Philippines ended, and he was shipped back to the States, where he had met Daffy when he signed up for her reading class. He had learned to be a fairly decent cook and was thinking about opening a diner, but he knew whatever he did, he would have to read better and know the basics of math.

She was in her first year as an elementary school teacher in San Diego, California, and earned extra money from the government under a provision of the GI Bill which provided self-improvement opportunities to all illiterates receiving an honorable discharge from the Armed Services.

After the children left her classroom to go home in the afternoon, it was filled to capacity with former sailors from Coronado, the city's sixty-five-thousand-acre Navy base. Air-conditioning hadn't arrived yet, and the school was sweltering hot by that time of day. San Diego was in the throes of an unusually warm summer.

And not all the heat was generated by the southern California sun, many of the men attended only as a pretense to spend some time with the prettiest girl they had a chance to be around since returning stateside.

Mason's determination to master the new skill set him apart and caught his dedicated teacher's eye. Daffy patiently urged him on as he struggled through the words in her students' first grade book, reading little kids' stories, like the one about Dick and Jane and their dog Spot going up the hill to fetch a pail of water.

His childlike enthusiasm and wonder, so unexpected considering his rugged appearance and the awful wartime things he had seen, touched her, and over a period of time they fell in love.

After Mason and Daffy were married, the same GI Bill financed the down payment on a small farm in Michigan, a location chosen so they could be within a reasonable driving distance of his widowed mother. He also thought that now he was married, he would do better as a farmer than a short-order cook. His parents had been part of the great migration of blacks from the southern states to Detroit for work in the automobile plants.

Daffy had found teaching work at the nearby Lapeer State Home and Training School, the state-run institution for the mentally handicapped, through her high scores on the civil service test that applicants were required to take. It was primarily her steady income that allowed them to meet the mortgage payments on their fifty acres.

With her light skin and delicate facial features, she could have easily passed for a Caucasian in the all-white community, but she never tried to. Proud of a family heritage of success in the teaching profession—both of her parents were teachers in the San Diego school system—she never felt a need to appear to be anything different than what she was.

When their home farm was fully paid for, they mortgaged it again to buy a second one. By that time, it wasn't necessary for them to depend so much on Daffy's salary, because Mason had become an expert in commercial agriculture.

He vigorously embraced the newest progressive concepts of the science as they came along, such as contour plowing to reduce erosion of precious top soil, and placing selective herbicides in the ground next to the seeds at planting time to eliminate the need for weeding.

They had become wealthy. The thousand acres they had accumulated, through the acquisition of one farm after another over the years, had a state equalized valuation for real estate tax purposes of four hundred thousand dollars. Local realtors customarily figured market value at about twice the SEV.

Today, Mason was plowing a field to get it ready for the planting of winter wheat with what farmers call a "three-bottom plow" because it has three plow shares rather than the old-fashioned single one. A cloud of screaming seagulls, bright white against the clear blue sky, followed along behind his tractor to feast on the earth worms being newly uncovered.

He had noticed the fast-moving small brown automobile after he made the turn at the end of a row. As he watched, it pulled off onto the shoulder of Mount View, the gravel road that bordered one side of his field, sending up a plume of dust.

He continued his work, carefully laying down three new furrows parallel to the previous ones, but he couldn't resist glancing in the direction of the car. He saw a blond woman in a dark business suit get out of the driver's side, hurry around the back, and start out across the field towards him.

Mason knew that crossing the gently rolling terrain would be harder than it looked because of the uncertain footing. She stumbled in the soft, freshly-turned earth of the first furrow she encountered, falling to her knees not more then ten feet into her journey.

Mason smiled in admiration, involuntarily nodding in her direction when he saw the woman immediately get back up, remove the city shoes she wore, and pitch them over her shoulder in the direction of her vehicle. She continued on her way then, obviously undeterred by her unladylike tumble.

He stopped his tractor when she reached him, noticing how her creamy white slender ankles looked so young and beautiful.

"I'm Barbara Hemion," she began, "with the state Attorney General's office in Lansing. Are you Mason Ducker?"

"Yes, I am, ma'am." Then he added, "And now that you tell me you are from the capital, I have to ask if you have you met this county's most famous person in Lansing, Michigan Supreme Court Justice Robert Preston Foster?"

"I tried, unsuccessfully, to get him to hear a case of mine once," Hemion replied, but then quickly added, "but the social niceties will have to wait, Mr. Ducker. There is a question I have to ask you, and your answer is very important to me. Why didn't you chair Deep Creek Township's Board Of Zoning Appeals meeting yesterday?"

"Well, speaking of Lansing, that's where I was, tending to my mother's funeral. She lived in the Pines Healthcare Center, a nice place my wife, Daffy, found for her on the Internet that specializes in Alzheimer's patients.

"She was what they call a 'runner,' kept wandering away into the woods and fields when she lived with us here. We just couldn't stand the worry of it any longer and placed her there. She was 98 years old when she went home last weekend."

"Went home?"

"That's one of the few good things that came out of our slavery, Ms. Hemion, a comforting term many of us blacks use to describe death."

* * *

161

They talked for a long time, standing across from each other on a tiny island of wild grasses, that had been spared from cultivation through the years on account of the sugar maple growing at its center.

Hemion had commented on the perfection of the tree's confirmation, its thick foliage was a pale green cloud that crowned its brown trunk like a big ball of cotton candy on a cardboard handle.

Mason had explained that its beautiful symmetry was due to its isolation in the middle of the field, where it had no competition from other trees for the sun. And, he suggested with a smile, human beings might grow to be more perfect too if they weren't always jostling with each other for a more advantageous position in the world.

Gradually she shared everything with him, her suspicions about the suicide, the threatening note in her book, and finally, her reluctance to trust the local law enforcement establishment.

All the while, she watched his dark, handsome chiseled face carefully for clues about what he might be thinking and feeling but not saying, though she saw nothing in his expression beyond a genuine non-judgmental interest in her story.

"Go to the state police post in town, Barbara," he said when she was done, the use of her first name confirming for her something she had sensed at the moment he reached down from his seat upon his tractor to shake her hand; they were somehow bonded with each other, both of them warriors in the same good army, fighting for fairness and decency.

"Ask for Detective Sergeant Keller," Ducker continued, "the state police just transferred him here from the Copper Harbor Post in the Upper Peninsula of Michigan, so his slate should still be clean. I don't think we should talk about your concerns to anybody else but him for now."

* * *

"So who do you think is leaving you mysterious notes saying they're not taken in by you?" a red-haired, freckle-faced Detective Sergeant Stanley Keller asked an hour later, after she had finished her rather long-winded account of her story in his private office. Before she had time to answer, the middle-aged officer added, "Let me guess: the randy bartender that you're not giving any encouragement to, your hot pal Francine that you left in a snit, or even the Mexican maid who found that blond fall you add to your hair when you want to look more sexy?"

Hemion was impressed with his recollection of the details of the story she had just told him, and his attempt to put a sexual spin on everything made her laugh, in spite of a trace of fear that had been trying to find a home in the pit of her stomach. There was no blond fall, of course, it was just part of his shtick.

Then he spoke again, still not giving her time to reply, which was his manner, "All three of those potential suspects were in the same building your room was in and could have easily planted the note in your book while you were out.

"There was plenty of time to do that while you were at Pitt's farm reporting his death to that young stud from the Sheriff's Office, and then hugging and kissing the other Scragg chicks at your little Millville Landing reunion.

"The security in motels is practically nonexistent when the rooms in those places are being cleaned," he rattled on, "because the custodial staff work as a team on several rooms at once for efficiency, leaving the doors open to speed things up. After all, there are better things they would rather be doing with each other than picking up after somebody else's tryst. "I'm sure you—"

"There is someone else," Hemion said, interrupting him this time, and finding it necessary to take a deep breath to steady herself before continuing. It wasn't every day, after all, that an outsider like her accused a pillar of the community of stalking, and possibly murder.

Chapter Twenty-Three
Show Me Some Proof

Detective Sergeant Stanley Keller's whole demeanor changed when Hemion revealed to him her suspicions that Matthew Pitt had been murdered, and that Melvin Peebles had a motive to do the killing.

For one thing, he was more serious and the sexual implications in his casual remarks to her disappeared, and she was surprised to find that she missed it. She figured it was probably an outlet for his libido, and the thought crossed her mind that she had never enjoyed that kind of verbal banter before. Yes, she admitted to herself, she had been thinking more frequently lately about what sex would be like, and asking herself what she was waiting for.

The salacious tease had been the casual aspect of his personality that had lifted her spirits, which were at a low ebb because of worry about Danny. These constant worries distracted her from another new feeling she was experiencing, having nothing to do with sex; she might be in some real danger of physical harm for the first time in her life.

She was sure she had made her share of enemies prosecuting criminals as an attorney for the state, but this was different. Unlike the defendants in her cases, the murderer of Matthew Pitt was still at large, not in a holding cell awaiting trial.

The killer had already targeted her with a threatening note and still had complete freedom of movement to do more serious harm. And she wasn't at all sure that she had convinced Sergeant Keller that a murder had actually occurred.

But he had begun to listen to her with more concern, not interrupting her constantly to answer his own questions before she had a chance to. Most important, his initial reluctance to send the note to the crime lab to test for fingerprints was no longer valid.

He had first suggested that it was against department policy to make such tests in suspected stalking cases, citing budgetary considerations. Now that there was a possibility of a murder one criminal charge, he seemed eager to do so.

What impressed her most about him was his total recall ability for details she had previously supplied to him. That had been an amazing mental skill he had exhibited from the beginning of this meeting, even though at that point he had seemed only mildly interested in what she had to say.

"You've consistently demonstrated a remarkably good recall of what I've been telling you," she complimented him, "even when you weren't taking me very seriously. I'll put in a good word for you with the right people in Lansing."

"Thanks, but I'll do my best for you without all that political bullshit, Ms. Hemion. Catching criminals is my bag, just like yours is getting a jury to convict them and a judge to send them to off to prison."

"I believe you will do your utmost to solve this case, Sergeant Keller. You certainly are all business now and I'm delighted with the change. But before we leave the old you behind completely, I suggest that you tell him to watch the racy double-entendres, to think twice before he comes on to women with that sexy stuff.

"While it didn't bother me a bit," Hemion continued, "sooner or later, some little twenty-year-old you're working with here, fresh out of the State Police Academy, is going to scream sexual harassment and you'll be out of a job. You're not exactly Arnold Schwarzenegger, you know."

* * *

Then they went to work as a team on the note in the book before carefully placing it in a plastic evidence bag, using great care in its handling so that it would be admissible as evidence in a murder trial.

"I hope I didn't smudge the prints by closing the book on them," Hemion said.

"That was OK, paper on paper doesn't hurt them."

Wearing latex gloves, he pressed the bag closed, remarking, "It won't be back from the crime lab with their report on the fingerprints until next week. The same laboratory will report to the Sheriff's Office on what they found at the homicide scene about then, too, if the guys over there sent their request out in a timely fashion. So, you might as well go on your canoe adventure for a few days and relax while you can."

Working with Keller had made her feel closer to him. She wasn't attracted to him in a romantic sense, it was more that he was a surrogate for her brother. She figured that they were about the same age, and Danny had planned on going into police work before the shooting.

On impulse, she said, "Someday, I'd like to serve on the United States

Supreme Court. I know that's pretty ambitious, but I think that it's good to have a life goal, don'cha think so? What are your goals in life, Sergeant?"

"This, what I'm doing right now, I'm really content, happy as a clam in sand."

"Mason Ducker thinks highly of you, Sergeant Keller," she continued to gush over him. "He's the one who suggested I come see you."

"You don't have to butter me up, Ms. Hemion. All your charm is wasted on me. Ducker doesn't even know me, although I've heard many good thing about him and his wife, Daffy, since I arrived in Lapeer two months ago. Their reputation in the community is very fine.

"I'm a new face at this post," he continued, "and that's all Ducker could have said about me to you, isn't it?"

Hemion was taken aback by his frankness and accurate assessment of her conversation with Ducker. This man had the ability to see through bullshit, as he called it, and to ferret out the truth, she said to herself.

Somewhat flustered, she then continued, "Well, he did say he figured I could trust you."

"You're supposed to be able to trust all of us lawmen, Ms. Hemion. Didn't your mom tell you as a child to just find a policeman if you were ever lost?

"Why don't you just go ahead and tell me the rest of what's on your mind?" he continued in a patronizing tone of voice. "Since the Sheriff's Department responded to the 911 dispatcher's call to Pitt's farm, and did the initial crime scene workup, they were the ones, logically speaking, you should have taken your note to. Why didn't you, Ms. Hemion?"

"Because the deputy sheriff had already concluded that it was a suicide and tried to sell it to me as such, saying Pitt's motive was heartbreak after his friends and neighbors refused to support him," Hemion replied with a scowl.

"I saw the deceased in action just hours before I found him dead," she continued. "He was angry, not depressed.... He was a real fighter. I just don't think he was the kind of person to play lollipop with a shotgun barrel at the first setback he encountered."

"I respect your instincts in criminal matters, Ms. Hemion. Don't be afraid to tell me what you believe really happened. You honestly think the Sheriff's Department has been corrupted by the Guililand Group and Melvin Peebles, don't you?

"And you were reluctant to tell me that for fear I would bail out; the new kid in town afraid to go head-to-head with the law enforcement establishment in this county. You greatly underestimate me, Ms. Hemion."

She paused to weigh her words and then replied, "Let's put it this way, some Sheriff Department complicity is enough of a possibility that I'm not placing any further trust in them."

Then she added, "I wouldn't be telling you that now if I hadn't grown confident in you since I've been here, regardless of what Ducker said about you."

They looked at each other for a moment, the gravity of their conversation forcing them both to silently explore their own thoughts. Sergeant Keller was the first to break the silence.

"Let's go over the details of the position of the body on the bed one more time. I want to make sure I've got it pictured right before I give you my opinion."

* * *

Hemion had worked with many police officers in prosecuting criminals and most of them took their responsibility seriously. But she found none more thorough than Sergeant Keller when it came to the documentation of the minutest details.

He wrote furiously on a yellow legal pad as she described the grisly scene in Pitt's bedroom again; the acrid smell of brain tissue exposed to air, the gore on the wall that looked to be the horrible concoction of some mad abstract painter, and the shotgun with its polished walnut stock nestled between Pitt's thighs.

What she had expected would take ten minutes stretched into an hour, and only about half that time was spent conversing. Sergeant Keller, deep in thought, stared out the window for such a long interval at one point that Hemion became fidgety, and she excused herself to go out into the hall of the building for a stretch break and cup of coffee.

It was a corridor that served the jail portion of the state police post as well as the suite of offices she had been in, and signs for prison visitors were everywhere.

Hemion went from one to the other, her curiosity aroused. "No Weapons Beyond This Point" was printed on one next to a door that appeared to lead further into a cell area.

"Only Items Accepted for Inmates Are Cash and Paperback Books" she read on a piece of paper taped to the bulletproof glass of what Hemion supposed was a cashier's window. Next to it, a "$15 Booking Fee" sign was a reminder that it cost money to go to jail.

An ATM machine had been placed against one wall for the convenience of those being booked. Even after you were incarcerated, the money needs were apparently many and varied. You could choose your purchases from a list of what looked to Hemion to be about two hundred items, all were "available through the commissary on Sundays" according to the note at the top.

She felt her face flush slightly at the sight of "gas ban" and "hemorrhoid cream", which were the first two items on the list. *Welcome to the real world, sweetheart,* she said silently to herself.

Toward the middle of the list, "child's birthday card" caught her eye, and tears came suddenly and without any warning for the second time that day. Being a father was another joy Danny would never have.

* * *

"It definitely was not self-inflicted," Sergeant Keller announced when Hemion had dried her eyes in the ladies' room and returned to his office. "The 'kick', as hunters call it, from the shotgun when the shell goes off would have thrown the weapon half way across the room, and probably Pitt's finger with it, ripped off by the circular trigger guard."

"But wouldn't the young deputy sheriff that talked to me...." Hemion began, but she let her voice trail off into silence.

"Of course he should have known that, and that's the part of all this that really bothers me," Sergeant Keller said. "But as usual," he continued, "there are a variety of possible explanations, although it takes some painful stretching of the mind to come up with any.

"Maybe their homicide guys were all out sick," he suggested, "and they sent their vehicle traffic control expert, who had never seen a gunshot victim before.

"Or the kid that took your statement out at Pitt's farmhouse knew what a shotgun would do, but was afraid he couldn't handle all the questions you would dump on him if he shared that with you. After all, he probably was aware you were an Assistant Attorney General by then, because you had already revealed that to the 911 dispatcher that called the Sheriff's Department in the first place."

Keller paused for dramatic effect, then said, "Or your wild suggestion of Sheriff Department complicity might have something to do with it. In any event, I suggest you go canoeing with your girl friends, but watch your backside."

"There he is again," Hemion said, pointing to him with a laugh, her first one since Sergeant Keller had turned so serious after realizing he might be dealing with murder. "We just got a return visit from your old self," she

169

teased. "You really must tell him to say 'back,' not 'backside,' when he is warning ladies to be careful."

"I'm serious, Ms. Hemion, the Lapeer State Game Area isn't just a vast, pristine hideaway for nature lovers. Many of the local people grow drugs there in hidden places on the state-owned land, to avoid having their homes confiscated if they got caught growing the stuff in their backyard.

"They call the concealed growing spots their 'gardens,' marking them with their handheld Global Positioning Systems at spring planting time to locate the plants later for watering and harvesting. It could get nasty if you were out picking daisies and stumbled into one of their marijuana or psychedelic mushroom plots.

"And," he continued with a serious expression, "there was that incident not too long ago when that Chaldean party store owner from Detroit caught his wife cheating on him in there and disemboweled her on the spot. I guess it's an ancient Iraqi home remedy."

She studied his face for a moment and decided he wasn't joking, he didn't seem to realize that what he had just said could easily be mistaken for an attempt at humor by some people.

"And then—" his voice trailed off.

"Enough!" Hemion interrupted him. "I don't want to hear it. Anyway, the state police will protect us, you guys are good at that, right?"

"It's all we can do to cover the populated sections of Michigan."

"But somebody has to be out there watching out for disembowelers."

"Only the Lapeer County Sheriff's patrol, the game area is their baby."

She looked at him without speaking for a moment, feeling the recurrence of fear in her stomach. Then they bid each other goodbye, agreeing to meet again the following week, when the laboratory results were in.

* * *

It was late in the afternoon, Hemion realized suddenly as she left the state police post. She expected the others would be furious with her for delaying their departure, and she was pretty sure that it would be dark by the time they reached Oxbow Landing. Even though she was exhausted, she quickened her steps as she left the building.

But at last, she rejoiced to herself, she was free to rejoin her dear Scraggs, and let the Flint River carry them all away on a carefree trip into the wilderness.

Chapter Twenty-Four
Nightfall Changes Things

When she arrived back at Millville Landing, Hemion was pleased to note that nothing seemed to have been finalized toward their annual trip in her absence; it eased the guilt she was feeling about being many hours later than she had expected to be.

Camping gear remained where it had been dropped by the Scraggs when they had first arrived there. The two canoes the ranger had pulled from the storage shed and had waiting for them on the riverbank, had yet to be loaded.

All she got in the way of greeting besides a few glances in her direction, was a perfunctory, "Hi, girl", that Janis said over her shoulder without looking away from the fan of playing cards she was holding in one hand and scrutinizing intently for the game they all seemed to be so interested in at the moment.

Not that the fun part of the extended-weekend vacation hadn't already begun with the playing of strip poker with a tree stump for a card table; and the ranger, down to his boxer shorts, was losing.

"That's it, she's back," he announced, throwing his hand of cards onto the make-shift table and jumping up from his folding chair, his lively behavior emphasizing the lack of the others' enthusiasm for quitting the game just when it was getting interesting.

None of the four Scraggs were even close to him in terms of progress in their state of undress, which surprised Hemion, considering that at least one of them, Mildred, was so inept at card games that some people were hesitant to play with her a second time.

Hemion suspected that her pals had been cheating, especially Francine, or that maybe the ranger had let them win hoping that his state of undress would act as a turn-on for the women.

"But we're not done, Eddie," Francine shouted in protest, her face flushed. "The game's not over yet," she bellowed.

"Oh, yes it is!" he answered firmly. "We agreed to play until she got back," he added as he headed for the building, his bunched-up uniform clutched in one hand, using the other to carry his leather hiking boots by their high tops.

"What in the hell happened to you?" Paige demanded of Hemion, as if she had just realized that the missing Scragg was now back with them at the ranger station.

"I'll tell you on the river."

* * *

"I hate to say it, but he really can be boring," Janis whispered to Hemion as the Scraggs went about the business of loading the canoes.

Eddie Kildare, the ranger, had been alternately giving them more information than they wanted, and trying to dissuade them from starting until the following morning.

"He loves his Lapeer State Game Area," Hemion whispered back.

"'Lapeer' is the Anglicized version of 'La Pierre,' the French fur traders' name for the area," Kildare told them. "That meant 'rock' in their language and was inspired by the many prehistoric stone artifacts they found while traveling along this river buying beaver pelts from the Potawatomi Indians.

"The Flint is one hundred and forty-two miles in length, with an average gradient of two and nine-tenths feet per mile, and drains a watershed of approximately thirteen hundred and thirty-two square miles. Much of its basin has been channelized for drainage, changing lotic habitat to lentic, and exacerbating unstable and event responsive flow."

"Good Golly," Mildred said, "what does all that mean in plain language?"

"It boils down to this," Kildare said, pausing for dramatic effect and then adding, "don't leave until the storm has passed."

"What storm?" Paige asked, her voice quivering slightly.

"The National Weather Service has posted a severe thunderstorm warning beginning at midnight tonight," the ranger replied. "I heard it when I went inside to put my clothes on," he added, with a shy smile. "It was a radio dispatch from the Sheriff's Office.

"I would recommend that you ladies put up at the new Best Western Motel in Lapeer and try again tomorrow morning. It's very nice; in fact, my cousin, Melvin Peebles, is a part owner. Perhaps you've heard of him, he's our town's richest man."

Hemion made a mental note that Peebles could have gained access to her motel room by virtue of his ownership, and then, not hearing anything from the other Scraggs, said, "I think we'll go ahead, we're experienced campers." With that, the women climbed into the canoes.

172

The ranger was about to shove them off when a sound of rubber tires on loose gravel was heard coming from the hill behind them. The flag man was heading toward them at full speed, skillfully negotiating the steep, uneven logging road from the parking lot.

"Apparently, he wants to see you off," the ranger said.

They watched the expert cyclist apply his coaster-brake by reversing the direction of the foot pedals, causing the familiar metallic scraping noise. Skidding to a stop ten feet from them, he hopped off the bike, propped it up with its kickstand and, striking a military pose beside it, delivered a snappy salute.

"Please give us a shove, Kildare," Paige said, adding under her breath, "I want to get out of here, right now too."

He nodded and gave each canoe a hard push to get them away from the shore and out into the current. "I'll notify the Sheriff's Department that you're on your way," the ranger said loudly, to be sure he was heard across the widening distance between the canoes and the riverbank.

Startled at his words, Hemion called back to him, "Don't do that!"

"It is my orders," he yelled. "I have to report the position of everybody going into the game area since that Chaldean woman was murdered by her husband there this past spring."

Then, turning Dr. Phil with his advice, he added shouting between hands cupped around his mouth, "Use that stuff I gave you for mosquitoes with Deets in it to avoid West Nile Disease. And remember, you can't use what's left of it on the kids when you get back home."

"None of us have children," Janis hollered, but not quite loudly enough for him to hear.

"What?" the ranger yelled, cupping one ear with his hand.

"No kids," she shouted at the top of her lungs, and then more quietly added for the Scraggs' ears alone, "and we probably never will have."

"Speak for yourself," Francine said from the other canoe a few feet away, causing all but Hemion to look at her in surprise. But her face was expressionless, and she dug her paddle into the swiftly moving water without saying anything more.

* * *

Although Eddie Kildare had assured them that a sunken bridge was the only real hazard for experienced canoeists between the ranger station and Oxbow Landing, it had been decided that the canoe with only two people, Paige and Francine, should take lead. Being the lighter of the two, it would be the

173

easiest to maneuver in searching out the best course through the glacial-boulder-laden channel.

The other three Scraggs followed in the second canoe. Hemion took the rear seat in that one so as to do the steering with the jay stroke, while Mildred paddled in the bow seat. Janis sat on the floor between them, stabilizing their craft by lowering its center of gravity.

The sun was hanging just above the horizon now, sending its horizontal rays under the branches of the trees that grew along the river.

The golden light from the west filtered through waist-high shore grass and was divided by it into layers. A hatch of May flies streaming skyward through the different planes of light seemed to flicker, strobe-like, as if each was a tiny nightclub dancer.

Janis was facing forward to see better, and over her shoulder she said, "See how the evening light changes the color red, Barbara?"

"What do you mean?"

"Look at that cardinal perched in the white birch tree over there. Now isn't that a pure fire-engine red color if there ever was one?"

"That's for sure."

"If we had passed by and seen him two hours ago, his feathers would have been scarlet, but with an orange cast to them. He wouldn't have been half so pretty as he is now."

"Really," Hemion said with surprise, "I never noticed that the time of day made such a difference."

"It's my job to notice things other people don't, and then tell them what they're missing so they won't anymore."

"Well, it's my job to gather evidence," Hemion said, laughing. Then she continued in a more serious tone of voice, "Let me tell you what nobody seems to have noticed but me."

"And that is?"

"There aren't any herons."

"The great blues written up in the brochure?"

"Right."

"I noticed their absence," Janis said, "I just hadn't said anything about it yet."

"You did not."

"OK, I didn't; after all, Mildred's the bird watcher in the group."

Hearing her name, Mildred called to them without turning around to face them, "Talking about me again, ladies?"

"No, dear," Hemion replied.

"Just keep paddling, sweetie, we love you," Janis added.

174

"It's like they have been scared away from the river by something," Hemion continued, "but we haven't encountered another soul on the water."

"Do they have natural enemies, predators I mean?" Janis asked. "I glimpsed a mink running along the bank just after we left the ranger station. It was a glistening deep brown in color, almost black. They're gorgeous, but vicious killers, I understand."

"The ranger told us no, that nothing bothers full-grown herons except mankind, which is the most savage destroyer of life, unfortunately."

"Perhaps another canoe party went through ahead of us," Janis suggested. "They might have scared the herons downstream ahead of them a ways."

"There weren't any others signed in at the ranger station, and they are supposed to leave a travel plan there as a condition of receiving their camp-site permit."

"So what you're really saying is that there must be a wilderness camper on the river ahead of us who's not interested in using the game area's improved campsites. So what's the big deal? Barbara, why do I get the feeling there is more at stake here than I know about? I get the impression that this is a lot more important to you than a few photogenic birds that have gone AWOL."

"I'm just tired, pal. It's been a long and trying day. I can hardly wait to get a tent over our heads at Oxbow Landing and then crawl into my sleeping bag."

* * *

It was close to dark by the time they came upon the sunken bridge that the ranger had warned them about. The sound of the rapids reached their ears well before they could actually see the froth of white water that lay directly over its submerged timbers.

On a grassy bank to the right, overlooking the noisy rapids, there was a small tent with a canoe beached upside down beside it. The campsite was barely visible under a canopy of tree branches that contributed to the darkness of a rapidly advancing nightfall, and there was no sign of life around it.

In order to discuss the best way to proceed on downriver to Oxbow Landing, the Scraggs brought their canoes alongside each other at the foot of the bank, no more then ten feet below the tent's half-circle-shaped window that faced the river. They held themselves in place in spite of the strong current by gripping cattail plants that grew in clumps at the water's edge.

"I saw something back there," Francine said, "silhouetted against the

175

setting sun. A man, I think, running along even with us at the top of the ravine."

"Oh please, Francine, don't do that," Paige said, her voice already quivering with nervous concern, "this place is creepy enough as is with that certified loony prowling the woods."

"A patriotic, red-blooded, disabled American riding his decorated bike," Janis corrected her. "He's not prowling either, just showing off his exceptional riding skills in plain view. And furthermore, he obviously likes us."

"Yeah, right. It's that last part you said that worries me the most," Paige said.

"Wait, there's still more to my report," Francine insisted. "Like I said, all I got was a quick glimpse, like a flash photo, but I think he was naked."

"Francine, that's pathetic," Paige said derisively. "The whole weird story is a product of your horny imagination and a childish desire to scare people. I refuse to take you seriously."

Mildred began to speak, "You don't think that the ranger, Eddie Kilgore, would follow us, do you…." but her voice trailed off into silence as a sound came from the riverbank directly above them.

It was the noise of a zipper being closed, seeming extraordinarily loud in the eerie silence that had fallen upon the forest at the day's end.

The wind that earlier in the evening had made the leaves on the trees rattle and scrape against each other had died out so completely that the river's summer odor hung above its surface undisturbed, a pungent blend of smells from sun-warmed water, rotting leaves, and mud flats exposed to air.

The Scraggs lowered their voices and made an attempt to continue talking while glancing upward now and then in the direction of the silent campsite above them. While they had no idea it was Preston Foster's, they presumed somebody had been watching them from it, and perhaps following them out of sight along the shore as they progressed down the river.

They struggled to keep their focus on the question of whether to portage around the sunken bridge in front of them in the river or set up camp right there. The portage would be somewhat hazardous in the darkness with all their equipment plus the canoes. But their voices gradually became softer, until they were conversing in whispers, and finally they fell silent.

Again the sound of a zipper reached their ears, but this time it sounded different and lasted longer. "They've closed the window and now they're coming out a door facing away from the river," Paige whispered under her breath, looking in the direction of the tent.

After a long moment had passed, during which nothing could be heard but the murmur of the rapids, Francine whispered, "Let's run the sucker."

No one replied, but moved to action by her decisive words, the women let go of the cattails and paddled furiously toward the center of the river. Only there did the surface of the water that was boiling across the sunken bridge appear at all smooth, promising at least a few inches of depth.

* * *

A huge, crackling fire lit up the center of Oxbow Landing.

At the outer edge of their campsite, Eddie Bauer's largest umbrella-style tent waited for the Scraggs, but now they were enjoying themselves so much that none of them wanted to go to bed.

After their arrival at the landing, they had been delighted to find a generous supply of firewood waiting for them, and a pit to burn it in that was encircled by a continuous bench constructed of rough-hewn planks nailed across the tops of two-foot-thick sections of tree trunk.

The night air remained so still that the smoke slowly spiraled skyward toward the stars, allowing them to enjoy the evening without the discomfort of getting it in their eyes.

Frangelico nightcaps were being sipped from speckled-blue Coleman tin cups. Feeling safe in camp now, the friends were finding amusement in what had seemed to be such a desperate situation only two hours before. "I didn't know what was going to step out of that tent with us at its mercy while we were stuck on that sunken bridge," Mildred said. "So, here's to our new hero, Janis, the bookworm turned action figure."

Janis stood and took a deep bow, saying in a deep voice, "Thank you, Your Majesty, but it would have been impossible without the aid of my sturdy companions here."

She had climbed out on the bridge with rushing water halfway up her calves and pushed the canoes free, then, with arms outstretched on either side for balance, walked on the slippery moss-covered timbers to the riverbank opposite the tent, rejoining the other Scraggs a short distance downstream.

"Not to change the subject, but will the Audubon Society refund my contribution if I complain about the lack of herons?" Paige inquired with a giggle to no one in particular.

"So someone else besides me did notice," Hemion said.

"I told her that I did, but she didn't believe me," Mildred complained, with an exaggerated pout.

"Their executive director told me that this place was world famous for them," Paige continued, "and he was really cute."

"This here neck of the woods ain't world famous for nothin'," Mildred proclaimed loudly, straining to make herself sound backwoodsy, Davy Crockett style.

"Well, don't be too sure about that," Hemion said, continuing with, "What about the Imad Abbas case? Eddie Kilgore mentioned it back there when he shoved us off, explaining that it was the reason he had to tell the sheriff that we're in the game area."

"I read about that murder on the Associated Press wire service in the *Chicago Trib*'s newsroom just a couple months ago," Janis said, her voice taking on a serious tone, "they found her hanging by her feet in a tree in this very woods. She had been gutted like hunters do with those poor deer they shoot."

"Oh, God, don't talk about that now," Paige said, more than a hint of fear in her voice.

"Don't worry, her loving husband is in jail for killing her," Mildred said soothingly. "That's one reason I stick to women, they're not quite so violent, usually, when it comes to adultery."

They sat in silence for a time until Paige said uneasily, "It gets so quiet when we're not talking. Aren't there supposed to be frogs croaking or crickets chirping or something?"

"I'm going to step over to the river to take a PTA bath," Francine announced, getting to her feet. "I'm too tired to walk to the pump. It looks like it's quite a ways back in the woods according to the map attached to our camping permit."

"I haven't heard that in a while," Hemion said.

"What?" Francine said.

"Parent Teacher Association," Hemion replied, adding, "My mom belonged to the PTA when I was in middle school."

"We appreciate your quaint remembrance of times past, Barbara, but I think Francine means pussy, tits, and ass," Janis explained in her most patient manner, to gales of laughter from the others.

When it finally became quiet enough for her to be heard, Francine spoke again, her wash cloth and towel in one hand and her drink in the other, "Seriously, have you ever thought about what it must be like to be a man? I mean, one minute it's a battering ram and the next a faucet, it's so weird...."

She was interrupted by a metallic, scraping noise coming from the dense forest that began a short distance to the east of their fire on the river's edge.

"Oh, my God," Janis said softly, then pressed her fingertips against her lips as if to shush everyone up.

"It's him!" Paige whispered, her eyes wide with fear.

178

A different sound reached the women's ears as they stared out into the darkness, coming from a much greater distance away than the first; it was a low-pitched rumble of thunder giving advance notice of the approaching storm the ranger had warned them about.

Chapter Twenty-Five
Oxbow Landing

The bald eagle soared so high above the Flint River basin that it could see both Assistant Attorney General Barbara Hemion's tent at Oxbow Landing and Justice Robert Preston Foster watching the women's campsite from the forest. The two adversaries were now only a quarter-mile apart.

Though its telescopic eyes were capable of spotting a field mouse from a mile up in the sky, today it was looking for bigger game; carp trapped in shallow pools on the river flats as the flood waters from the storm of the previous night slowly receded, their protruding dorsal fins a come-and-get-me sign to predators.

So intent was the great bird of prey upon its quest for food for her two ugly gray down-covered eaglets waiting for breakfast in their tree-top nest of sticks, that it paid little attention to the blond-headed man and woman, both extraordinarily good-looking, and who could have passed for brother and sister, as they moved closer to a confrontation in the bright sunlight of a new day.

* * *

The night had been a difficult one for Preston. He had watched the erratic movement of their flashlights from the dark woods as the Scraggs struggled to get their canoes across the sunken bridge, realizing that it was almost time for the conversation with Hemion that he had been planning for so long.

Stress from that knowledge accelerated the frequency of a violent obsession that had begun to plague him a few days before when he became bored with the unexpectedly long wait for Hemion and, for diversion, had begun following the ongoing murder trial of the Duvall Brothers.

Preston had first heard about the case that had attracted national attention when listening for the weather report on the small but powerful digital radio he had brought into the wilderness with him for that purpose. WWJ, an all-news station in Detroit, gave the statewide forecast every ten minutes, which made it easy for Preston to catch it without being forced to listen at length.

The brothers lived in the woods in a region in Michigan similar to the Lapeer State Game Area and were charged in the beating death eighteen years before of two young men from Detroit that had come there to hunt deer, victims whose bodies had never been found.

The defendants were but two of a tightly knit clan of seven brothers known as hard-drinking, hot-tempered brawlers. Witnesses at the trial testified that the accused had bragged of the killing to their relatives and friends, telling them that they had disposed of the evidence of their crime by cutting the corpses into pieces and feeding them to hogs.

When Preston heard that, an image of himself doing the same to Hemion, her blood mixing with the mud and manure of a pigpen, had come immediately into his mind. And just as his psychiatrist, Rachel Childs, had warned him, the harder he tried not to think about the apparition, the stronger the image became.

His farm background made things worse. As a child, it had been his job to "swill" the pigs, pouring leftovers from the farmhouse kitchen, including raw meat, from a big steel pail into the animals' "slop trough," to be voraciously gulped down to a cacophony of excited grunts and squeals. He had no doubt that hogs had enjoyed the Duvals' offerings.

In desperation and against his better judgment, he experimented with putting the images out of mind by doing something four times. That was the self-defeating way of temporarily displacing obsessions that he had used with his legal work, a method so time-consuming that it had eventually destroyed his career as a Justice.

As a test, he choose washing up in the river. On his fourth trip back up the bank, with what he jokingly contemplated were the cleanest hands in Michigan, the violent obsession was gone.

But past experience had taught him that the respite would be short lived. So while still free of the dreadful images and able to reason with himself, he quickly made up his mind not to find relief that way again, knowing that if he gave the compulsive repetition an inch it would take a mile, and eventually engulf all his waking hours.

Over the course of the several days that passed before the arrival of Hemion, the involuntary mental images had returned periodically to besiege him. Preston had made no effort to stop them. Instead, he let the dreadful mind pictures come and go as they pleased, strengthening himself with the reminder that they signified nothing, just as Dr. Childs had directed him to do.

* * *

Hemion had been awakened early that morning well before the other Scraggs by the sound of coyotes howling. It was the noise a pack of them make when fighting over a kill, sounding like women and children crying hysterically with both grief and joy.

Intending to find the well indicated by the drawing of a hand-pump on their map, she quietly crawled out of her sleeping bag, undid the Scraggs' security precautions from the night before, and slipped outdoors.

After hearing the metallic noise coming from the woods, the frightened women had hurriedly double-staked their tent in preparation for the approaching storm and gone to bed. They had closed the nylon door and tied its zipper down with a shoelace looped around a heavy log laid crosswise on the floor at the foot of their sleeping bags.

There hadn't been any of their customary lighthearted chatter before going to sleep, for fear of being unable to hear the footsteps of an approaching intruder. All that seemed a little silly to Hemion now in the daylight, and she smiled to herself as she hoisted up the backpack containing her toiletries and began walking briskly down a trail leading in the direction of the well.

* * *

Preston had chosen an old deer-hunting blind as his observation post. It was located on the crest of one of the game area's high banks, the almost-vertical cliffs formed when the river cut its ravine through massive mounds of glacial gravel thousands of years ago.

Below him lay a picturesque, panoramic view of a river winding through green hills that rolled gently towards the horizon. And most important for his purposes, it was a view which included all of Oxbow Landing.

The canoe encampment's well, with its bright red-painted hand-pump, and cement block privy were located in a clearing several city blocks—in distance—inland from the riverside tent sites. Preston knew that the women would eventually need to use those facilities, so he expected that there would soon be an opportunity for him to be alone with Barbara Hemion.

His main concern was controlling the insidious rage he knew he would experience upon his first glimpse of her. The violent obsession of feeding her to the pigs had already entered his mind more than once since he awoke that morning, but he had steeled himself and simply tolerated the powerful feeling it aroused within him according to Dr. Child's explicit directions.

It was the simple but had-to-do concept that was at the heart of her cognitive behavior therapy for OCD. His painful bearing of the tension of non-response was richly rewarded since after only ten minutes or so, the nightmarish image passed.

It was to be expected, he told himself in way of preparation, that the sight of Barbara Hemion would probably trigger the return of the obsession and might considerably strengthen it. After all, he reasoned, she alone stood in the way of his judicial comeback. Anybody in the same situation would feel some anger toward her, that was only natural.

Dr. Childs had explained that his OCD would probably never go away completely. She made it clear to him that the power to resume his legal career had to come not from a cure of the illness but, instead, from a total refusal to respond to it in his old, self-defeating ways.

That had been what their therapy sessions had been all about, purposely exposing himself to what triggered the obsessions and then being able to ignore them. Their tolerance did get a little easier through desensitization.

An acquaintance who was a decade older than him had told Preston the same thing about his experience in Viet Nam insofar as the sound of the first "incoming" artillery shells was the most frightening sound in the war. He had said that you never got fully conditioned to the eerie whistling noise, although with the passage of time, it became slightly easier to function in spite of it.

Preston knew that he, too, like the gunner under fire in combat, somehow had to be able to compose himself enough to function in spite of the distraction of obsessions in order to survive life's endless battles.

Dealing with Barbara Hemion today would be good practice for his future with OCD, he told himself with a grim smile, wincing at the thought that he probably would be living with that invisible handicap during the rest of his years.

He decided to approach her in plain view once he determined from his lookout spot that she was alone. He focused his Bushnell 7X-21X40mm zoom-lens binoculars on the red water pump and waited.

* * *

Hemion laughed out loud when she heard the metallic grating noise that came with her first down-stroke on the pump's handle. The sound told her that it wasn't the bicycle man after all that had sent the Scraggs scurrying into their tent. She supposed, smiling to herself, that it had been just another camper getting some water in the middle of the night.

She kneeled upon the sandy ground to catch the icy cold liquid in her cupped hands, taking a quick swallow of it before the balance leaked unto the ground. Filling her hands again, she closed her eyes and splashed water on her face, enjoying the refreshed feeling it gave her.

When she opened her eyes again, she saw walking towards her a tall man dressed in Levi's and a matching blue denim shirt. Startled by his presence when she thought she was alone and struck by his blond hair, good looks, and slim build, she didn't recognize him at first as the former Supreme Court Justice. Standing up, she waited for him to get closer before she spoke to him.

"What a surprise to see you, Justice Foster."

"I wanted a chance to talk privately with you, Ms. Hemion."

"Not now. I'm on vacation with friends."

"You are blocking my appointment by the Governor to the Michigan Supreme Court under the guise of an investigation into Chief Justice Woodward's handling of my illness. Why do you hate me so?"

"Call my office next week and I will try to work you in."

"You know that I've already done that many times, to no avail. Your secretary always says you are in a meeting. Also, you don't return the calls that I leave on your voice mail either."

"So this encounter didn't just happen by chance. We figured somebody was shadowing us down the river."

Ignoring her candid observation, Preston continued with a serious expression on his face, "Imagine for a moment how good it would feel for you to let go of your debilitating animosity towards me. We have more in common than the color of our hair, you know," he said with a smile. Then he added, "An intense interest in law and politics for starters…. We might even become friends.

"Welcome to my territory." He beckoned suddenly with his arms spread wide before she had time to respond to his suggestion. It was as if he was starting their conversation over again, with a slight tilt of his head and a broad smile that revealed even white teeth. "Let me show you around while you think about what I've said. I live a ways up the river and I've roamed this place since I've been a kid."

"I've seen all there is to see just fine without your help."

"Everything?" he replied, a tone of friendly challenge in his voice. "So let's play twenty questions then, okay, Ms. Hemion?"

"I suppose," she agreed, suppressing an impulse to smile a little at his engaging confidence.

She was struck by how attractive he was in the outdoor setting, even more so than when she had sat across from him at the Judicial Tenure Commission meeting she had chaired. What would he have to say if she told him the truth

185

about the cause of her dislike of him, she wondered.

"So, what do you think those horizontal lines are on the trees?" Preston asked.

"Where?"

"I'll show you," Preston said, stepping over to a large, smooth-barked beech tree nearby. He reached up, touching what appeared to be a scratch made crosswise on its trunk by a sharp object.

Hesitantly, she suggested, "Maybe a lumber company, contracted by the state, marked trees to be cut in order to thin out the woods for better growth?"

"Hey, I'm impressed. But no, it would be a treeless wasteland when they finished the removal, like the face of the moon," Preston seriously replied, "because you can see that every tree in sight bears the same mark.

"I'll go easy on you and give you a hint," he continued. "Ask yourself why all the marks are at the same height, and you'll probably easily figure out what the right answer is."

"So now you've made me out a big dummy if I don't, right?" Hemion said sarcastically, but with a slight lilt to her voice. And now that her interest had been piqued, she indulged herself in finding pleasure in problem solving similar to being on the popular quiz show *Jeopardy*.

She struck an exaggerated pose of being deep in thought, chin in hand, and didn't speak for several minutes. "O.K., I give up, tell me," she said at last, a hint of a smile finally appearing on her face for the first time since their conversation began.

"Thin ice...." he announced matter-of-factly.

"On floodwater in the early spring," Hemion added immediately, interrupting him to prove that she didn't have to be told the complete explanation, and forgetting herself long enough to give Preston a quick, triumphant thumbs-up with a big grin.

"You got it," he said enthusiastically, adding, "When the wind blows, the trunks sway and mark themselves."

"End of game," Hemion said, her facial expression turning serious once again. "How much do I win?"

Then she added, "I need to make a call now on my cell phone, away from my friends, the last thing they want to hear is shop talk."

"I'll leave you by yourself for privacy, but please wave me back when you're through and we'll walk together to the river. There's a doe with triplet fawns that comes down to drink about the same time every afternoon. I'll show you a place where you and your traveling companions can hide in order to see them. It's quite a sight ... one of nature's wonders."

186

* * *

"A raccoon got that one," Preston said. He and Hemion stood beside a shallow pool of muddy water, looking down at a partially eaten carp that lay in the grass at their feet. They had walked from the pump towards the river, but were still some distance from its edge.

"Why would Mother Nature be so cruel as to trap them like that?" Hemion said, adding, "They're at the mercy of their enemies, and unable to get away. It's hopeless."

"You're crying," Preston said gently, having looked closely at her face after noticing a tone of profound sadness come into her voice. "Does it have something to do with me?"

"Danny Hemion," she replied quietly, "You refused to hear his appeal of his wrongful murder conviction. And, now he's serving a life sentence without parole. I'll never forgive you."

Startled, Preston thought for a moment and then said, "Give me more, to help me remember the case."

"The rape and murder of a nun, his former teacher at St. Alphonsus, the Catholic school we both attended, he's my brother."

He thought for a few minutes before he responded. "Now I recall the facts of that file, because I was the only Justice on the Michigan Supreme Court who voted to hear his appeal when it came up to us from the Michigan Court of Appeals."

"I don't believe you."

"Check it out."

"I intend to, and if I'm wrong I'll be the first to apologize, because I will have done you a terrible injustice."

Preston looked at her for a long moment and then said, "Are you saying that you have been working against my appointment to the Michigan Supreme Court because of that?"

"Something else, too, but it's silly ... of no real consequence."

"What is that?"

"No, really, I'm embarrassed to tell you, especially now that I realize I may have been horribly off base about your role in the Supreme Court's refusal to hear Danny's case."

"Get them both off your back, you've got better things to do than carry that heavy load around with you."

In spite of herself, Hemion smiled at his apparent concern.

Then she spoke again, suddenly feeling young and shy, "Well, do you remember that Lapeer High School played St. Alphonsus once in football

187

when you were quarterback?"

Preston paused briefly and then answered, "Yes, I do. It was an away game for us. The St. Alphonsus Cathedral next to your school was magnificent. In Dearborn, Michigan, if I remember correctly."

"Yes."

"We won."

"You seem to be able to remember that part easily enough."

"What's wrong with winning?"

"This is embarrassing."

"What is?"

"I can't do this," Hemion said, blushing.

"If it's bothered you for all these years, then it must be important."

"Important?" Hemion asked, then, breaking into laughter, added, "Not hardly. And I don't really know whether I can tell you…. It's … it's so silly."

Smiling broadly, Preston said, "Hey, what can I say? It would take a lobotomy to get all that stuff out of us."

Squeezing her eyes tightly closed as if to make her confession easier, Hemion rapidly blurted out, "You wouldn't dance with me at Homecoming when I asked you to after the football game."

"That's it?" Preston said, astonished, straining not to laugh.

"I was just fifteen years old," Hemion said. "You were this oh-so-fabulous high school football star," she added, sarcasm briefly putting a hard edge on her voice. "I asked you on a dare from my girl friends, and I was mortified in front of them when you said, 'No.'"

"I hope I said, 'No thanks.'"

"Nope, just plain 'no,' you were awful, so stuck up and everything!"

"Wait a minute, there was a reason for that, too."

"Yes?"

"Nanette Stocker was wearing my class ring, wrapped with adhesive tape to make it small enough to stay on her finger. That was called 'going steady,' almost the same as being engaged today. I couldn't dance with anybody but her. She would have killed me, literally."

"You have an answer for everything."

"Don't I wish."

"I need to make another business call."

"I thought maybe the one you made back at the pump was for backup, that perhaps you were afraid I was going to harm you."

"I'm trying to reach my colleague, Donna Pendergast, the best Assistant Attorney General in our office. She's hasn't lost a case yet."

"She's representing the state against the Duvall Brothers,"

Preston acknowledged.

"Right. The jury came in this morning with a guilty verdict. I was calling to congratulate her. It said on the radio that she was so moved by the jury's decision that she broke into tears.

"So did Detective Sergeant Robert Lesneski, the state police officer who worked together with her on the case," Hemion continued, adding, "We all call him 'Bronco.' He's a terrific investigator and never gave up on nailing those horrid guys, even after all those years had passed since the murders actually took place."

Preston looked at her for a long moment and then spoke, "I'll say goodbye and let you use your phone. I've enjoyed our little talk. Don't forget my offer to be friends."

When she didn't respond, he turned and started walking towards the river.

* * *

Hemion stood motionless and deep in thought, watching Justice Foster's tall figure slowly disappear down the trail.

He had been right about one thing, she admitted to herself, it had been a relief to talk to him about both of those things that had troubled her so greatly. The business about the dancing seemed about as silly to her now as the fear that had consumed the Scraggs at last night's campfire.

She would pay a visit on those people that had been trying to convince her to support Justice Foster's return to the Michigan Supreme Court bench. She would ask both Laura Hopkins and Chief Justice Woodruff Woodward what they knew about the Court's vote on whether or not to hear Danny's appeal.

She didn't really know Hopkins, having been introduced to her only once at some political event or other, though she remembered her as being quite the dazzler. But she figured she could rely on Woodward. She should be able to trust what a Chief Justice of the Michigan Supreme Court told her.

She noticed that Justice Foster had changed direction. Turning away from the river, he was now walking towards another one of the small pools of water that dotted the river flats.

She watched him closely, her curiosity aroused as he sat down on a log and removed his footwear. Then he waded into the pool, leaning over to scoop up a fish. She figured it had to be a very large one for her to be able to make out what it was from such a long way away.

She smiled to herself as she saw him return to the river with the creature struggling in his arms, then bend down to slip it back into the swollen waters that were still mud-colored from the storm in the night.

189

For just a moment, Hemion allowed herself to imagine how she would feel about this person if she confirmed his story about his voting in favor of hearing Danny's appeal. As if she suddenly found the answer, she was seized by a powerful emotion she had never before experienced—jealousy—the fear of a possible rival for a man's affection.

Composing herself, she decided not to involve Laura Hopkins after all.

Chapter Twenty-Six
Mars Approaches

Preston invited Rachael Childs, M.D., the psychiatrist that had successfully treated him for OCD, to accompany him to the news conference at which Governor Jennifer Granholm announced his interim appointment to fill the vacancy on the Michigan Supreme Court created by the death of Preston's friend, Justice Fredrick Walberg.

After confirming that Preston had voted to hear her brother Danny's appeal, Assistant Attorney General Barbara Hemion had dropped her efforts to derail the appointment. Ashamed of the serious mistake she had made, Hemion attempted to make amends.

She not only withdrew her request for an investigation by the Michigan Judicial Tenure Commission of Chief Justice Woodruff Woodward regarding his handling of the matter of Preston's illness, but in addition joined Woodward's effort to assure the Democratic Governor that Preston was extremely well qualified to be returned to the Michigan Supreme Court in spite of being afflicted by OCD for two years.

The first woman elected to the position, Granholm was eight months into her first year in office following the end due to term limits of Republican Governor John Engler's long reign. Her "honeymoon period" over, she had begun to receive a small amount of criticism, inevitable for people in public office, and it caused her to be increasingly circumspect regarding her decisions.

Dr. Rachael Childs had joined Preston at the podium to accept Granholm's appointment in the Lincoln Ballroom of Lansing's Kellogg Hotel and Conference Center. They had taken the opportunity presented by the Governor's news conference to jointly announce their formation of The OCD Foundation of Michigan to help other people whose lives had been devastated by the strange but relatively common psychiatric condition.

Preston had briefly described his form of the disorder to the attentive audience. In response to an inquiry about OCD's impact on Preston's competency from a reporter who was a stringer for *Time Magazine*, during the question and answer period near the close of the press conference, the doctor referred the media to her article about Preston's successful treatment in the current issue of *Psychology Today.*

Preston had shrewdly judged the press conference as a perfect opportunity for a moderate Republican to go on record as being an advocate for better mental health care in Michigan. It established a beachhead for himself on solid political turf that up to now had been the exclusive domain of liberal Democrats.

In crossing traditional party lines, he was taking a page from the notebook of Republican President George W. Bush, who was claiming credit for the No Child Left Behind Act and the Medicare Prescription Drug Act. Both were social welfare types of legislation, historically within the realm of the Democratic Party platform during the past several presidential elections.

* * *

Now doctor and patient sat together at the empty table they had shared with Governor Jennifer Granholm during a luncheon. But the press conference had ended several minutes ago. The Governor had excused herself to return to her office in the Capitol several miles across town, reminding them in the small talk of taking her leave to be sure and watch Mars that night.

"What was she talking about?" Dr. Childs asked Preston after Granholm left the table.

"Maybe you're working too hard to help OCD folks like me if you don't know what she's talking about by now. The story has been on TV and in all the newspapers for the past several weeks," Preston smiled, then quickly added, "Just before dawn, Mars will be closer to Earth than it's been since prehistoric times.

"Speaking of your wonderful service to the OCD community," he continued more slowly, in a serious tone of voice, "you know, ever since my final appointment with you for treatment, I have tried to find the words to thank you for turning my life around."

Reaching over to take her hand, he added softly, "They tell me I'm fairly good with words, but my gratitude to you is so great that it seems beyond my capacity to express myself adequately."

Dr. Childs gave his hand a quick squeeze and then abruptly withdrew hers.

Preston looked at her in surprise.

"I want to think clearly," she said by way of explanation.

"I can't imagine you doing otherwise."

192

"There is something I have put off telling you, Robert, until your treatment was complete."

"In the name of professionalism?" he asked matter-of-factly.

"Yes. I didn't want anything to interfere with your recovery."

There was silence between them for a few seconds, punctuated by the crashing of tables and chairs being folded up and stacked against the walls of the room by Kellogg staff people in order to clean the floor for the room's next use.

When she spoke again, it was so softly as to be barely audible above the din around them. "I've made the mistake of falling in love with one of my patients."

"It's not your fault, Rachael, we don't have control, generally speaking, over who we fall in love with."

"I know that, Robert."

"You have my greatest admiration—" Preston began but was interrupted by her rush of words.

"Would you please be my husband?"

Gently, he reached for both of her hands again, this time looking deep into her wide-set dark brown eyes. Holding her hands firmly as if to let his strength flow into her, he spoke to her almost in a whisper, "I can't, Rachael, but I'm so honored that you would ask me. You see, I'm already engaged to be married to Barbara Hemion."

* * *

Barbara, at the age of 38, had shyly confided to her man that she wanted to make their first lovemaking extra special. She had chosen the passing of Mars, the instant of planetary closeness, in fact, as the precise moment in time to give up her most prized possession, her virginity, to him.

Mars and Earth were, indeed, on a course that would soon bring the two planets closer together than usual. The last humans, or human ancestors, to gaze upon Earth's nearest neighbor in the Solar System at such close range were feral creatures that had still been some fifty thousand years away from inventing farming.

The planets' elliptical orbits around the sun would not bring them so near each other again until the year 2287, when current earthlings would be long dead. The once-in-a-lifetime view from Earth's perspective would take in Mars' southern hemisphere where it was turning into summer.

USA TODAY had recently advised, "Sky watchers are gearing up.... Mars will be the closest it has been to Earth in 60,000 years.... For a close-up view, plan to use at least a four-inch telescope to see features such as polar caps.... Bigger telescopes should identify shaded regions of Mars that fooled early astronomers into thinking that the surface featured canals."

The *Detroit News* a few days later observed wryly, "Overall, the planet is a cosmic clock moving at the pace of nature, not at the speed of modern society. And its current swing by Earth is something of a heads-up as humans face a series of world crises such as AIDS and terrorism. Modern humans have not only gotten themselves into a stew, they did it in a remarkably short time."

Commenting on the approach of the planet that was usually sixty million miles away, the *Lapeer Area View*, the local newspaper for the county where Red Moon was located, suggested, "If you're planning a trip to Mars, you might want to schedule it for this Wednesday, August 27, 2003. On that day, airfares are sure to be low as ... Earth and Mars will be less than thirty-five million miles apart at 5:51 a.m. Eastern Standard Time...."

* * *

Barbara Hemion awoke to the ringing of her travel alarm clock at 4:00 a.m. and couldn't remember where she was for a few seconds. Then she heard the soft lapping of waves close by and reached out into the darkness in the direction of the pleasant sound. Her fingertips touched rough-textured fiberglass, reminding her that she was aboard *The Wings of Morning*, Bobby Foster's sailboat, on the lake at Red Moon.

Swinging her feet off the narrow bunk onto the slanted cabin floor, she sat quietly for a few minutes in the warm darkness, composing herself before going out on the deck. She expected that Bobby would be using the telescope they had set up together on the bow at sunset, enthralled with his view of Mars.

Or perhaps, she hoped, smiling to herself, he would be in the water, swimming naked nearby. She had never met anyone so intent on knowing the world of nature and choosing to be part of it, at every opportunity. It was reflected, even, in the name he had chosen for his boat.

She thought for a while about all that had happened between them since their eventful forest confrontation at Oxbow Landing a month before.

Immediately upon her return to Lansing after the Scraggs' canoe trip was over, she had met with Chief Justice Woodruff Woodward and learned that Bobby had argued vehemently in favor of hearing Danny's appeal when it came up to the Michigan Supreme Court, their heated discussion having taken place in an unrecorded closed-door meeting of the Justices.

She then invited Bobby to lunch and profusely apologized to him. The powerful chemistry of her repentance and his gracious forgiveness had provided an unexpected shortcut to closeness between them, and they began dating several weeks ago at his suggestion.

As she sat quietly in the dark cabin, she replayed in her mind his sensitive acceptance of her regret for her vindictiveness in attempting to block his reappointment to the Court. "Nobody does everything right," he had said, continuing, "I stopped looking for perfect people—including myself—a long time ago."

She hoped that she could hold the memory of his serious manner as he forgave her. His warm smile had revealed even white teeth and made tiny laugh wrinkles appear around his arresting, Pacific-blue eyes.

He was definitely a knockout in the looks department, she acknowledged to herself, with a full head of blond hair, too, when so many forty-year-olds like him had receding hairlines or were completely bald. Having a body like Michelangelo's "David," only huskier, it was no wonder that Red Moon, his expensive hideaway for successful career women, had been a hit with him as the lucky ladies' male companion and sexual partner.

Possible aftereffects of that venture, she recalled, had been one of her biggest concerns as she felt herself falling in love with him. She had been able to put that worry aside when, without being asked to do so, and appearing rather embarrassed about it, he had told her that a blood test had shown him to be free of sexually transmitted diseases.

She smiled to herself as she recalled the look on his face when he hesitantly handed her his internist's letter containing the good news. His expression had been that of a little boy showing a school report card to his mother, relieved that he had passed all his subjects and would therefore be excused from any punishment.

At that point, she had confided in what she hoped was not too embarrassed a manner that she too had consulted with a doctor, her gynecologist, and he had recommended not only KY Jelly but also that Ortho Evra, a contraceptive patch, might relieve her anxieties about getting pregnant if she chose to become sexually active.

Then she thought about what was planned by her to take place with Bobby very soon and immediately felt a tidal wave of apprehension sweep through her. They were such a mismatch when it came to the intimacies of sex. She knew that all she really had going for her was the fact that she was an avid reader.

Getting up from her seat on the edge of the bunk, she moved through the cabin door and out into the open cockpit area where she could see the sky.

* * *

Preston had anchored *The Wings of Morning* in the center of the one-hundred-acre lake on his ancestral farm. A chorus of crickets reached Barbara Hemion's ears from the distant shore. He had told her that a few months earlier the "background music," as he called it, would, instead, have been provided by frogs.

Far from city lights and with nothing else on the water to obstruct the view, the sight was a spectacular one. Barbara Hemion caught her breath at the panorama of thousands of stars sparkling overhead in the last hours of darkness before dawn.

Turning to face the bow of the boat, she felt a west wind softly caress her face with its balmy warmth. She saw that Preston had indeed taken off his clothes but, instead of being in the water, was standing out at the farthest point of the deck with his back to her. She guessed he was looking at Mars, which now was not far above the horizon, the planet having passed overhead from east to west while she had been sleeping.

He was leaning slightly forward into the pre-dawn breeze, and it occurred to her that in the pale light from the luminous sky, his motionless form, with his perfectly maintained six-foot-two-inch muscled physique could have passed for one of the carved, wooden bowsprits that graced the Flying Clouds, the revered sailing ships of the nineteenth century.

He wasn't using the telescope, which sat on its tripod next to him. Climbing up out of the cockpit and onto the deck that covered the front two-thirds of the boat, she was the first to speak.

"Bobby, why aren't you enjoying a close-up view with this?"

"Take a look through it and you'll find out. I think I know now why they build observatories on bedrock."

Before putting her face to the eyepiece, she commented, "Mars seems much brighter than when it first appeared over the trees on the other side of the lake last night."

"That's because it was surrounded then by other bright objects, including the constellations of Pegasus, Aquarius, and Pisces. Now it's more alone."

"Where did they all go?"

"Nowhere. Mars left them behind to cross the sky. Not everything rises and sets like Mars does. Take circumpolars like the Big Dipper, for example. It doesn't go anywhere, just spins in place over the North Pole, once every twenty-four hours. That's how slaves escaping the South always knew which way freedom lay, they followed what they called the Drinking Gourd."

Fixing the 4.5-inch Meade Polaris reflecting telescope on Mars, Barbara

Hemion was startled to see that the planet had grown a wiggling tail. Then, feeling Preston's arm gently around her shoulders, she turned and faced him.

"Good morning!" he greeted her warmly, as if they hadn't spoken yet. She remembered him doing that sort of thing at Oxbow Landing and several times since and supposed it was a rather engaging idiosyncrasy of his that she might as well get used to.

"All that stuff about planets and constellations," he continued, "makes me feel like some dry, old astronomy professor, and that's not what I'm here for today."

"Yes, well, first tell me why Mars was round when seen by us through this very telescope six hours ago, and now it's wiggling around and looks like...."

"Go ahead and say it. We have to start somewhere in getting rid of your inhibitions."

"Okay, a sperm," Barbara Hemion said, feeling her face flushing.

"The wind's shifting directions just enough to swing the boat back and forth on the anchor rope, like a pendulum on an old-fashioned clock," Preston explained, adding, "so it's impossible anymore for a still view that would get rid of the tail. I might as well stow the scope away in a locker, and that will give us more room up here anyway."

Looking around the triangular space where they were standing, a small bow deck ahead of the craft's single mast, she noticed that two sleeping bags had been zipped together to make a double one. It lay at their feet along with several pillows.

* * *

After what seemed an eternity, Barbara Hemion finally felt Preston's breath part the fine blond hair of her pubic mound. She closed her eyes to the blanket of stars above her in order to better focus on the incredibly delicious sensations rippling through her lower body.

She had hoped for, but hadn't really expected, the multiple orgasms that seized her, and her extensive reading of how-to sex books hadn't prepared her for the shuddering loss of control that came with them. Reaching behind her head, she grasped the base of the thick, aluminum mast firmly in both hands to steady herself as she raised her pelvis to accommodate his warm, thrusting tongue.

"You shouldn't, Bobby," she gasped, "I came straight from sleeping without washing down there, the odor—"

"That makes it even sweeter for me, it's a wild, musky smell that

197

completely turns me on," Preston looked up to say toward her upturned chin, all he could see of her face between his hands on her breasts, adding, "With you, I feel totally uninhibited."

"You're telling me."

"It's almost time for the big, cosmic event, and I want us to change positions," he said then, adding, "Why don't you turn on your side so we can lay like spoons?"

After she did as suggested, he slid his body up behind hers, putting his left arm under her head so she could pillow it on his bicep. Bending his elbow and wrist, he used the fingers of that hand to gently squeeze the nearest of her hardened nipples.

He moved his other hand downward between her shoulder blades, resting it for a time in the small of her back. Then he reached over her hip to slowly trail his index finger up and down the crease of her vulva until it began to open like a flower to his gentle caress.

When her clitoris became exposed, he extended his journey of exploration to softly rub that special place, pleasuring it with the feather touch of his fingertip. At the same time, he used his tongue to part the moist, golden curls on the side of her head in order to find and trace the outer rim of her ear, whispering, "I'm in love with a beautiful woman."

"Do I know her?"

"You're beginning to, you just need an open mind and a gentle push in the right direction."

"From behind?"

"Yes," Preston said, laughing in spite of himself at her dry sense of humor, then he added, "It's shallower that way, so it won't be quite so uncomfortable when your hymen breaks."

"What time is it?" she murmured.

"It's our time. Open your eyes, Mars is straight ahead."

Chapter Twenty-Seven
A New Day

"It's a good thing I didn't know what I was missing all these years. I would never have held out this long if I had," Barbara Hemion laughed, then added exuberantly, "I'm just so pleased with my body—I didn't know it could do those wonderful things! And I just love giving myself to you, my darling Bobby."

"You were so pent up, but don't move yet," Preston said softly, continuing, "Now it's time to share our afterglow. In some ways, it's the best part of making love."

"I've never felt so relaxed," she replied. "So completely at peace with the world."

"That won't last."

"It feels like it will, like it could go on until the end of time, and that there's just the two of us and the rest of the world has gone away."

"That's an illusion."

"Pooh on you. What's with this negativism all of a sudden, Bobby?"

"I just want you to appreciate your mood's fleeting nature, so you'll savor it to the max while you've got it. It's an extraordinary serenity that lasts for only a little while after orgasm. It's the most wonderful feeling in the world."

"And all I have to do to start over and get it again is take hold of this handle?" she giggled, reaching down toward his groin.

"Until I die or it stops working, whichever comes first."

"I think we should give it a name, like 'Herbie,' maybe."

"Well, Herbie is sleeping for a little while," Preston laughed, adding, "You wore him out."

"Can we talk about something while he takes his nap, or will it break the spell of our short-lived tranquility?"

"We can try. What are you thinking about right now?"

"One of my cases."

"You've got to be kidding."

"Sorry. It would take a lobotomy to get all that legal stuff out of my head."

"Shop talk is sure to put an end to our precious moment."

"Please."

"No."

"If it makes you happier, we'll call it 'pillow talk for lawyers.' You be Rock Hudson, I'll be Doris Day, okay?"

"That sounds just dreadful. We don't need other people right now. It would only be an intrusion on our privacy. Is this what our future holds? I'm having second thoughts."

"Don't you dare, mister," she warned with exaggerated fierceness, then, softening her voice, she continued, "It's about Matthew Pitt, the farmer I found dead in bed."

"Okay. What about him? In ten words or less."

"Why would a successful man like Melvin Peebles, a township attorney and all, go so far as to kill Pitt and try to make it look like a suicide?"

"There's nothing much to talk about when someone like Peebles is concerned."

"What do you mean?" she asked, absent-mindedly running her fingers through Preston's hair.

"Greed as a motive to kill has been around since the beginning of recorded history. Matthew Pitt was all that stood between Peebles and a fortune in real estate. His fingerprints the crime lab found on Pitt's shotgun and also on the note to you that he placed in your book at the motel will convict him.

"As a matter of fact," Preston continued, "just yesterday I talked to Nate Lewis, Lapeer County's Prosecuting Attorney, and he told me it was an open and shut case."

"It's sad," she said wistfully. "Matthew Pitt was the sort of person you meet only rarely, that you want to know better. I think he knew things about life that I could have learned from him, and now I can't."

"That's how I feel about you," Preston said, adding, "and, fortunately, you're still around."

* * *

"The show is about to begin," Barbara Hemion announced, pointing to a line of trees on the eastern shore that were silhouetted against a lavender sky. An almost blinding patch of red-orange sun, its edges made ragged by branches, was showing through a towering white pine.

She sat on top of the sleeping bag with her back against the mast watching the sky, wrapped in one of the soft robes that Preston had handed up to her through the forward hatch along with a steaming mug of hot chocolate, large enough for both of them to share.

"You must have the right connections," he said. He had left her briefly to switch the sailboat's anchor rope from bow to stern so the wind would have them facing away from Mars and towards the sunrise. But now he had returned to sit between her legs, reclining against her, with the back of his head pillowed upon her breasts.

"What do you mean, Bobby?"

"You got us the best seats in the house."

She rested her arms on his shoulders as he took a swallow from the mug that she held to his lips.

"You certainly have this down pat," she observed wryly.

"Don't hold it against me."

"What are you thinking about right now?" she asked, as he had asked her not long before.

"Uh-oh! What's good for the goose is good for the gander, right?"

"I'm not up on all your barnyard sayings."

"It means 'your turn to ask me what I just asked you,' and my answer is 'the Flint River,' it reminds me of your body, curve after lovely curve," he replied lovingly.

"Remember the sunken bridge that you and your Scragg friends got your canoes stuck on?" he continued. "Water is rushing over it right now, even though we aren't there to hear it. Maybe something else is standing by it, listening to its music. That doe with triplet fawns, perhaps. Her babies would be a lot bigger by now."

"Or one of those dreadful-sounding coyotes."

"You really love the out-of-doors, don't you, Barb? Just like me!"

"Of course, my darling Bobby," she whispered in his ear, putting the drink down in order to wrap her arms around him.

Both were silent for a few minutes as they watched the climbing sun gild the wave-tops, forming an ever-advancing path of shimmering golden light. When it reached *The Wings of Morning*, Preston got to his feet and extended his hand to her.

"Now what are we doing, Captain?"

"Herbie woke up and told me he's getting bored," he laughed as he led her gently downstairs into the cabin. Just inside, she sunk to her knees and loosened his robe.

Epilogue
One Year Later

The Michigan Republican Party had chosen the beautifully restored historic Detroit Opera House for its final fund-raiser in the presidential campaign of 2004. A black-tie night at the ballet, it was being held just two months before the election in November.

"I can't believe how beautifully they move, Bobby," Barbara Hemion whispered to Preston Foster as they sat holding hands in his patron's box in the darkened theatre. Below them on the softly lit stage performed the world-famous Kirov Ballet from the Mariinsky Theatre in St. Petersburg, Russia.

The dancers were engaged in the flawless execution of what is regarded by many as the most exquisite single scene in all of classical ballet; the opening of Act III, famously known as The Kingdom of the Shades, a realm of ghosts, in the one-hundred-twenty-seven-year-old "La Bayadere."

It started with a lone dancer, elevated on a six-foot-tall platform with a ramp leading to the stage. Emerging from the darkness, she began an arabesque consisting of a half dozen steps forward on her toes with her arms in a circle above her head. She paused, arched backwards for a brief moment and then, as she started it all over again, a second dancer appeared out of the shadows behind her.

Within seconds, there was a third dancer. And a fourth and fifth until, minutes later, the slow, halting single-file processional of perfect arabesques had filled the stage with thirty-two women wearing classic white tutus, all of them moving in unison. The capacity audience was mesmerized by the hypnotic power of the repetitive choreography, as if they were sitting on a beach instead of in a theatre, watching waves roll to shore.

"When did you know that I was the person you were looking for to spend the rest of your life with?" Barbara whispered under her breath, leaning against Preston seductively.

"When I saw you kneeling by the red pump to splash water on your face. I had expected to be angry when I saw you, but all I felt was admiration for your beauty in that outdoor setting.

"It was an unforgettable vision," Preston continued, "like what's taking place down there on the stage."

At the conclusion of the Kirov's program, a reception line was formed, extending across the theatre's main lobby under its massive chandeliers of Austrian crystal, their centers loosely wrapped in a swirl of red velvet.

President George W. Bush, running for re-election, and his wife, Laura, headed the line followed by the former President from Michigan, Gerald Ford, and his wife, Betty. Next to them was Max Fisher, a millionaire friend and supporter of generations of Republican politicians, and the increasingly influential Betsy DeVos, the Republican Party's state chairperson.

Standing directly to the left of Barbara and Preston in the line was Barbara's boss, Mike Cox, the current Michigan Attorney General and, according to the buzz, the Republicans' next gubernatorial candidate.

His popularity caused many of the guests to pause for an extra word or two with him. That gave Preston and Barbara a welcomed though sporadic chance to talk with each other.

"I have a surprise for you," he said during one such break in their seemingly endless handshaking and exchanging of pleasantries with guests. Reaching into the inside pocket of his tuxedo jacket, he retrieved a white envelope and handed it to her.

"Bobby?" she asked enthusiastically, tearing it open, then adding after a moment, "Are these really two tickets for the *Queen Mary 2*'s voyage to Rio de Janeiro in Brazil? And, during carnival time, as well?"

"It sure is, and Carnaval, as Brazilians call it in Portuguese, is ten times better than our Mardi Gras in New Orleans."

"Oh yeah, Bobby. You know for a fact that it's exactly ten? You're sure it's not eleven or twelve?" she teased.

"Don't give me a hard time about lingering visages of my OCD, or I'll tell the Scraggs about your wearing red snuggies that I discovered the first time we made love."

"You'd better not," she laughed, adding, "See this?" as she made a fist and held it up, as if for his inspection.

"I guess none of us would want our entire life story put up on a screen for all to see, Barbara," he said. "We are all learning, finding our way, and, hopefully, growing. You and I—"

She interrupted him impatiently, "I appreciate all your profound stuff, hon, but I just thought of something. Isn't Rio's Carnival just before Lent?"

"Yes, it's around the clock for four days ending on what we call 'Fat Tuesday.'"

"I'm not sure Mike will let me be away long enough to go by ship, our

204

office is super busy in the spring," she said, frowning in disappointment.

"He will when you tell him it's to be our honeymoon."

"Oh my God, we are full of little surprises tonight, aren't we, Justice Foster? And now I've got one for you," she announced with a big grin. Stretching up on her toes to reach his ear, she whispered, "There's going to be a little Bobby Foster."

The End